IMMORTAL
IN
SPLASHED INK

A THRILLER OF INTERNATIONAL INTRIGUE

LONNIE M. GARBER

IMMORTAL IN SPLASHED INK
A THRILLER OF INTERNATIONAL INTRIGUE

iUniverse books may be ordered through booksellers or by contacting:

iUniverse
1663 Liberty Drive
Bloomington, IN 47403
www.iuniverse.com
844-349-9409

ISBN: 978-1-6632-2485-9 (sc)
ISBN: 978-1-6632-2486-6 (hc)
ISBN: 978-1-6632-2487-3 (e)

Library of Congress Control Number: 2021914410

Print information available on the last page.

iUniverse rev. date: 07/29/2021

For Jeffrey

*"It takes two to speak the truth:
one to speak, and another to hear."*

Henry David Thoreau

PROLOGUE
MARCH 2014
Malaysia

PERAK REGION, MALAYSIA

A hammer blow to the back of her head, the headache struck suddenly on the train ride, midway between Ipoh and Kuala Lumpur. The woman, a Chinese tourist about thirty years old, pulled the zipper on her knitted jacket up to her chin and wrapped the hood tightly around her neck. She closed her eyes and tried to rest, but the pain had become constant, and she felt nauseated.

Taking a vacation before starting her new job at a wind turbine factory, she had flown from Beijing to Kuala Lumpur and continued by train to the Perak region in the western part of Malaysia. She was traveling alone and had chosen western Malaysia because she thought she would feel comfortable with its large population of ethnic Chinese people who had originally gone to Perak to work in the many tin mines that dotted the region.

She was an enthusiastic hiker and had looked forward to exploring the area's limestone cliffs, which sheltered many caves and hidden shrines that had been carved into the jungle over the course of centuries. Trail map in hand, she had made her way along narrow paths beneath the jungle-topped mountains, stopping to peer into jagged crevices that contained tiny metal or enamel statues of Buddha.

After a vigorous walk, she had reached her primary destination, the famed Sam Poh Tong Temple, which was set in the largest cave in the valley. The site had been discovered by a Buddhist monk from China in the early twentieth century, and the jungle shrine within had taken him over two decades to build.

Exploring the temple grounds, she had walked through impressively landscaped gardens surrounding a large, babbling pond before entering the temple cave. There she found a small altar area containing beautiful statues of Buddha.

Behind the altar, she entered a passage leading out to another smaller garden notched into the hillside. It was highlighted by a red pagoda set beside a small pond filled with turtles of a variety of sizes and colors.

Looking more closely, she had seen that the pond water was filled with cloudy plumes of debris, and she noticed a strong and unpleasant chemical smell. With a jolt, she realized that most of the turtles in the water were dead and simply floating among the few that were living. She studied the far shore of the pond and saw more turtles that also appeared to be dead.

Quickly heading away from the pond and the noxious odor emanating from it, she stepped through an arched opening in the garden wall that led to an area surrounded by rough, unkempt grass. She walked toward the perimeter but found mounds of animal droppings rotting in the humid heat. Avoiding a messy patch, she stepped back and then struggled for purchase when her foot landed on a soft surface. Thrown off balance, she thrust one arm toward the ground and barely managed to stop her fall. She was disgusted to see dead bats strewn about the grass and realized that the unstable surface that had caused her to stumble had been detritus from their decaying carcasses.

She used a tissue pulled from the pocket of her jeans to wipe off the brown debris clinging to her hand and arm as best she could, but it left a stain on her skin.

In anticipation of her trip, she had read about the bat population of Malaysia and knew it was among the most prolific in the world. There were more than one hundred species represented in the rainforests and caves, she had learned, sporting exotic-sounding names and descriptions like flying fox bats and giant fruit bats. At dusk every evening, millions of the flying mammals exited their shelters in the huge, limestone caves to spend the night foraging for insects before returning to the dark sanctuary before dawn to sleep away the day.

But bats never flew during daylight, she had read. If they were sick, they did not leave for the night flights and stayed behind to die inside the caves, not outside. So, she wondered, how did these bat carcasses happen to be outdoors in an open patch of grass?

Disenchanted with the jungle, she revised her itinerary for her final three days to focus on more traditional sites and to experience Malaysian food, which she found to be excellent. She determined to purchase a cookbook and prepare a Malay meal for her family when she returned to Beijing.

On her final day of vacation, she took a bus back to Ipoh and spent several hours browsing the Old Town, an atmospheric area dotted with Chinese mansions and historical buildings reflecting the importance of the city's large mainland Chinese population. She picked up some souvenirs for her family in the outdoor stalls and at 4:00 p.m. boarded the train to Kuala Lumpur where she would catch her flight back to Beijing.

When she had begun to feel ill on the train, she thought it was the result of dehydration. She pulled a water bottle from her backpack, but nausea overcame her and she dropped the bottle on her seat. She dozed for a few moments, lulled by the rocking of the train, but was jolted awake when she began to shiver uncontrollably. She tried to signal for the conductor circulating through the cars but found it too difficult to call out. People sitting in nearby rows seemed not to notice her as she slumped against the window.

When the train pulled into the station at Kuala Lumpur, the other passengers gathered their belongings and left the car. She found herself alone and tried mightily to gather her backpack and stand up, but her knees buckled and she sank down in the seat. Fighting to think clearly, she waited.

At last, a conductor entered her line of sight and announced loudly at her, "Kuala Lumpur, final stop!"

She raised her arm in his direction and whispered, "I am ill. I need help. Please help me. . ."

He stared at her for a moment and approached. "What's the problem, miss?"

She said softly, "I don't know what happened." She struggled to think and murmured, "It must be from the turtles. . ."

He adopted a stern expression and stared down at the Chinese tourist for a few moments. Finally he said in a harsh voice, "Turtles, huh? Are they in a cigarette or powder? Disgusting, miss. I'll call the police to help with your 'turtles.'"

Even in her fevered state, she knew the conductor was accusing her of drug use, an activity for which Malaysia was well known to impose severe criminal penalties. She mustered the strength to look directly at the man and said, "No, sir. It is not that. I became sick and need a doctor."

"We'll just see about that," he replied with a smirk. He turned his back on her and disappeared.

Too ill to do anything else, she remained slumped in the seat as fear began to ripple through her already trembling body. Tears slid silently down her cheeks, and more than anything she wanted to call for her mother.

After a time, two uniformed policemen entered the railway car accompanied by the conductor. One of the policemen leaned over her and said, "What seems to be the problem, miss?" He spoke pleasantly, unlike the conductor.

"I am very sick," she whispered. "I don't know what happened to me, but it must have to do with the turtles," she said so softly that only he could hear her. Her eyelids drooped, and saliva was pooling at the edges of her lips.

The policeman frowned and turned to his partner. "She is speaking Mandarin, and I don't understand her well, but I don't think she made sense. These Chinese tourists are a misery. Can you inquire?"

The two men exchanged places, and the second officer leaned over her. In a sharper tone than his partner, he said in Mandarin, "Miss, what's going on? What drugs did you take?"

She tried to respond, but no words came out. After a few moments of silence, the policeman turned to his partner and said, "I'll call for a medical team to transport her and figure out what kinds of drugs are involved. Then we can see if there is a source we can pursue."

She listened and processed what was being said, panic overtaking her. When she spoke in a louder voice fueled by adrenaline, all three men heard her clearly. "It must be the turtles," she said and thought that this made perfect sense. "Or the bats. More likely it was the bats because I touched them," she said as she slipped into unconsciousness.

The three men looked at one another and started to laugh. The two Mandarin speakers confirmed for the other policeman that what he thought he had translated was, indeed, correct: the woman had blamed her condition on turtles and bats!

They called in a request for a medical team and agreed that Chinese tourists were nothing but trouble.

PART ONE

2021

Long Island, New York

CHAPTER 1

I hear the argument in my waiting room heating up, and sitting in my office with the door closed, I am still hopeful that my secretary can resolve it. I have told her to inform Jack Cedar that I cannot speak to him directly, that I represent his wife and he must have an attorney contact me on his behalf. Nonetheless, he loudly demands that I meet with him immediately, that the woman who retained me is not what she seemed.

I try to recall the woman in question: In my mind's eye, I see her sitting across from me at my desk two weeks ago, an Asian beauty dressed in a navy blue silk skirt and an elegant blue-gray tweed jacket. She does not have the finely etched, pale features I associate with Japanese women, yet as she serenely relates a litany of her two children's accomplishments without conveying a trace of pride, I wonder if she is in fact a tiger mom, driving her children to ever greater achievements that never quite manage to impress her. She has the look of Southeast Asia, I think: a creamy, olive complexion and beautiful, slanted eyes, deep brown, that stare at me without emotion as she describes her children. I admire her taste in clothes and wonder if the look would suit me as well with my lanky physique.

I only half listen after she enumerates the first few awards and trophies that her children have garnered. Unlike their mother, I am duly impressed with these kids, but I am far more interested in hearing the details of her husband's threat to remove the children from the country without her consent. Although she is in my office to prevent this and although she expressed fear of her children vanishing when she requested an immediate appointment to see me, she now is surprisingly calm and displays no agitation.

I am an experienced divorce lawyer and have had other cases of threat and removal of children by an angry parent. I conclude that her story does provide sufficient justification to ask the court to restrain the husband from taking the children out of the jurisdiction without either the written consent of his wife or a court order. Restricting travel is particularly important because the Covid-19 pandemic is not yet in the rearview mirror and people still are skittish about leaving the country even for ordinary travel reasons.

I lay out the terms of my representation of her to obtain a divorce from her husband of fourteen years, whom she says is a research chemist and professor at New York University in New York City. She tells me that he has become increasingly volatile in recent years and she suspects that he has a girlfriend whom he spends time with during his speaking trips to professional conferences in Europe and Asia. It is those connections, together with specific statements he has made, that cause her to fear he will abscond with the children.

My retainer is $25,000, higher than usual, but I will need to set aside my other cases and make an immediate application to the court to restrain the husband and seal his safe deposit box, which is where his wife tells me the children's passports are kept. She says she found notes in his desk at home referencing a specific flight to Dublin departing JFK only ten days after our initial meeting, so time is of the essence. After politely listening to my standard explanation of the specifics of the services I will and will not provide, she signs the retainer agreement without comment and, to my surprise, counts out $15,000 in cash from the designer bag on her lap. She assures me that she will provide the remaining $10,000 when she returns to sign the paperwork in three days, which she does.

At our second meeting, she is serene and again beautifully dressed, this time in brown. She confirms the factual details I have set forth in papers prepared for the court, including her and her husband's full names, residential address, date of marriage, birthdates of children, etc., and assures me that the description of events I have incorporated accurately reflects what she has told me about his deteriorating conduct and threats to remove the children from the country.

If we are successful, I assure her, her husband will not be notified of the allegations until after the judge assigned to her case has signed a temporary restraining order barring the children from being taken out of the jurisdiction. I add that the bank has been directed to seal the safe deposit box containing the passports.

But now Mr. Cedar is in my waiting room raising hell. I assume that he has been served with the court order that I was successful in obtaining in time to prevent the children from boarding the flight scheduled for this evening. My secretary's insistence that Cedar leave my office and have his attorney contact me apparently has the effect of pouring a flammable substance on his open fire. His voice grows louder and angrier. Recalling his wife's description of a scary temper, I decide it is time to intervene, although I realize it is entirely possible that giving my support to my secretary will just give him two women to bully instead of one.

I stand to my full height of five feet, four inches, and throw open my office door, giving me a clear view of the scene unfolding in the waiting room. He is leaning over the secretarial desk and shouting.

"Mr. Cedar," I say angrily in a voice I hope sounds commanding, "you need to move away from my secretary and calm down!" I know he is forty-eight years old, and he is trim, tall, and looks fit enough to indeed be dangerous. He has a full head of sandy gray hair, more typical in a man ten or fifteen years older, but it does not diminish the aura of vitality that he exudes. He is a good-looking man, and I think in passing that the grad students he teaches must gravitate to him.

My appearance in the doorway has startled him, and he stares at me. "You are Aruba Jones?" he says incredulously. When I answer affirmatively, his body language and demeanor shift drastically, and I think he actually may laugh.

"You're the lawyer who wrote these papers?" he says, smirking at me. "With the name Aruba, I was expecting some giant, scary dude who is either stupid or easily bribed. Not a petite female lawyer who is either stupid or easily bribed." He tries to hide his chuckle, obviously thinking he is quite the card. He is no longer menacing, only obnoxious.

"I can assure you I am neither of the above," I say. I am used to condescending male quips and endless jokes about my name. I am unmoved. "And I can also assure you that the court order that was served on you is serious and binding. I suggest that you retain an attorney immediately to respond. And now, Mr. Cedar, it is unethical for me to speak to you since I represent your wife, who is your adversary in this proceeding, so I ask you to leave my office immediately."

"The bank just denied me access to my safe deposit box, Ms. Jones," he sneers, "and I need to get some things out of it right now! So I'm not going anyplace until we take care of that." His body language conveys that the joke is over. He straightens up, and his iron will is on display. I can picture him barking at an irate student, "You got a C, and you're keeping a C."

He continues. "I don't know who you represent, Ms. Jones, but it is not my wife. You need to clear up your mistake—your incredibly stupid mistake!—in the next thirty minutes, or I will miss my flight to Dublin because my passport is in the bank vault that you had sealed and I cannot get it out. If that happens, Ms. Jones, I will have a big problem. And I promise that means that you will have an even bigger problem." He glares at me.

I stare right back. "Mr. Cedar, I understand that you are shocked that your wife has taken this serious step to get a divorce and protect your children, but it should have been predictable in view of your recent threats against her. You need to get a lawyer, and you'll be able to tell the judge your side of the story." A look of fury creases his features, and he tries to cut in, but I raise my voice and continue with authority. "And on Monday your attorney can ask the judge to let you get your own passport and other items out of the box, which the court may do if you have a good reason. I am pretty confident, though, that the kids' passports will be withheld until your domestic problems are resolved."

Now he takes a step in my direction and growls. "Ms. Jones! Shut up and listen. I don't know who you think I am, but your 'client' is not my wife."

"This is ridiculous, Mr. Cedar. You need to leave—" I say, but he cuts me off and roars in fury.

"I am not married! I have never been married. And I certainly do not have any children. What I have is a plane to Ireland in a couple of hours that I cannot miss!"

I am thunderstruck by this claim and don't respond. I stare at him and process this information.

He continues. "Obviously, you have the wrong Jack Cedar. So you need to contact the judge *right now* and get it straightened out."

"Your wife gave me your photograph for the process server, and it's definitely a picture of you," I tell him. "Marsha"—I nod at my gaping secretary, who is sitting at her desk listening—"pull the Cedar file and bring it to me."

I walk back to my office and gesture for Jack Cedar to follow me inside. He shouts, "Whoever this woman is, she is *not* my wife!"

"Did you read the affidavit?" I ask him as Marsha puts the legal file on my desk. "Is your home address correct? Your date of birth, employment?"

"Give me the papers," he snaps and grabs them from my hand. "I received them just before I went to the bank to get my passport and only glanced at them." He rifles through the first few pages that set forth the relevant details to identify the parties involved. "Yes, yes," he says, "those things are all correct. But I have never even heard of 'Aimee Cedar' and certainly do not have children with her, or with anyone for that matter. Did you see a marriage certificate? Or birth certificates for these children?"

I urgently review the intake notes I have taken out of the file on my desk. There is nothing unusual. In my fourteen years of practicing matrimonial and family law, I have learned to take a client's version of personal events with some degree of skepticism. But there is nothing to cause me to question the accuracy of the basic facts Mrs. Cedar had provided. In fact, I realize that I have never asked a client to provide a marriage certificate. Who, I wonder, would invent a marriage for the purpose of trying to obtain a fake divorce?

"Look," I say to Cedar, "my client was here twice and gave me all of these details about you that you acknowledge are correct. I cannot just accept your statement that none of it is true." I sit back in my chair, formulating a plan. It is almost four o'clock on Friday, so I say, "I'll call my client and have her provide a marriage certificate and birth certificates for the kids on Monday, and we'll take it from there." I buzz Marsha and ask her to get Aimee Cedar on the phone.

Cedar is visibly deflated but does not respond for a moment. The situation appears to be wearing him out. "Ms. Jones, I'm not being clear enough," he finally says in a tough, measured tone. "I am scheduled to fly at 9:00 p.m., which means I must get to JFK by seven o'clock, which is in"—he glances at his watch—"about three hours. I don't suppose this. . . woman, your client, happened to mention that I am traveling with a colleague on this flight and that we are attending a prestigious, international conference at which I am presenting a keynote address that is crucial to my professional resume."

Aimee Cedar has not mentioned this at all, not any of it; she only said that he was planning to snatch the kids.

I stare at Cedar and find it hard to believe that he is making up this story. He is clearly very angry, but he continues to project an intelligent and stable demeanor. He seems to be a man who wields some degree of authority. He has acknowledged that the details provided by my client are accurate, but he is not concerned that this admission will undermine his claim that the big story is false. He is accustomed to being believed.

But what should I make of Aimee Cedar? Her bearing had been, in truth, so calm that it might have been contrived. Her description of her children was so impressive yet lacking emotion that it might have been scripted. And yet, what possible motive could anyone have for making up such a story? And she had placidly paid me $25,000, a pretty rich sum to get a phony divorce.

Marsha knocks on the door and then steps in. "I'm afraid the number we have for Mrs. Cedar is out of service," she says. "I tried it three times to be sure I dialed correctly. I also looked online but could not find any other phone number for her name. And it appears that someone named John Walker lives at the address we have on file for her." She waits and finally says, "What would you like me to do?"

Cedar leans forward, ignoring Marsha, and says to me, "Well, Ms. Jones, that might be a little hint about the credibility of your client." He says it with strained patience, as if speaking to a child who has not yet developed the analytical skills to distinguish hamburger meat from fillet mignon. He restrains himself. He will not argue or berate me yet because he has a more important matter to attend to. He asks, "How do you get the judge to lift the order?"

I am chastened and doubting what I have done, but I am not ready to call the court. I am not sure myself if I hesitate because I am not fully convinced of his story or because I simply cannot admit the magnitude of the fool this woman may have made of me. "How can you prove to me that you're not the husband of Aimee Cedar?"

"Oh my God!" Cedar thunders, jumping out of his seat. "The burden is on me? Shouldn't you have mentioned the matter of documentation to your client? How can anyone possibly prove they are *not* married!"

He has a point. "Give me the phone number of your office," I say.

He hesitates, wondering if I can possibly make things any worse by spreading this information to his colleagues. Of course I can, but he decides to trust me on the request. He writes down the phone number on a yellow Post-It he takes from my desk, and hands it to me.

I place the call and ask the receptionist who answers to connect me to Professor Cedar's admin, which she does. A professional-sounding woman comes on the line and introduces herself as Harriet. When I ask for Cedar she advises that he has already left for the day and will be out of the country next week as he is speaking at a conference in Europe. She is momentarily flummoxed when I ask in a confident voice, as though I know her, if Mrs. Cedar will be traveling with him.

"You mean his mother?" she asks, chuckling. "I really don't know, but I doubt that a woman in her eighties would be making this trip. Would you like to leave a message?"

"Actually, I meant his wife," I say.

She does not respond for a few moments and then says cautiously, "Who is this? Can I have your name and contact information, please? I'll email your message to Professor Cedar." I give her my email address and ask if she can have him contact me ASAP.

Without a word, Cedar pulls out his cell phone and watches the inbox, which, sure enough, within two minutes notifies him of a new message from his office. It relates my call back information and message and then, "She clearly does not know you since she asked if 'your wife' was traveling with you! Sorry I failed to weed out the call."

Cedar hands me the phone so that I can read the email for myself. To his credit, he says nothing and gives me a minute to respond.

I look at Marsha who is still standing in the doorway, speechless now, and ask her to get Judge Simon's chambers on the phone. It is now after four o'clock on a summer Friday, and I know, even as I ask her to make the call, that the chance of getting anything done before Monday is slim to none. In a few minutes she returns, and I can see from her expression that she has no one on the line. I tell her to call the administrative judge's chambers, and we have the same lack of success.

Cedar follows the proceedings in silence. I conclude that he is a practical man. He stares at an imaginary spot on the ceiling, and I think he is deciding whether to jump up and sweep everything off my desk in a burst of fury or to stoically accept the emerging reality that nothing can be accomplished until Monday. I wait and think.

"Can't you explain to the bank that this is a mistake?" he asks. I am ahead of him on this idea and instruct Marsha to get the bank's legal department in New York City on the phone.

Amazingly, a senior attorney is still there, and he listens patiently to my story that we may have served the wrong man. He does not hide his condescension for Long Island attorneys like me, whom he deems to be essentially unsophisticated country lawyers. Of course, my story only reinforces his disdain, but I am doing it to impress Cedar with my effort, not because I think it will actually accomplish anything.

"Ms. Jones, you surely know that only a judge can lift the restraining order. The bank cannot possibly, based upon your claim of 'mistake,' simply disregard it."

"Of course, of course." I press on with Cedar watching me intently, but since he can hear only my side of the conversation, he doesn't know the bank's attorney is speaking to me as though I am a high school student playing lawyer for the day. I say into the phone, "The only thing we sought to restrain are children's passports, and

Mr. Cedar only needs to remove his own passport and some business material. We can arrange to have a police officer present to ensure that he does not take any other passports, if there are any, or anything else at all from the box." Even I know that I sound like a fool.

When the lawyer on the other end responds only with "Oh my God!" I end the call.

But Professor Cedar's angry grimace lets me know that he is not finished. "What happens if a criminal is on the loose after four o'clock on Friday?" he lectures me, waving his arm in my direction. "Do they just tell him he can keep it up until Monday?"

I explain that a judge is indeed on call to deal with emergencies, but these involve life-and-death situations where there is imminent risk of irreparable harm. No judge would deem a missed flight by a man who cannot prove his story to be in that category, particularly when we cannot even reach the complainant, Aimee Cedar, who has raised the issue of irreparable harm to her children.

Finally, I say stupidly, "Look, it's possible I may have been duped. But why would someone do this?" He makes no response. "Can you think of anyone who would come up with such an elaborate scheme to hurt you?" Again, no reaction and I start to think he is meditating or something.

I try again. "She paid me *twenty-five thousand dollars* to do this. *In cash!*" This gets him to swivel around and look at me. "She's a beautiful Asian woman, olive complexion, brown eyes, impeccably dressed and cool as a cucumber. Have you had a dispute with anyone who fits that description? Do you even know anyone who fits that description?"

"No," he says flatly. "Maybe it's someone trying to get *you* in trouble, not me." But he knows this would only make sense if he were a violent type, which he does not appear to be, or the kind of person who would involve the bar association with a grievance against me, which he may be.

With remarkable self-possession he finally says, "I need to use a desk privately to try to reach my colleague and let him know I won't be making the plane."

I am relieved by his pragmatic request, clear the paperwork from my desk, and vacate my seat. "Please," I say, "sit here and feel free to use whatever you need for as long as you want. I'll be in the conference room." I usher Marsha out ahead of me and leave the office, closing the door behind us. Marsha wants to talk and dissect what has happened, but I am so humiliated by this catastrophe that I cannot even look at her.

CHAPTER 2

I bring a stack of work into the conference room but find I am unable to focus and complete the motion papers I had been preparing for a client before Jack Cedar burst into my office. I consider what my liability would be in the event I have wrongfully obtained a restraining order that caused Cedar to miss his flight and incur who-knows-what damages. Would my legal malpractice insurance possibly cover such a bizarre event? I decide it is useless to ponder potential outcomes until I have more information, and resolve instead to take care of a few phone calls while I am waiting for Cedar to finish whatever it is he is doing.

I leave two messages for clients asking them to call me about the status of their cases. My third call connects and my client, Luis Matero, answers in a glum-sounding voice.

"Luis," I say, "I heard from the court, and everyone needs to appear next week. The judge wants to see you all in person before he proceeds." This includes Luis and his ex-girlfriend Sofia who is the mother of his seven-year-old daughter, Jazmin. The judge also wants the child brought to court, together with her law guardian, who is a lawyer the court has appointed to represent her. Luis moved out on the girlfriend when his daughter was only two years old, and he has not been much of a father, seeing her only every few weeks. But he has voluntarily paid child support out of his modest wages as a receiving clerk at a local supermarket, which he continued even when he was furloughed for a couple of months during the pandemic. He has provided her with medical insurance and followed with some degree of consistency her progress in school.

The mother, never very impressive in a parental role, seems to have gone completely around the bend since the Covid lockdown ended, drinking and carousing with men whom Jazmin describes as "scary." The child reports that she has even been left alone overnight in their low-income apartment. Luis now feels it is his duty to intercede and try to have his daughter live in his home, where his sister and his own mother will care for the child while he works. He knows it will not be the best situation, but it should be an improvement over the current conditions.

Luis hired me with a minimal retainer, and in this case I know I will never get paid enough to even cover my time. But that is the way my practice works: the average of the fee from Luis and the fee from Mrs. Cedar will work out all right.

"I told you I can't go to court," Luis says. "I'm scared and I can't do it. You have to figure out something else." Luis is from Honduras and has confided to me that he sneaked into the US two years before Jazmin was born. When she was four, he says he happened to be in a local bar minding his own business when a brawl erupted and he was swept up in the arrest of everyone present. Unable to afford good representation, he eventually pled guilty to a reduced charge based upon the DA's promise that his sentence would be "time already served" while awaiting trial. I do not really believe Luis's story, but it makes no difference with respect to the matter of his daughter's welfare at the moment.

What does matter, however, is that following his plea deal he was peremptorily deported and sent back to Honduras. It took Luis only two weeks to find his way back into Arizona and another two to get from there back to Long Island, where he picked up his former life as if nothing had happened. He is right to worry about going to court, although in a liberal state like New York it is less likely that a judge will blow the whistle on him, especially when he is needed to help care for a seven-year-old child. But I am not an expert on immigration, and I have warned him of this.

"Luis, I told you from the start, there is no other way unless we can get Jazmin's mother to agree to give you custody. See if you can think of something that will persuade her, like paying her some child support to cover when Jazmin visits her."

"You know I got no money to do that! If Jazmin lives with me, I can't be paying her mother too!"

The conference room door opens, and I see Jack Cedar standing there. I hold up a finger to indicate just a moment and say, "OK, Luis, think about it and call me on Monday." We hang up.

"Jack," I say, "were you able to reach your colleague?" He stares at me stonily, and I realize I sound too friendly, like we are now old pals. I ask, "May I call you Jack?"

"Seeing as you probably have destroyed my career by making me a no-show at the most significant speaking engagement I've ever had, why not? I guess someone so influential in my life should be treated on a more intimate basis than 'Professor Cedar,'" he says, barely managing a civil tone.

I do not know how to respond. I understand his anger, and yet, if the story is what he claims, it is I who have been used and made a fool of for the purpose of hurting him. More than likely he knows this Asian woman who retained me or, at the very least, he has done something or is involved in something that warrants such an extreme and clever, not to mention pricey, plot against him.

Or, I think, perhaps it is his own claim of mistaken identity that is the snow job here, and his admin had been briefed in advance to bolster his story. He is trying mightily to get me to buy his farfetched claim and help him defeat the restraining order that I myself obtained on behalf of Aimee Cedar. He is so persuasive, so solid in his presentation, that I believe him. And yet I don't.

I inform him that nothing more can be done to unseal his safe deposit box until Monday. I urge him to take steps to mitigate problems evolving from the delay in his travel. But when he begins to angrily relate details of the trip and the conference he is supposed to attend, I stop him cold. I am tempted to find out if his trip matches the details my client had provided, but until this is sorted out, I still represent Aimee Cedar, and I already have gone way out on a limb by even listening to his story and speaking with him directly rather than through an attorney.

I tell him that over the weekend I will continue to try to reach my client and will let him know if I succeed. He assures me that he, too, will be on the lookout for any explanation or further developments that might emerge. We exchange cell numbers, and to my relief he finally departs my office.

I crumple into my chair, feeling drained and exhausted. Either Aimee Cedar's entire story was fiction, or Professor Jack Cedar has just given a performance that qualifies as a masterwork. I go through my file in detail and reread the papers I submitted to the court. It is a carefully constructed story replete with all the necessary supporting details. Aimee Cedar is completely believable.

Marsha comes into my office and announces that she has made another failed attempt to contact our client. It is now after 5:00 p.m. on Friday, yet she makes no move to leave. She has been with me for almost five years, and she knows that I am a serious and careful lawyer. We both wonder why a mistake of this magnitude simply walked in the door.

She looks dejected, and I say, "Go home. Nothing can be done with the court until Monday, so there's no point in just staying here being upset. I'll keep trying to get in touch with Aimee over the weekend, but that's really all we can do. We'll sort it out on Monday and do whatever needs to be done." I try to sound upbeat, but I am thinking about my malpractice insurance.

Marsha leaves, and after letting several friends know that I have a headache and won't be joining them for dinner, I head home, wondering if I should have been a teacher as my mother suggested.

CHAPTER 3

It is a warm autumn day, and the lowering sun casts pools of deep yellow through maple trees that are still full with leaves. I find my BMW in the parking lot and steer onto the Meadowbrook Parkway heading south. My office is in Garden City, the legal and professional hub of Nassau County, which is located on Long Island and accessible to New York City. The midrise office buildings are filled with lawyers, financial firms, and doctors, and there is a shop for every retail merchant you can think of within a couple of miles. Everything was shuttered and deserted for many months after NYC commuters delivered the coronavirus to the suburbs. Even now, although most schools, businesses, and retailers are open, crowds are noticeably thinner, and restaurant reservations, once tough to snag, are readily available. Everyone is still mystified that our way of life simply disintegrated so quickly.

After about ten minutes I turn off the Meadowbrook onto the Loop Parkway, which connects the mainland to a slim barrier island running parallel to it. A mile or so farther east is Jones Beach, a huge complex of public beaches with an array of facilities and services that, on a hot summer day, offers thousands of people from the city enough space to socially distance in the sun.

But over the Loop where I have driven is the beach community of Point Lookout, where there is only a small beach for local residents and an ambiance not unlike a bygone New England whaling town. A few miles west are pricey homes set on a dozen streets that end on an expansive, private beach, and beyond that is the small city of Long Beach, full of restaurants, funky bars, and a boardwalk that tracks the shore. Surrounding the town are tiny beach bungalows crammed together, many used as summer rentals or shared housing for college students.

I head to my favorite hangout in Point Lookout, The Pocket Watch. The interior bar is dotted with socially distanced people, and the bartender spots me and jollies a few people around to create a six-foot opening for me. "You're not looking very happy tonight, Ms. Aruba," he says with a smile and a wink. "I think you could use a really dirty martini."

"You read my mind, Jim. That sounds great," I say and try to force a smile. But I am, indeed, feeling crummy, and when my drink is poured, I take it behind the building, where a wooden deck skirts a quiet bay. Scattered around it are high top tables and Adirondack chairs, a few of which are occupied by laid-back-looking people sipping cocktails. I find a spot at an unoccupied high top and survey the scene. Projecting into the water are a couple of small fishing docks with a half dozen or so modest boats tied to them. On one a young couple, laughing, fiddles with fishing rods as the setting sun turns the water crimson. The scene and the drink help my spirits somewhat, but I am in no mood to socialize, even though three or four people I know gesture for me to come over and join them.

Instead, I finish my drink and head down the road to the small beach house I purchased about two years ago. It is a charming three bedroom, decorated in nautical style, with pretty beach landscaping in the front and rear yards. But the real allure is the Atlantic Ocean just down the block and the roof deck I had built shortly after I moved in. Every room has windows that catch the ocean breeze, and from the roof you can see the sun rise in the east and set in the west and the stream of ships heading in and out of New York that seem to float on the horizon in all types of weather.

I don't reply to two messages on my landline's machine, eat leftover Chinese takeout stashed in the fridge, and then spend an hour flipping through a ridiculous number of TV shows, mostly awful, that the cable company has provided for me to choose from, none of which capture my attention. I go up on the roof and with binoculars study four ships parked along the horizon, trying unsuccessfully to determine the type of cargo they are hauling. I call Aimee Cedar three times, still unsuccessful.

Finally, I decide it is a respectable hour to go to bed. Surprisingly, I fall quickly into a peaceful sleep.

My vibrating cell phone startles me, and I am instantly wide awake. My clock says 5:22 a.m. I think this is either a family health emergency—my mother?—or a burglar trying to determine whether anyone is in the house. I grab the receiver and bark, "Hello?"

There is no response, and I am vacillating between relief and fury when I hear a man's voice say tentatively, "Ms. Jones?" The voice is familiar, but I cannot quite place it. Then I do.

"Professor Cedar?" I say in disbelief. "It's five thirty in the morning. Has something happened?"

Silence. Then he says, "Turn on your TV." Obviously this is a ridiculous request under the circumstances, but his voice is strange and choked, with none of the confidence or authority of the prior afternoon.

I hesitate and ask, "Why?" and again, "Has something happened?"

"Just do it," he says with more authority. "CNN if you have it. . ." It takes me a few minutes to turn on the lamp, find my TV remote, and operate it in my unnerved state. He waits without speaking, but I can see the seconds ticking by on my phone. I know that we are still connected, and he is there waiting for me to react to whatever he thought was important enough to call to my attention at five in the morning.

Finally the screen comes to life, and I see a news reporter in front of a large building with lights illuminating the scene in front of it: police cars and news trucks everywhere. I begin to feel a pounding in my chest as I recognize Kennedy airport, only recently beginning to revive after the pandemic receded. The reporter is in midsentence, and the non sequitur makes no sense to me. "What's happened?" I say urgently into the phone, but in the pit of my stomach I already know.

Cedar says in a subdued, almost inaudible voice, "The plane. . . the plane has vanished. Just disappeared."

Before I can react to him, I hear the CNN reporter say, "To recap for viewers who may have just joined us, at approximately 1:15 a.m., Emerald Air flight 12 heading from John F. Kennedy Airport in New York to Dublin, Ireland, with one hundred and seven passengers and crew aboard, disappeared from radar. As of now, there are no further details."

I try to breathe normally as the reporter continues. "Emerald Air has set up a dedicated area of their terminal in JFK and a hotline for affected families."

I hit the mute button on the TV and say into the phone, "Oh my God! You would have been on that plane!" but Cedar interrupts.

"My colleague," he says, and the effort he musters to speak is palpable. I remember he was meeting someone on the flight. Whatever his personal relief at having missed the plane, I realize he is dealing with the tragic loss of a colleague, possibly a friend.

When he cannot continue, I say, "I am so very sorry," and I am truly overcome with empathy and shock.

He is silent for a moment, and then he says, "It's not just that. There's more." I wait silently, and finally he says, "The person I was traveling with is a friend of mine." He pauses. "George Hong, earth science professor at Columbia University."

"Oh, how terrible—" I begin, but he cuts in.

"No, not that. Not just that. I couldn't sleep and was watching TV when the news bulletins started coming in around 3:00 a.m. When I was sure it was the flight on which I was booked, I called my friend's wife to either comfort her or tell her what happened before she saw it on TV." He takes a breath that is audible over the phone.

"She said her husband called her shortly before the plane was scheduled to depart. He told her he was at the airport *with me!*" I listen to this statement and try to think through what connection there could possibly be between Cedar's passport trouble and his colleague's false statement to his wife.

"Aruba," he says, sounding for the first time as though he might trust me, "she said her husband told her he was having a drink with me before we boarded, exchanging science jokes, and he would call her from Dublin. So she went to sleep."

"I don't understand," I say. "He told her that you were at the airport, having a drink with him and getting ready to board together?"

"That's exactly right. But obviously not true, as you and I know."

I am speechless, and, I think, so is Cedar. The phone is silent. For the second time today, he has given me information that is impossible to decipher.

PART TWO
2014
Asia

CHAPTER 4
March 2014
Kuala Lumpur, Malaysia

Noting that his patient's vital signs were steady, although she remained unconscious, the hospital staff physician, Dr. Anshar, exited the room. He had been treating the woman, a Chinese tourist, since she was brought to Prince Court Medical Centre four days earlier by two policemen convinced that her symptoms were drug-related. He had concluded that they were fools and that Kuala Lumpur could not even manage to train the police to recognize basic medical emergencies. The triage team at the hospital had found the patient to have a fever over 103 degrees and an oxygen level of less than 55 percent, indicating a respiratory deficit that would have put an older person in grave danger of imminent death. As it was, it took about forty-eight hours to stabilize her condition sufficiently to think she had a reasonable chance of survival. There had been no material improvement since.

Anshar could not determine exactly what was wrong with the woman and had been unable to formulate a solid treatment plan. It was clear that she had severe respiratory illness with dense pulmonary consolidations. However, she had tested negative for all known bacterial agents that caused pneumonia, influenza A, influenza B, influenza H1N1, H1 seasonal, and the emergent strain of H7N9, the so-called avian flu that had recently caused panic in China.

Anshar leaned back in his chair, fingers tented in front of his face. He pulled out his contacts file and located the number for Dr. Keiji Takama, his Chinese acquaintance from medical school who was now a respected specialist in emerging infectious viruses at a prestigious virology institute in central China.

In recent years, the study of emerging infectious pathogens had become a major research area, and the Chinese institute at which Dr. Takama worked was at the forefront of the field. It was well known in the medical community that his team had logged great progress in tracing the animal origins of severe acute respiratory syndrome (SARS) and avian influenza viruses.

After holding for a connection and then speaking to two receptionists and finally Dr. Takama's own secretary, Anshar heard his schoolmate's hardy greeting on the line. Speaking in Mandarin, the language of their school days in Hong Kong, Drs. Takama and Anshar chatted for a few minutes, catching up on news about their wives and children.

Anshar turned to the question at hand and related the details of his patient's Chinese citizenship and her present medical status. He told Takama that, although she had been unable to communicate at the hospital in Kuala Lumpur or disclose her history, the passport in her backpack when she was brought in had enabled the medical team to contact her family and establish that she lived in Beijing and had travelled to Malaysia for a vacation before starting her new job. She was twenty-eight years old, and to the best of anyone's knowledge, she had been in excellent health and was physically fit. That was about it on patient background.

Thinking over the innocuous story and the litany of lab results, Dr. Takama said there was little he could do to help since she was negative for all known viral and bacterial pneumonias.

Finally he asked, "You are sure of the lab results? There have not been any documented cases of avian flu outside of China, but still, you are sure the test results are accurate?"

Anshar replied, "Yes, I actually ran the H7N9 twice since it is a new strain, both negative." He added, "Is there any possibility that this profile could be the result of drug use?"

"Not likely," Takama said. "Respiratory symptoms are not usually associated with drug use, but did you find clinical evidence of substance abuse?"

"No, we found nothing. But the policemen who brought her in thought she had a drug overdose." Anshar chuckled and added, "They said that, before passing out, she blamed her illness on bats and turtles, which they concluded meant she had taken something." Dr. Takama was silent for so long that Anshar finally said, "Are you there?"

"Yes, yes, just thinking of possibilities," came the reply in a clipped tone.

Dr. Anshar waited until Dr. Takama continued. "Do you have knowledge of her activities before she fell ill? Do you know where she was? Was it Kuala Lumpur the whole time?"

"I don't know her itinerary, but she arrived in Kuala Lumpur by train from Ipoh and was so ill that she couldn't exit the train without help. I don't know what she did in Ipoh. . ."

"Ipoh is in Perak, right? The northwest peninsula?" asked Dr. Takama, and without waiting for an answer he said, "I can't think of anything drug-related, but I will check around with my colleagues and let you know if I get any ideas." He abruptly ended the call.

Dr. Anshar sat staring at the phone and wondered if the obvious change in Dr. Takama's demeanor could have been related to the mention of Ipoh. There had been rumors about an undiagnosed respiratory illness appearing in western Malaysia near Ipoh, but it was nothing more concrete than the possibility that a small number of pneumonia patients might be linked in some unknown way. It seemed farfetched to think his patient might be one of them.

Dr. Keiji Takama replaced the landline phone on which he had spoken to his colleague. When the call had come in, his staff had located him in the secure animal research section of his facility. Cell phones were not permitted in the high security area since they could not be adequately disinfected for return to a nonsterile environment.

He strode down the corridor and exited the ward by entering the sterile transfer room where he removed the protective suit that covered him from head to toe. He deposited it into a metal, revolving canister that carried it directly to a sealed unit two floors below, where it would be sterilized. He then stepped into the small shower and scrubbed himself carefully with liquid antimicrobial soap that was stacked in individual packets on the shelf. Finally, he exited the other side of the shower into a changing room, toweled dry, and put on a clean medical uniform hanging in the closet. He used his ID card to open the doors of the infectious disease area and walked to his office.

He reviewed a few messages and then told his secretary he would return in an hour. He took an interior staircase to the basement and pressed the chip on his ID card to the locking system on a metal door, which swung open, admitting him to a brightly lit white corridor. A uniformed guard sat inside the door and nodded a greeting to him.

Keiji strode down the hallway past closed doors on both sides, many displaying bold, red signs reading "DO NOT ATTEMPT TO ENTER WITHOUT TODAY'S CODE." He stopped at a doorway marked "Special Communications" and pulled out his cell phone. He logged on to a secure website, entered his numeric credentials and then two passcodes that were changed weekly. He held the camera on his phone to his face and waited. In a moment, a six-digit number flashed on his screen. He punched it into the keypad on the door and heard the locking mechanism click open.

The room was empty except for a desk with four landline telephones in a row and a basic assortment of writing materials that might be needed to make notes. Bypassing the first phone, which was marked "North America," and the second, which indicated "Europe," he picked up the receiver of the third phone marked "Southeast Asia." An operator requested the details of his identification, confirmed that he was authorized to use the line, and requested the location and the person he wished to call. All the information would be preserved in an electronic log in case questions arose in the future.

He waited for nearly ten minutes until the operator finally said, "Dr. Den Chin is on the line for you."

"Dr. Takama," came the greeting. "I have heard excellent reports about work progressing at your facility. What can I do for you?" While not harsh, Dr. Chin's tone was businesslike and did not invite a cordial response.

"My apology for taking you away from your work," Dr. Takama said deferentially. Dr. Pao Den Chin was his superior by several levels and controlled the government committee for the study of environmental and infectious epidemiology. He was well known as a disciplined scientist who did not engage in personal conversation. In fact, he remained so private from his fellow scientists that no one even knew whether he had a family or any personal life at all. Nonetheless, Keiji Takama's research center specialized in the study and treatment of emerging infectious diseases, and Dr. Den Chin had an almost fabled reputation at the facility. Communication with him was considered a measure of professional prestige.

"Something has happened that I thought I should relate to you immediately," Takama began. There was no response, so he continued. "I had a call from an old colleague at Prince Court Medical Center. It's there in Malaysia, where you are, in Kuala Lumpur on Jalan Kia Peng—"

Den Chin said impatiently, "I know the facility. What about it?"

Keiji Takama rushed his words, attempting to hold the senior doctor's attention long enough to relate the information. "He has a patient, a thirtyish Chinese woman visiting from Beijing, with classic viral pneumonia symptoms, very ill, possibly critical, but she tests negative for all common bacterial and viral elements. He thought I might know of something else to test for—"

"Well, you don't, do you?" Den Chin did not raise his voice, but he might as well have for the annoyance he conveyed. "You surely don't expect to get any ideas from me about an individual patient," he said.

"Well, no, sir, it's not that. But the reason I felt I should advise you of this right away is that he told me she had been in Ipoh—you know, in the northwest peninsula?—and she said something very strange to the policemen who brought her into the hospital." Takama paused, waiting for encouragement.

After a moment Den Chin barked, "Are you planning to tell me what that was or let me guess?"

"Yes, of course," Takama said. While not on the level of Dr. Den Chin, he was respected in his own right and unaccustomed to being spoken to like a minor functionary. "She said, 'It must have been the turtles. . . or the bats,' before she became unconscious."

There was no reply, and finally Takama said, "Bats, sir. She said it must have been the bats. I thought you would want to know that right away."

In a more modulated tone Den Chin said, "Yes, of course. Thank you, Dr. Takama. We know of nothing else for which your colleague might test his patient, so do not respond to him any further. I will investigate the matter, and, needless to say, the local physician is not to know that our team is here in Malaysia. And please do not discuss the case with anyone else." He clicked off, leaving Keiji Takama staring at the silent phone.

———

Dr. Pao Den Chin remained in the secure call room of Kuala Lumpur center for several minutes, considering his course of action. Since he had been elevated to the head of Foreign Actions in Environmental Epidemiology, or FAE, by the chairman's special committee, he had broad authority to formulate and carry out activities in foreign countries, including his current mission in Malaysia. He was not certain if he was permitted to exercise the same authority within China, but this new development expressed by Dr. Takama was rife with ominous implications for the mainland.

Den Chin knew that contacting the chairman's special committee could lead to serious consequences for him. He had had enough experience with the group to know that he was likely to be blamed for the situation even though he was merely the one who had stumbled upon the trouble almost by serendipity. Reaching his decision, he picked up the secure phone and requested the administrative clerk for sensitive communications who was on duty. "Miss Ting," he said when the line connected, "I need to send an encoded message to the chairman's committee." When she indicated that she was ready, he dictated: "Must meet with member for Developing Export Strategies and member for Environmental Options as soon as possible after my return to Beijing from Kuala Lumpur Wednesday evening. Urgent. Please provide time and location."

He waited until Miss Ting encoded the message and then continued. "I need a flight booked from Kuala to Beijing on Wednesday afternoon."

Den Chin ended the call and followed protocol to leave the secure wing and return to his office.

CHAPTER 5
March 2014
Kuala Lumpur, Malaysia

Dr. Pao Den Chin sat back in his desk chair after making notes summarizing his conversation with Dr. Takama. He thought about how to best present the revelation to the committee members he had arranged to meet in Beijing, knowing that they would be reluctant to recognize its gravity. How fortunate, he thought, that Keiji Takama had followed his instinct that the information was important and that he had persevered in relating it to Den Chin, who knew that he had not made it easy for the younger man. He regretted that he had been unnecessarily harsh and made a mental note to send Takama an email expressing a few words of praise.

Den Chin picked up the small, framed print of a seventh-century Chinese painting that he kept on his desk, and gazed at it for a few moments. *Immortal in Splashed Ink*, painted on a paper scroll, depicted an immortal, ancient deity, his open kimono flapping about his mighty chest and abdomen, striding forward with power and purpose. A few outlines in fine, black ink formed the facial features, ears, and chest, but the rest of the figure was rendered with a haze of wet ink, merely suggesting the deity's manly features.

As always, the artwork calmed his mood and enabled him to organize his thoughts. The original was in the National Palace Museum in Taiwan and had held special meaning for his father, who had been an expert in Chinese ink painting. Den Chin knew that his own love of Chinese art had come from his father, but so had the distant and aloof nature that prevented him from connecting easily with others. In so many ways, Den Chin knew that his own character had been determined by his father's experiences.

1949
Taiwan

With the army of the Communist People's Republic of China storming across China toward Shanghai, Pao Den Chin's father had joined more than a million of his Chinese countrymen in a desperate retreat across the East China Sea to safety in Taiwan. There, the defeated Republic of China nationalists, led by Chiang Kai-shek and his Kuomintang (KMT) Party, had re-established their government.

Called Formosa for centuries before becoming commonly known as Taiwan, the island had been handed over to the Republic of China after Japan's fall at the end of World War II. Already battered by a brutal Japanese occupation, the Taiwanese had been hopeful that the newly arrived nationalist government would usher in better conditions.

Den Chin's father had been a minor museum curator in Shanghai, specializing in the history of Chinese ink drawing. He had believed the nationalists to be more culturally enlightened than the brutish Communist insurgents and so had volunteered to accompany the KMT's ships, hastily loaded with the greatest art treasures of the overrun Forbidden City, to Taiwan. There, a new Museum of Chinese Culture had been promised by Chiang Kai-shek, and Den Chin's father had dreamed of the opportunity to participate in this lofty undertaking to safeguard the artistic riches of the cultural history that he loved.

However, he had not anticipated the White Terror unleashed in Taiwan by the KMT. Desperate to retain the island as their remaining outpost of power, Chiang Kai-shek had led the nationalists on a brutal campaign to root out Communist spies and sympathizers among the local populace and even among the Chinese who had fled the mainland along with them. With the declaration of martial law, mass imprisonments on trivial charges became commonplace, as did brutal beatings and summary executions. No one was interested in a Museum of Chinese Culture.

Running out of money, Den Chin's father had eventually taken a job as a waiter in a Taipei restaurant, which served mainly wealthy Shanghai gentry who had escaped the mainland. They had treated him like a personal servant, tossing offhand demands for food and drink in arrogant, loud voices. And that was far better than the treatment they handed out to the Taiwanese.

Patiently waiting for work on the planned museum to begin, he had used his meager earnings to rent a room in the modest apartment of a Taiwanese family near the restaurant. They were a pleasant and old-fashioned couple who squeezed into one bedroom together with their seventeen-year-old daughter so that Den Chin's father could occupy the second bedroom. They all shared the bathroom and kitchen, and Den Chin's father, who was an unfailing gentleman, had been treated with kindness and the dignity that he was denied at the restaurant where he worked.

He had fallen in love with the couple's daughter, Mai, whose shy and demure temperament enchanted him. When they married, Mai moved across the apartment to share the room of her new husband, who continued to pay rent to his new in-laws but now shared the dinner table with them whenever he was not working at the restaurant.

In 1953, a wealthy Chinese patron of the restaurant threw a plate of steaming noodles at Den Chin's father, accusing him of delivering the wrong menu item to the table. The plate had smashed against his shoulder, causing an injury that bothered him for the rest of his life, and he had fallen to the floor in a shower of broken glass and food. The restaurant owner stormed out of the kitchen and ordered Den Chin's father to "clean up the mess you made, stupid dog!" which he did, as the table of rich former Shanghainese looked on.

Den Chin's father had never returned to the restaurant, causing a year of great financial hardship for the family. There was no information about plans for the museum, but finally he was able to secure a job as a street cleaner in Taipei. He had reasoned that working for the city, even in this lowly capacity, might enhance his chances of hearing about the museum and obtaining an entry position when construction finally was to proceed.

In 1956 Pao had been born, and his parents squeezed closer together in the bedroom they continued to occupy in the apartment of Mai's parents.

Finally, in 1963, Den Chin's father heard that the opening of the museum finally had moved up on the nationalist agenda. It was to be named the National Palace Museum after the original one in Beijing, and committees had been formed to plan the construction of the building and to curate thousands of ancient artifacts that had been crammed into storage since 1949.

After years working as a street cleaner, Den Chin's father had found it difficult to put on proper clothes and assume the confident demeanor necessary to apply for a dignified position at the museum. Even worse, his long-ago education and experience as a curator had taken on the aura of a dream or perhaps, he thought, it had occurred in one of his prior lives. After all, there was not one person in Taiwan who had known him then or could share or validate his memories.

Pao Den Chin loved his father, who was gentle and solicitous if somewhat aloof. Even at seven years old, Pao had sensed that his father's absent manner was born of personal defeat and not from disappointment with his son. Pao, a strong and confident boy, had begun to feel protective of his father. Now, as an adult, he realized that in some subtle ways he and his father had begun to exchange roles when Pao was still a young boy.

When through persistence and luck his father had surprisingly managed to secure an interview for a position on the museum's initial staff, Pao knew instinctively that it was fraught with danger. He watched with trepidation as his father had carefully dressed in the cheap, ill-fitting suit he had purchased for the occasion and tried to practice a confident facial expression in the mirror. Mai did not share Pao's worry and felt sure that her husband's potential would be recognized and rewarded by the museum committee. She had led a sheltered life shaped around her family and had no experience that would have enabled her to evaluate the likely outcome of such a situation.

Den Chin recalled that the man who returned from the museum interview was a different person than the one who had left only three hours earlier. Pao had begun to cry silently after one look at his father's face, which had taken on an ashen tinge and a remote expression.

"My dream is gone," his father said in a monotone voice to his wife, ignoring Pao. "They laughed at me for seeking a curator position. 'A street cleaner!' they said. 'Show us your degree. Give us a reference from your job in Shanghai.'

"I said, 'I will tell you the history of ink painting in China and explain how it is done with different techniques from fine lines to splashed ink. That is my reference,' but they had no interest, would not let me demonstrate any of my abilities or knowledge. Instead, they asked if my family had contributed money to Chiang Kai-shek's culture fund and told me that was the only way I could hope to get a position. I told them that I am a loyal nationalist and support Chiang Kai-shek but do not have the financial means to contribute.

I got nowhere. Finally, I saw that it was hopeless and gathered my things to leave. One of the committee men took pity on me and offered me a position"—Mai's face brightened until Den Chin's father continued—"as a janitor. He said I had good experience for that job." He turned his back to Mai and Pao and stared out the window of the apartment. "I accepted. At least I can see my beloved art treasures that I followed across the sea."

Pao had run to his father and wrapped his arms around his legs in a childish gesture of comfort to which he received no response. An unfamiliar emotion overtook him, causing his neck to prickle.

I hate the nationalists, he had thought solemnly, and I will punish them.

Den Chin's father eventually accepted that his aspirations would never be realized and had been at peace with the lowly job he muddled through almost every day. To young Pao's amazement, his father had remained loyal to Chiang Kai-shek, and attributed his mistreatment by the regime to the strain of never-ending war with the Communist mainland.

The museum finally opened in 1966 to tremendous fanfare, but Den Chin's father had not even been permitted to be present at the official ceremony since attendance was limited to those in Chiang Kai-shek's favored circle.

Den Chin's father did not complain, but it was clear that he had been emotionally defeated. He had never again communicated to his wife or son enthusiasm for the future or even for living. The family remained in the small apartment, and Mai took in laundry to make additional money.

When Pao was fifteen, his father had been run down by a bicycle when he left the museum to head home after work. His head hit the pavement in an unfortunate way, and he had been unconscious when he was transported to the hospital. No one from the museum had contacted Mai to tell her what happened, so she only learned after waiting at the door for the museum to open the next morning why her husband had never come home.

When Mai and Pao finally arrived at the hospital, Den Chin's father lay in the middle of a ward crowded with patients without money or connections. He had fallen into a coma and died that night without ever knowing that his family was beside him. Mai had not seen or spoken to a doctor, although Pao saw white-jacketed professionals going in and out of the private rooms across the hall, reserved for wealthy nationalists.

With almost unbearable bitterness, Pao concluded that his father had chosen the wrong side when he had followed the nationalists across the sea.

He had vowed to take care of his mother and grandparents and mimicked his father's calm and polite demeanor as best as he could, but anger gnawed at him constantly. He had tried to become the man of the family and be supportive of Mai, but in her sorrow her naturally quiet temperament turned into virtual silence. Pao had been essentially alone even when his mother was present.

When he was sixteen a fellow student with whom he had become friendly cautiously asked Pao if he was interested in attending a secret meeting of the youth division of the People's Republic of China, the now firmly entrenched Communist government on the mainland that had long ago prompted Den Chin's father to flee. His friend assured him that the PRC hated the nationalists as Pao did. He said yes, he would like very much to attend.

CHAPTER 6
2014
Beijing

"The rare earth mine at Bukit Merah in Perak is likely to become an international issue yet again. The pollution it generated has been well known since the 1980s," Den Chin told the two committee members with whom he had requested a meeting. "But there are recent aspects of it that are not public. In fact, I believe that at this time only my lab in Kuala Lumpur has drawn a definitive connection between the rare earth mine and the new issues."

They were sitting in a private dining room of the refined Aman Summer Palace hotel, drinking French wine and enjoying a luncheon of perfectly prepared Peking duck that had been carved tableside by the chef. Den Chin was still surprised by the personal excesses of the committee members who, all in the name of strengthening Communism and on the tab of the party, enjoyed lavish lifestyle benefits that would be unimaginable to rank-and-file members. Den Chin thought in passing that his father, who had been loyal to the nationalists because he believed the Communists were lacking in refined taste, would have been amazed at the quality of the committee's palate and the budget spent to indulge it.

"It sounds uncertain that there is a direct connection," said the member for environmental options. "The scenario you are describing hardly indicates cause and effect."

After joining the party as a teenager, Pao Den Chin had been brought to the attention of the leadership in Beijing, which was always seeking ways to infiltrate the KMT in Taiwan. Recognizing the potential of Pao's impressive intellect coupled with his serious, even mournful nature and his ties to Taiwan, the party brought him to Beijing and provided him with a superior education at university and medical school. His lack of easy interaction with others, however, made him unsuitable for treating patients, and he gravitated to research. He designed and completed a series of biomedical projects and gave presentations to senior committee members who were consistently impressed. Now, having been elevated through the party hierarchy for decades, Den Chin was a high-ranking and respected member.

"We have limited data at this point, but I nonetheless feel it is a virtual certainty," Den Chin said. The committee members waited for him to expound on his statement, but he remained silent and sipped his wine. When no one spoke, he added, "The Peking duck here is unparalleled. What an excellent choice of venue." The committee members nodded their agreement.

When they finished dining, the three men strolled outside to reach the secret gate providing access from the grounds of the hotel to the emperor's summer palace. Rather than an actual palace, the area was an extraordinary park covering hundreds of acres of classically landscaped gardens and water features and numerous historical buildings. Originally intended to serve as a summer resort for the emperor, the area was now a magnificent tourist attraction offering garden walks, boating, and historical tours through the buildings.

The usual crowds had been dispersed by the security detail accompanying them, and the men were able to walk pleasantly along the shore of Western Lake to the Dragon King Temple. The member for environmental options had indicated he had a special appreciation for the temple, which had been reconstructed in the eighteenth century as a place to pray for rain. For a time, it had been called the Temple of Extensive Moisture.

"What is your recommendation?" asked the member for developing export strategies once they were inside and the temple had been cleared of others so they could speak in privacy.

Den Chin turned and faced his comrades. "As you are aware, the Malaysian government has been . . . convinced. . . to look the other way while we have surreptitiously excavated the supposedly closed rare earth mines in Perak for more than a decade," he said. "We also have had our teams in place for almost two years to generate public opposition to the new Australian refinery near Kuala Lumpur because of 'environmental hazards.' If allowed to reach full production, that facility would significantly reduce our own control of worldwide rare earth supplies."

Den Chin paused and saw that he now had the rapt attention of the two men. "Our mining program in Perak was conducted under the very noses of the Japanese who apparently, amazingly, still believe that the tunnels have been dormant since they completed their so-called remediation, which was performed without scientific basis. The method they employed could only have been thought up by the lazy and ignorant Japanese who tried to bury the problem, literally."

Den Chin explained to his colleagues that the "cleanup" had consisted of loading eighty thousand metal drums containing nuclear waste and other poisonous material from the original rare earth mine into the interior of a blasted-out mountain in Perak. That mountain, he told them, was now irreversibly compromised as a result of the deterioration of the drums, which allowed the poisonous contents to leach into the soil and water of the mountain. He believed that the contamination was very likely connected to the unexplained deaths of bat populations in the area as well as other serious issues. And now there was a possible connection to human illness in the Perak region.

"Yes, yes," said the member for environmental options, his face taking on a grim expression. He waved his arm impatiently at Den Chin and said, "That much is obvious. But how do you recommend we handle it now?"

Den Chin continued. "There are two aspects to address. First, the supposed cleanup that most likely caused the environmental disaster was done by the Japanese, not by us. Nonetheless, if our presence in the region is discovered, we will no doubt be blamed for the environmental problems in addition to having our covert mining operations exposed."

"You said there are two aspects to consider. What is the second issue?" asked the member for environmental options.

"Second," he replied, "it is imperative to eliminate evidence that it was our own team that generated social agitation among Malays to oppose the new Australian refinery." The members stared at him in silence. "Inasmuch as we operate the largest rare earth facility in the world in Baotou, Inner Mongolia, it would not be very helpful for us to be stirring up opposition to that very process based on health and safety concerns."

"Do you really think anyone will care enough to look into that?" asked the member for environmental options, more as a conclusion than a question.

Den Chin continued in the same modulated tone. "Until the Chinese tourist was hospitalized, I did not expect the matter to draw wide attention. After all, the other eight cases of pneumonia of unknown cause were all local Malays, and the Perak medical services, fairly primitive, did not draw any connection among them." He looked directly at the other men. "But the critical, possibly fatal illness of a young and healthy Chinese national on vacation in Malaysia, that is a different matter entirely. The Malay medical services will be defensive, and their inability to provide a reliable diagnosis will likely be reported internationally, particularly in light of the recent avian flu scare. The publicity will focus suspicion on the area of the supposedly closed mine in Perak, which is where she spent most of her vacation."

Den Chin noted that his companions were now listening intently. "At that point," he said somberly, "it is a distinct possibility that someone will notice the similarity of her case to the eight cases among the Malays. Who knows what will happen after that? And who knows what connection may be drawn between her illness and the environmental catastrophe surrounding the mine?"

Den Chin waited for a response, but the two committee members were silent. After a few moments, the member for developing export strategies stared hard at him and said, "And, Dr. Den Chin, I repeat, what exactly do you propose to do about it?"

"At this point," Den Chin said, "the waste material hidden in the mountain by the Japanese has been chemically blended with the soil and cannot be separated back into original components. There is nothing at all that we, or anyone for that matter, can do about it. All we can do is erase all evidence of our presence there and hope it will not be linked to us by circumstantial suggestion."

The two committee members stared at him, aghast. The member for environmental options cleared his throat. "Circumstantial suggestion? What are you talking about? We are not supposed to be mining or doing anything in Malaysia at all! Why would this have any link to us at all?" he asked.

"Because," said Den Chin calmly, "at this point our surreptitious use of the mine is the least of our problems. Although the mine and the abominable 'cleanup' were Japanese, the subsequent actions we engaged in involve us in the matter without doubt. Furthermore, we *discovered* this problem, putting a burden upon us to determine a course of action that will have significant consequences. The initial question, sirs, is do we reveal the problem and address it? Or do we simply vacate the area, erase evidence of our presence, and hope for the best?"

The two committee members stared at each other grimly, ignoring Den Chin. They appeared to silently reach agreement on the matter, and without a word to Den Chin, the member for developing export strategies signaled his senior administrative clerk who had been standing outside the temple with the security officers. He instructed the clerk to arrange for their immediate use of a private meeting room in the hotel, which they would need for the balance of the afternoon. They also required a secretary approved for secure meetings to be transported from Beijing as expeditiously as possible.

Over the course of the ensuing meeting, the three men agreed on an action plan. They hammered out the exact goals of the operation and its procedural details. The secure meeting secretary recorded notes and was discharged with instructions to complete a list of tasks.

The two committee members summoned their car to drive them back to Beijing, and Den Chin arrange for a separate car to take him directly to the airport.

Before leaving the meeting room in the hotel, he called the secure line to Beijing and instructed the operator who came on the line, "I need you to connect me to Dr. Binh at the Beijing Center now." He hung up and reviewed his notes for about ten minutes until the phone rang.

"Dr. Binh," he said after they exchanged formal greetings, "I need you to arrive in Kuala Lumpur with a secure medical transport team as early as possible tomorrow." Binh asked how long Den Chin anticipated that he would be needed in Kuala and said it would be difficult to travel immediately as he was in the midst of a pharmaceutical evaluation. "*My* matter takes precedence over anything, everything else," replied Den Chin curtly. "Feel free to indicate it is my order to anyone who questions your leaving. Kindly advise my staff of your travel arrangements, and we will schedule a meeting at the Kuala Center's secure rooms as soon as possible. I will explain the issue to you then."

Den Chin got into the car waiting for him at the hotel entry and got to the airport in time to board a private jet by early evening. He was back in the PRC residence maintained in Kuala Lumpur in less than six hours, in time to have a few hours of sleep before his early morning meeting with Dr. Binh.

CHAPTER 7
2014
Kuala Lumpur, Malaysia

As instructed by Dr. Den Chin, Dr. Binh and his team arrived at Prince Court Medical Centre before noon and met with the medical director of the hospital in his office. Twenty minutes later, the director summoned Dr. Anshar to provide an update on his most challenging patient, the Chinese tourist with an undiagnosed respiratory infection.

The director's office was standing room only with two Chinese doctors sitting in the guest chairs and a third standing at the window when Dr. Anshar arrived. The director stood to greet him and gestured at one of the men seated in front of him. "This is Dr. Binh," he said. "This team has been dispatched from Beijing to take your Chinese patient home to her family."

Dr. Anshar raised his arms in a questioning gesture and his facial expression displayed shock. Without moving farther into the cramped office, he told the assembled group sternly that his patient was gravely ill and that a plane trip would seriously diminish her chances of survival. Moreover, he told them, she had a respiratory illness that very likely was contagious, and it seemed foolhardy to move her into a public setting where others could be exposed.

"Such a trip would directly jeopardize her life," he said firmly, staring at the director. "If her family is anxious to support her, they certainly can come here to Kuala and be with her," he suggested.

The director said nothing but instead motioned deferentially to the man he had introduced as Dr. Binh, who said, "Yes, I understand your concerns, Dr. Anshar, but with no disrespect intended, the family would feel more secure if she were treated in China." He smiled pleasantly to diffuse any discomfort caused by his obvious condescension about Malaysian medical standards.

Dr. Anshar replied that he was a medical man and had little interest in politics, but that he found this to be a shocking statement. "The People's Republic of China is hardly known to indulge requests for special treatment based on family sentimentality," he said. "Is the patient from a rich family?"

"Oh, no," responded Dr. Binh, appearing undisturbed by Dr. Anshar's provocative question. "I know that Malaysia may have different operational norms, but in China we do not consider the status of persons when we render medical care. It is merely a kindness to an ordinary family." His tone was quiet but conveyed that the removal of the patient to China was not open to discussion.

The hospital director focused on Dr. Anshar with a penetrating stare, and with a grim expression nodded for him to continue.

Dr. Anshar paused and after a moment appeared to have made his decision. He said to Dr. Binh, "I see. When will you be removing her? Will you be needing an intensive care team to accompany you or any equipment?"

"Oh no, no, but thank you for your kind offer, Dr. Anshar." Dr. Binh gestured at his two associates, neither of whom had uttered a word or displayed any emotion throughout the exchange, and said, "I have brought my team, so we are all set. I have arranged to transport the patient to Beijing tomorrow on Malaysia Airlines, and my colleagues will be removing her from the hospital first thing tomorrow morning."

Dr. Anshar's expression openly conveyed shock, and the director quickly interjected, "Yes, that will be fine, Dr. Binh. I will prepare the discharge paperwork for tomorrow and alert the nursing staff to have the patient prepared to travel."

They discussed details and concluded the meeting. Dr. Binh and his associates departed, never having asked to see the patient or review her medical records. Dr. Anshar started to point this out to the director, but he was quickly ushered out of the director's office and instructed that there would be no further discussion of the matter. The director made it clear that Prince Court Medical Centre would not get into a dispute with the government of China over the care of a Chinese national. He told Dr. Anshar, "You did your best; now forget it and get on with your other patients."

CHAPTER 8
2014
Kuala Lumpur, Malaysia

Den Chin paced about his office at the PRC's Kuala Lumpur center, mentally reviewing the emergency action plan he had devised with the committee members in Beijing. He was responsible for implementing the action and coordinating its moving parts, and he again ticked through each step to be sure he had not neglected any details. Time was short, and execution had to be flawless.

It was critical that the administrative staff at the Kuala center not know that a coordinated action was underway, which would make the plan far more difficult to supervise. Bypassing the clerks and secretaries who normally would handle arrangements of this type, Den Chin personally assigned a different team leader to each segment, making sure that they operated independently and would never have sufficient information about other teams to realize that they were part of a coordinated plan.

Dr. Binh already had reported to him that transport of the gravely ill Chinese tourist together with three medical attendants had been arranged on a Malaysia Air flight from Kuala to Beijing. Transportation of the group to the airport was scheduled with a local ambulance company that knew only that a Chinese tourist had fallen ill and was returning to a Beijing hospital where she would be close to her family.

The leader of the foreign agitation group, the members of which had been installed in numerous residences in Perak and charged with generating Malaysian opposition to new rare earth mining programs, had been instructed to gather his team for immediate return to Beijing. All forty-two members had been provided with tickets for the Malaysia Air flight.

The Kuala center's administrative staff assigned to the mining operations, twenty-six people in all, had been informed that the action was complete and that they would return to the mainland on the same flight.

Six of the eight Malay patients with suspicious pneumonia already had died, each with a diagnosis of "infection of unknown origin." Den Chin investigated the medical records but found no indication that any link between the deaths was suspected.

Families of the two Malay patients who were still alive, both critically ill at different rural hospitals in Perak, had been offered "humanitarian assistance" from an Asian charity to pay for transfer of the patients to Beijing to receive more sophisticated treatment. The families were advised that the generous offer was at the instruction of the Chinese committee member for developing export strategies and was intended to foster better relations between Malaysia and the PRC. The family of the first patient declined the assistance, but the elderly patient had died overnight and eliminated the problem. When the spouse of the second patient gratefully accepted, the charity arranged transportation on Malaysia Air for the barely conscious patient, his wife, and a two-person medical team to accompany them.

Under the supervision of Den Chin, samples of soil and water from the limestone mountain in which the waste products from the Bukit Merah mine had been buried were delivered to the airport for transport to Beijing for analysis on the same plane. The cargo was marked as miscellaneous material and equipment belonging to the Kuala center.

Finally, detritus from the dead bats and other animals had been carefully preserved for transport on the flight. Once on the mainland, the samples would be transferred to skilled virology laboratories for exhaustive examination.

Soon after dawn on the morning of the flight, when bats and other nocturnal creatures would be asleep in their nests, a black-clad remediation team assembled by the committee member for environmental options swept through Perak and released deadly chemicals into the mine shafts and caves carved into the limestone. They used an odorless gas known to have a devastating effect on bats and other small mammals but that would dissipate quickly and have little effect on humans when used in outdoor or ventilated environments. Finishing its mission, the team was transported by bus to the airport to await boarding that evening on the Malaysia Air flight.

Den Chin completed his final review of each step of the action and was confident that everything had been done. He carefully packed his files into his travel case and returned to the PRC residence to gather his personal belongings.

He had expected to also travel on the flight, but at the last minute an envelope containing a ticket to Taiwan was delivered to him from the committee. The accompanying letter explained that since a number of the team leaders knew Den Chin personally, his presence might cause them to realize that there was a connection among the various groups traveling on the flight. The committee suggested that, to avoid that possibility, he instead visit with his mother in Taiwan for a night.

He was pleased to spend a night in Taipei. Mai, now elderly but in good health, still resided in the same apartment in which he had grown up, but she now had a caregiver, for whom Den Chin paid, residing in the second bedroom.

He asked his Kuala administrator to reserve a room for him at the Taipei Marriott, left the Kuala center, and hoped for the best. He had learned long ago that the most carefully laid plans still required luck—uncontrollable and unpredictable luck—if they were to succeed. He would not know if luck was with him until the action was complete and the various travelers on the flight had returned to China and resumed their usual routines.

CHAPTER 9
2014
Taipei, Taiwan

Den Chin woke at 7:00 a.m. in his suite at the Taipei Marriott and allowed himself the unusual indulgence of lingering in bed for a while to enjoy the sumptuous bedding and perfectly conditioned air, so different from his usual accommodations in Beijing.

His mother had been happy with his surprise visit the evening before, but she had seemed frail and several times lost her train of thought in the midst of an ordinary conversation. He took her to an unpretentious Taiwanese restaurant that he favored whenever he was in the city, and they enjoyed an excellent meal. Ironically, she had become more communicative since she spent most of her time with only her health aide, and was more likely to express interest in her son's activities now than she had been during his lonely childhood years. Indeed, in those days, Pao thought, she rarely spoke enough for there to be any possibility of her statements veering off track.

He wished that his father had lived to see the cruelty and excesses of the KMT fade away into history. After Chiang Kai-shek's death in 1975, his regime on the island had been whitewashed for Taiwanese history books, and he now was remembered with expressions of respect. Extravagant monuments in public squares were modelled after the ones erected on the mainland before the Communists took power. Although the PRC still claimed ownership of Taiwan, the island had steadfastly resisted its control and continued to elect liberal leaders who forged political and trade alliances with the West to the annoyance of the party.

Den Chin's ties to Taiwan and his feeling of ease when visiting remained a valuable asset to the committee, and he sometimes used a trip to see his mother as a ruse to investigate matters of interest to the PRC. He remained loyal to the Communists, but he never forgot the childhood dreams he had learned from his father of the fine Chinese society that might have been.

Planning to do some work before his flight to Beijing, he ordered a light breakfast from room service and turned on the local news channel as he booted up his laptop.

Den Chin was thunderstruck by what he saw.

The Malaysia Air flight on which his entire retinue was traveling had disappeared less than an hour after takeoff. Now, eight hours after the plane had vanished from radar, there was no sign of a crash and no sign of the plane. It appeared to be lost.

He sat down on the edge of the bed, holding his head in disbelief, and watched for additional news about the disappearance until he left the hotel to go to the airport for his own flight to Beijing.

Dr. Anshar stormed into the hospital director's office and, ignoring the startled expression on the director's face, blurted out, "Have you seen the news?"

"What are you talking about, Dr. Anshar? You no longer show the courtesy of knocking or checking in with my receptionist?" the director said angrily.

"The news, the news," Anshar said. "The plane with the Chinese tourist on board has vanished!" he said in an agitated voice. He was pale, and his eyes were red.

The director stared at him. "No, I haven't heard that news," he finally said quietly. "You mean the plane crashed?"

"It has vanished," Anshar said. "Simply vanished. So far there's no evidence of a crash. No evidence of anything!" he said and slumped into a chair. "They could have just left her alone. My patient was improving, but they couldn't leave her alone," he said.

The director rose from his seat and came around his desk to sit down next to Anshar. "It is a terrible coincidence," he said sympathetically, "and you are an excellent physician to care so much about the survival of your patient. But, of course, consider the greater tragedy of a plane full of people, each with a future and a family. In this context, our patient is but a small piece of a greater story of sadness and loss. Why don't you go home and take the rest of the day off to be with your own family?" the director said, and Dr. Anshar did.

PART THREE
2021

Long Island, New York

CHAPTER 10

I pull into the parking lot of John's Eggery near my office as the red glow of sunrise is merging into the light of day. As I walk into the restaurant where we have agreed to meet, I realize that I look disheveled and unprofessional, wearing gray workout pants and a black T-shirt and a black fleece jacket, my hair barely brushed and just a touch of pale lipstick on my face. Of course, after Jack's call, I could hardly concentrate on putting together an impressive appearance, but still, I should have suggested a meeting place farther from my office where I would be less likely to bump into anyone I know. Even on Saturday, John's is as busy as social distancing rules allow, with lawyers and businesspeople eating breakfast before heading to work.

I see Jack already seated in a plexiglass, sectioned-off booth in the corner, drinking coffee and staring out the window. He is lost in thought and startles when I slide into the seat opposite him, glad that my back is facing the main part of the restaurant. "Hey, Jack," I say somberly, and he nods in return. "Any further news?"

He stares at me for a moment, taking in the change in my appearance, and I am appalled that I can't help but rearrange myself somewhat in an effort to find a more flattering pose. I note that

Cedar doesn't look too hot himself. His wardrobe selection is better than mine, but he is unshaven, and his face has a gray pallor.

"We need to find this Aimee Cedar," he says without preamble, staring at me. "We need to figure out why this. . . woman. . . kept me off that plane." He pauses, then says, "And look, before we go any further, I have to tell you it has crossed my mind that you *knew* her story was bullshit, that you cooperated in this plot for some reason that I can't fathom."

I am completely nonplussed by this statement. It had not occurred to me that he might think I was complicit with Aimee Cedar, only that I might appear humiliatingly stupid. I decide to reveal my own suspicions, which have been roiling my thoughts since he called me at 5:00 a.m. "Well, I have to tell *you* something," I say harshly. "It has crossed my mind that you know Aimee Cedar and that you and she concocted this story because you wanted an irrefutable excuse to stay off that plane. Or, if not that, then you are involved in something nefarious and know exactly why Aimee Cedar did this and who put her up to it!" I glare at him, not sure how to proceed.

The waiter appears, short-circuiting our animosity, and we each manage to roll off a basic breakfast order of eggs with bacon and toast. I don't intend to eat mine.

"Look, we don't trust each other, we don't know each other," he says when the waiter is safely out of earshot, "but we both want—I should say we both need—the same thing: to find this woman. That is the only starting place I can think of to figure this out. We have to work together on this for now." He scans my face for a reaction, but I am a lawyer, and I know how to keep a good poker face. I reveal nothing, but my mind is racing. Whichever one of us declines to hunt down Aimee Cedar is as good as admitting some kind of involvement in the scam, which now may have some obscure connection to the mysterious disappearance of a plane.

"OK," I finally say. It is true that I need to find Aimee Cedar to protect myself, and I realize Jack's suggestion that we do it together supports his innocence regarding the plot. Unless it doesn't.

Still, we don't begin the discussion, so finally I say, "Let's each ask one question. I start. What is the group you were meeting with in Dublin?"

"The GCAC," he says, and when I look puzzled, he adds, "Global Committee of Applied Chemistry."

"Well, what is that?" I ask, and he smirks in response.

"That would be *two* questions. My turn, Aruba," he says, rolling my name off his tongue with condescension. "Did you ever reach Aimee on the phone number she gave you, or was it dead on arrival?"

I ignore his tone and tell him, "Yes, we reached her several times to confirm details for the paperwork and to arrange the appointment for her to sign them. She said she didn't have a landline and we should use her cell, which is not unusual these days."

"What does she look like?" he follows up.

I reply tartly, "That's two questions, but I think we need to relax the rules if we're going to get anyplace with this. Aimee is cool as an iceberg and stunning. Asian; not Japanese, but Chinese or Southeast Asian maybe. Articulate and expensively, gorgeously dressed. Does that ring a bell?" He shakes his head no. I follow up. "So, what is the GCAC?"

"It's a federation of international organizations dedicated to excellence and advancement of all phases of chemistry, very respected and prestigious," he says with a tone of intellectual superiority. "We pool research from all over the world to assure uniform scientific standards, document discoveries, report novel research, and all other things chemical." He looks at me to gauge my interest and goes on. "I have a fairly distinguished resume, you know. I'm the associate chair of earth and environmental science at NYU."

I smile politely but am hardly bowled over since I never took a single course in science. "So, why were you heading to Dublin?" I ask.

"The GCAC is hosting a conference on twenty-first-century approaches to four billion years of environmental damage. It's actually their first symposium in Europe since the pandemic hit, and Ireland has rolled out the red carpet for us. Scientists coming from all over the world, and I was to give the keynote presentation on twentieth-century disasters in mining rare earth elements." He pauses and, noting my blank expression, continues. "It sounds dry, but in fact it's a fascinating topic. You can't imagine how interesting rare earth can be."

Not to me, however, so I move on. "What about the man you were traveling with? Is he a chemist also?" I ask. But I am thinking that this topic is not likely to be the link to recent events that we are looking for.

"George Hong is a professor of earth sciences at Columbia, a friend. He asked to come to the conference as my guest, and he helped me to review and finalize my presentation." He pauses and looks at me to see if I am still with him. I am, but I am deep in thought about what he has said.

An interesting aspect of practicing divorce law is that I am called upon to understand all kinds of businesses being divided between warring spouses even when one or the other is trying to obscure the facts. I have become a quick study in figuring out different enterprises even when I had not been familiar with the underlying business before. But so far I am stumped on this entire subject.

"So, what exactly is rare earth?" I finally ask and can see on Jack's face that he is pleased to begin his Rare Earth 101 lecture.

"The term 'rare earth' encompasses a set of seventeen elements and metals—remember earth science and chemistry from high school?" He awaits my nod of agreement and continues. "Despite the name, most of these elements are not actually rare and are plentiful in the Earth's crust. However, they are rarely found in sufficient abundance in a single location for their mining to be economically viable, and REEs, as rare earth elements are commonly called, are needed for many important applications in modern technology for which there is no equal substitute." He tents his fingers in front of him as if he is at his lectern at NYU. He says that REEs are essential to the manufacture of more than two hundred applications, including tech and most green products, and even systems that are needed for defense, like radar and sonar.

"This is all news to me," I say, and Jack replies that he is not surprised because most people never give any thought to the components or manufacture of the everyday items they use, even the ones they consider indispensable. Some of the products that require REEs, he tells me, are cell phones, computer hard drives, and certain batteries, for example, and you cannot build a wind turbine or a Tesla without them.

It is obvious he would like to continue with the entire lecture, but I interrupt. "This is really fascinating," I say, striving for a tone of interest that I do not feel, "and I would love to hear more, but for the moment, can you think of anything about this topic or the conference that could be connected to this plane disappearance?"

He stares out the window as our food is delivered to the table and finally says, "No, I cannot. This is a bunch of chemists we are talking about. There are some political issues about the topic, serious environmental challenges, but this seems to generate interest only among scientists. I have never heard a single supporter of green technology address the substantial environmental and human health hazards inherent in the current methods used to manufacture those very items. And, in any event, we were just going to share information at the GCAC conference, not *do* anything that would make anyone angry. Certainly not any one government or terrorist group with the inclination, let alone the means, to . . . sabotage a passenger plane. It's not conceivable, Aruba. Come on."

I ponder his statement and think that perhaps they will find that the plane disappearance has nothing to do with terrorism, that it was caused by a mechanical malfunction or an accident. Maybe a cell phone battery caught fire or something. Maybe the plane landed safely on some Nordic island. I say to Jack, "I see your point that a bunch of chemists discussing minerals is not a likely motivation."

We eat in silence for a few minutes, and then Cedar says, "So, what could have motivated Aimee Cedar? I can't think of any reason someone would go to that length to prevent me from leaving the country, especially since I could still just go on Monday after you get the restraining order lifted."

That might have been true, I think but do not say aloud, if the plane had actually arrived at its destination. What might have been just a short delay now has entirely different and far more serious implications. And, I realize, we have no way of knowing if keeping Jack off that flight involved some bizarre motive of Aimee's, or, too sinister to seriously contemplate, she knew that the plane was doomed and for that reason prevented Jack from boarding. And what is the connection to George Hong lying about Jack's presence at the airport?

"OK, let's think along a different line. What is in the safe deposit box?" I ask.

"My passport and some materials for my presentation. My grad students have been compiling data and visuals on current REE extraction methods and how environmentally safe procedures can be introduced. It's mostly contained on flash drives in my apartment." Jack becomes animated, and it is obvious that he loves talking about this project.

"Isn't everything also in cloud-based storage?" I ask. I am a relative novice when it comes to technology, but I do have some knowledge of these storage and backup options.

"Of course, of course," he says quickly. "But I have actual charts and visuals, painstakingly prepared by my team, that make it easy to understand the complexities. I also have photos and other graphics to enhance the presentation. You know, sort of a high-tech display that

IMMORTAL IN SPLASHED INK

is part informational and part glossy sales pitch." He takes a gulp of coffee and shifts in his seat.

"Look," he says, "I think we're wasting time on this line of thinking. I can't imagine any connection between my role with the GCAC and this woman concocting a story to keep me from leaving the country, let alone my connection to the disappearance of a plane! We need to think of other motives she might have had for doing this and, most of all, how to find her." He stares at me and doesn't need to verbalize his scathing opinion of my failure to obtain any documentation of Aimee Cedar's story. His stony expression says it is my job to find my client, and of course, he happens to be right on that one.

"OK," I say, trying for confidence even though I feel none. "We need to see the security camera footage at my building to see if we can get a picture of her." I do not practice criminal law and am not familiar with this kind of evidence, but I am brainstorming now. "I'll figure out when she first called me and check my phone records of incoming calls to try to get the number she called from. And maybe the parking lot cameras will give us a lead on what car she was driving. I can contact the police and tell them I need help finding this woman who retained me but seems to have messed up on her contact information. . ."

Jack abruptly cuts me off. "No police yet," he says firmly.

Unexpectedly the back of my neck prickles, and my mistrust of him rushes back. "Why not? They can possibly help us find her," I say with nervousness that I hope is not obvious in my voice.

"Hasn't it occurred to you that this does not look good?" he almost shouts but then remembers we are in a restaurant and lowers his voice. "I was supposed to board a plane that has gone missing, possibly—it sounds like probably—as a result of sabotage, and the only reason I didn't board is that some woman who has subsequently vanished says she was my wife, which she isn't, and that my children, whom I don't have, need protection. Don't you suppose that story might seem a bit odd to whatever agency—The FBI? The CIA? Or whoever the hell it is?—investigates this? And *you* created the story!" He looks ready to lunge out of his seat and grab me across the table.

"You're right," I say and realize in a flash that whether my malpractice insurance covers this may be the least of my problems.

We leave the restaurant and head to my office where the weekend security guard informs us that he is not permitted to access the security footage unless the police require him to do so but that the building management staff can probably accommodate us on Monday. We go up to my office where I log into my telephone records and locate the initial call from Aimee. It is from the same cell phone number that she provided, which apparently is no longer in service.

I still hold out hope that Aimee Cedar is a real person, a real client, and that there is a real explanation for what has transpired. Accordingly, I inform Jack that he may not look at notes in my case file since I still consider him to be my adversary in this case. We agree to meet at the management office in my building at 9:00 a.m. on Monday in the hope of reviewing the security cameras, and neither of us can think of anything else to investigate at the moment.

When he finally departs, I sit down at my desk, unsure of how to proceed. I go through every line of my file and see nothing out of the ordinary. I reread the motion papers that resulted in the restraining order that kept Jack off the plane. They are well drafted, detailed, and credible. Based upon the content, the court acted correctly in issuing the order.

And yet my client has vanished. Her contact information has evaporated, and, since she provided payment in cash, I cannot even prove that she actually retained me. In fact, I realize, I would have no way to even confirm that she exists if Marsha had not interacted with her sufficiently to corroborate the events.

I cannot think clearly and know the best thing would be to try for a fresh perspective. I decide to throw in the towel for now and go home.

CHAPTER 11

The plane mystery is the major news story all weekend, and every media service scrambles to provide viewers with a fresh angle. The aircraft was not a Boeing, let alone the cursed MAX jet, which had finally been restored to service not that long ago. The passenger roster reveals no individuals with the background of the usual suspects: no Iranians, no Middle Eastern names, no one to galvanize suspicion. NBC reports a list of passenger affiliations including the GCAC, referring to it merely as an "international chemistry club" without even offering an explanation of the acronym. The reporter finds the group of little interest and makes no mention that at least one of its members did not actually board the plane. Perhaps investigators will not come looking for Jack after all.

Finding nothing helpful to solve the mystery, I turn to a different approach and relentlessly search for any online reference to the vanished Aimee Cedar, though I find none. Next I scour the GCAC website, reviewing bios of its members and lectures from past conferences. Then I try to find case law where restraining orders were granted based upon intentionally or unintentionally false information but find nothing remotely relevant.

Late on Sunday afternoon, I walk down to the beach, the air too cold for sunbathers but perfect for walkers like me, and head west along the ribbon of dunes that was buttressed by the Army Corps of Engineers after Hurricane Sandy devastated the entire shore in 2012.

The waves are quiet and lap in long crescents along the edge of the sand. The magical quality of the sea air does not fail me, and my spirits begin to lift. Things will work out, I tell myself. I have been duped but did nothing illegal or even unethical. In fact, for some obscure reason, my naivety seems to have actually saved Jack Cedar's life.

I amble along pleasantly and spot a neighbor, Harry Shaw, wrapped in a red sweatshirt and sitting in a beach chair in front of the decking that traverses the dunes to his house. I don't feel like chatting with anyone, but he waves and stands up to greet me. About six feet tall and well built, he is a handsome, patrician looking man of about sixty who manages to exude good manners and good cheer without ever putting a sexual overtone on it. He has revealed to me that he was divorced a number of years ago, and I have no idea what he does for companionship or any other details of his personal life.

"How are you, Aruba?" he says in his affable, deep voice. "What a glorious day it is!" He is a dynamic guy.

I agree about the weather but have trouble mustering up any enthusiasm. Harry seems to notice my mood and fills the conversational breach. "Well, the pool guys finally finished the glass coping. It's a world-class event!" he bellows.

He purchased his oceanfront property almost a year ago, but the architectural masterpiece he envisioned is still not finished. He moved into the house a few months ago, but the construction on it continues around him, and on most weekdays, teams of workmen toil around the house and grounds.

It is obvious that money and time are of no consequence to Harry Shaw, and I marvel at both his temperament and his budget. Most recently, an eight-foot-high steel and cement fence, or more appropriately an impenetrable enclosure, has been erected, encircling his property. I cannot imagine why he feels a need for it in our crime-free neighborhood where a number of very wealthy people with well-known business connections maintain homes without the need for security barriers.

"Congratulations," I offer. "It would be nice if you actually could swim in it when summer arrives."

He studies my face for a moment and says, "You seem a bit deflated today, Aruba. Anything I can help with?"

"Just thinking over a few issues at the office," I say in a neutral voice.

"Well, that is a good lead-in to an episode of *Divorce Lawyer Stories*." He laughs and waits for me to begin, but I say nothing. "It's definitely your turn. . ." He prods me.

We have a bantering game between us: I tell him a divorce story in the "I thought I had heard everything" vein, and he counters by relating an anecdote about international shipping gleaned from his position as managing partner of Shaw Global, the international maritime company founded by his uncle in the 1980s. The firm is based in Switzerland, and in almost four decades it has grown to be one of the largest and most profitable shipping companies in the world. Its bright red logo with a bold arrow is recognized on every continent.

Harry is a Swiss national and still makes his primary home in Geneva where the firm is based, but for the last seven years he has served as chairman of North American Operations, leading the profitable division based in New York. He maintains a luxury apartment on the Upper East Side, but recently, because of the devastating impact the coronavirus and social unrest protests have had on New York City, he decided to buy the beach house. He told me that he chose the spot because he can see his ships steaming in and out of New York.

I am not up for the game but mentally run through some past divorce cases trying to come up with one that will be mesmerizing yet easy and fast to relate.

"OK," I tell Harry. "Got one. Even though we have 'no fault' divorce in our state, it's still important to set forth the reasons or grounds that someone wants to end a marriage. We do this in a proper legal format, called a 'complaint.'"

I explain to him that when grounds for a divorce are serious, it may affect a judge's thinking on the financial aspects of the case, on custody and visitation if there are kids, and on other issues such as who, if anyone, gets to remain in the marital residence. So as soon as a client retains me, I routinely instruct them to write out the reasons they want to divorce and put together "evidence," if there is any, to support those claims.

"You know," I tell him, "I have learned that in a marriage people can do all kinds of crazy things as long as they agree; if they stop agreeing, the same behavior can turn into grounds for divorce."

Harry listens intently and raises his eyebrows in my direction, inviting me to continue.

"So my client was the wife, a woman of about forty and very flaky. And from the minute she started to talk it was clear that she was not the sharpest knife in the drawer either. When she gave me her grounds for divorce, with tremendous melodrama, she handed me a wooden dowel that looked like a magic wand. She even waved it around in my direction and clearly expected me to understand its significance. When I shrugged, having no idea what it was, she turned the end of the dowel to face me and pointed it directly at my face. Still nothing from me."

I see that Harry is listening intently and continue. "'Look,' she said and pointed at the tip, which had engraved in teeny digits *666*. She whispered, 'The number of the Antichrist! It's my husband's wand, and when he thought I was asleep, he waved it at me trying to give me a curse. I saw him do it maybe six or eight times, but it didn't work.'"

Harry starts to chuckle, and I tell him that I thought using this baloney as grounds for divorce would likely give the court more sympathy for her husband, who obviously was married to a fruitcake. "So I asked the client if she had anything else to tell me. She did."

Good lawyers are at heart good storytellers and know how to present their client's tale to get the most mileage. I pause for effect until Harry finally says, "So?"

"Remember this was before the internet displayed everything to everybody, so we had to use other ancient methods of communication like newspapers. My client whipped out of her bag the classified section of a newspaper and pushed it across my desk. It was a full page of square ads of about an inch, and in each square was a photograph of a naked penis and, below it, a phone number! Some pictures were only a penis; some included nearby. . . anatomy. Some were fully erect, some flaccid, different colored hair surrounding different colored penises! Harry, I was speechless and struggling to suppress laughter when she leaned across the desk and jabbed her index finger at one of the pictures. In a loud stage whisper, she hissed, 'That's him! I would know him anywhere! And it's a classified *dating* page. He was looking for *dates!*"

I tell Harry that I stared at the photos for a few moments until I thought I could speak with a straight face and then asked her how she knew it was her husband. "I hate to tell you this, Harry, but they all looked pretty much the same to me. . ."

"Well," Harry comes back without missing a beat, "they may all look the same, but they don't all perform the same. . ." He smiles at me coyly.

"My client did not share the opinion that they look alike. She stared at me like I was a simpleton who had not mastered the fine art of penis ID from passport-size photos and said smugly, 'Oh, that's him without a doubt. I would know him anywhere!'"

Harry is laughing his good-natured, hardy laugh. "So, what did the judge think?"

"Oh, luckily I was able to settle the case without going to court. I have a feeling her grounds would not have garnered much special consideration from the judge. A woman, by the way."

"That's because we're in New York." Harry chuckles. "In much of Europe, actually much of the world, a female judge would be extremely impressed with those skills and want to know the secret! And men, of course, would think their 'equipment' was the biggest, the best, the most splendid, and that's why any woman would recognize them at once."

We share a good laugh, and I realize that I actually do feel much better. Harry promises to have a good maritime story for me in a few days. Most of his stories are grim, ships that run aground during storms, containers plunging into the sea, man overboard, but occasionally he slips in something funny like a sailor getting caught screwing in the cargo hold. I continue my walk.

I have always done my best work in the morning, so my office opens at 8:00 a.m. instead of the traditional 9:00 a.m. It works well for Marsha, too, since she is also an early riser. On Monday morning, after tossing around for half the night, I am lingering over a second cup of coffee when my cell rings. It's Marsha, already at her desk.

"When I arrived at the office, there were two FBI agents waiting at the door for you. I think you better get in here fast," she says in a tremulous voice.

I tell her I will be there in less than thirty minutes and she should offer them coffee in the conference room. A minute after we hang up, Jack Cedar calls. He tells me the FBI arrived at his apartment at 5:00 a.m. and questioned him for almost two hours. He gave them the legal papers and the restraining order that had prevented him from getting on the flight and told them what had transpired after he was served with them on Friday afternoon. He tells me I should expect the agents at my office, but of course I already know that.

CHAPTER 12

When I get to the office, Marsha jumps up to greet me, if you could call it that. Her face is drawn and worried, and she hustles me over to the side of the reception area, away from the conference room where she has stashed the FBI agents.

"These guys are the real deal, Aruba. They demanded the Cedar file to review while they were waiting for you. I told them that only you could turn over a file that is covered by attorney-client privilege and that I would lose my job if I let them have it. They all but laughed out loud at me."

She takes a few deep breaths, trying to calm down, and then continues. "The tall, blond guy said, 'You are dealing with the FBI, ma'am. You may have heard that we can do all kinds of things to get what we want. Ever watch any of those FBI shows on TV?' He was smiling, very affable, but it really was not funny, Aruba, not one bit. I finally gave them the file, and they have it in the conference room. I hope you understand," Marsha whispers, and I see she is close to tears.

"It's OK," I reassure her, "but while I'm meeting with them, find the building engineer and get him to review the security cameras to try to find a shot of Aimee Cedar. Figure out when she was here so you can narrow down the time for them. Hopefully the cameras have date stamping."

She stands frozen to her spot, processing what I have asked her to do. "Aruba, what is going on?" she says. "Is this a missing person thing, over state lines or something? Why would the FBI be interested in the Cedar divorce?"

I realize she has not connected the dots to link Jack Cedar to the missing plane over the weekend. "Marsha, the plane that went down." I pause, and she nods in acknowledgment. "That was the plane that we—I mean, I—kept Jack Cedar from boarding." Her jaw drops, and she holds her hand up to her face.

"Oh my God," she mumbles. "What does that mean, Aruba?"

"I don't know yet, Marsha," I say, "but I have to go in and speak to these agents right now. So you need to sit down for two minutes, get a hold of yourself, and then go find the building engineer and do what I told you." I put my hand on her shoulder and move her toward a leather chair in the waiting room. "OK?" I say and wait a moment until she nods and sinks into the chair.

I take my own deep breath, square my shoulders, and open the door to the conference room. I take in the two men seated at my table with my Cedar file spread out in front of them, as if it is their table and their file, and extend my hand toward them, saying in a confident voice, "Aruba Jones, gentlemen."

To my surprise I do not get a double take or any reaction at all to the disconnect between my name and my appearance and assume that Jack has already mentioned it to them. Or else they are seriously good at keeping FBI blank expressions. Unaccountably, it makes me nervous.

The blond guy rises from his seat and shakes my hand, and I note that he towers over me. He must be about six-foot-four, I think, and built like a linebacker. "Peter Drost," he says pleasantly. His buddy, a more ordinary five-foot-nine or so, with unremarkable features and brown hair, introduces himself as Hal Hamilton.

Despite their appearances, it immediately becomes obvious that Agent Hamilton is the boss of this team, and he does not bother to maintain a friendly, or even pleasant, demeanor. As soon as he begins to speak, I am on the defensive and know that I am being accused of something.

Hamilton tells me that they are investigating the Saturday early morning disappearance of the Emerald Air flight from New York to Dublin, and he obtains my permission to record the interview. He places a recording device on the table and tells me they are looking into three passengers who were scheduled to board the flight but did not. This is a typical starting point in such investigations, he says, since it is obvious that anyone with knowledge of potential danger to a flight would not wish to board.

The first passenger they interviewed stated that the business meeting in Ireland that he was scheduled to attend was moved to Vienna and that his secretary handled the cancellation of his Ireland flight. The second absent passenger is a housewife who missed the flight because her child contracted strep throat, confirmed by the pediatrician.

The third missing passenger, one Jack Cedar, he says, related to them a bizarre sequence of events that led to his missing the plane. Mr. Cedar was unable to explain his own story, which was strange at best, and directed them to me for details and confirmation. "So," he says, "Ms. Jones, why don't you just tell us what you know about this?"

Trying to maintain a modicum of compliance with legal ethics, I confirm for the benefit of the recording device that I am revealing privileged information only because I am being directed to do so by a government investigative agency and that, even so, I was not retained in connection with any illegal or criminal conduct by my client and do not know of any such conduct.

Then I give them a careful, detailed narrative of the Cedar case, beginning with the first phone call I received from Aimee in which she appealed for help to prevent her children from being removed from the country and concluding with Jack's phone call to me in the middle of the night to inform me of the missing plane. I end the story there, leaving out the interaction between Jack and me that followed his call, thinking it might imply that we had some common purpose when, in fact, I was retained to be his adversary.

Hamilton stares at me while Drost leans back in his chair and smirks. He jumps in and asks, "So, how do we get in touch with your client to confirm this?" I assume that Jack already has told them about this little problem, which no doubt provides a solid basis for the suspicious way they are treating me.

"Look," I say, fighting to stay calm although I know the story sounds bad. In fact, I admit to myself, it sounds very bad. "The contact info Mrs. Cedar provided to me apparently is incorrect. I have been trying to locate her nonstop since Jack Cedar came to my office on Friday. I have had no success with her cell number or the address she gave me, although we did reach her on that same number several times when I was preparing her motion papers."

They say nothing, and the silence stretches out, probably an interrogation trick, which I fall for. "I cannot explain it, officers," I finally fill the void. "I have no way of knowing if Mrs. Cedar intentionally gave me false information or if something has happened to her or if it is as simple as a clerical mistake. I really have nothing else to tell you, so if we can conclude now. . ."

Hamilton snaps forward so fast that I don't even register the movement, and he puts his open hand down on the table. He stares at me and says, "Ms. Jones, we will conclude this interview when I decide it's concluded, which I assure you it is not. So, are you ready to continue?" He smiles very slightly, like someone who has not actually smiled since the second grade, and I nod. He did not slam his hand on the table or lunge out of his seat or make any overtly threatening gesture, and yet there is something ominous about that hand sitting flat on my conference room table that causes my head to begin pounding.

"Of course," I manage to say evenly, trying not to show fear, which is now accumulating in every fiber of my being.

They take turns peppering me with questions, fast and furious so I will not have a chance to calculate a lie. They pull my file notes apart and ask what was Aimee wearing; did she have an accent; what is her level of education, country of birth; did she mention anything unusual about her children; did she tell me much about her husband's lifestyle and profession; how did they meet; how long did they date before they were married; and on and on. I am completely truthful but have no answers for many of their questions. I explain that I had no reason to be suspicious and that since it was an emergency application to the court I limited my intake to the immediate problem. Details of the marriage pertinent to continuing a divorce action would have come at later meetings, after the children's safety was secure.

They are incredulous that I did not ask for Aimee's ID or proof of the marriage, and in light of what has happened, I don't really blame them. But I don't waver from my explanation that I have never requested this of any client. I tell them what really is obvious: that it would make no sense for someone to make up a fictional marriage and hire a matrimonial attorney. Criminal lawyers disbelieve their clients from the first sentence, but while I always am suspect about my clients' versions of marital discord, which are likely to be subjective, I have never been skeptical about the existence of an actual marriage. Of course, that will now be a thing of the past, and I am wondering if it would be excessive to get fingerprints or a retinal scan for future clients.

"So, what was your overall appraisal of her?" Drost asks.

"She was smart, articulate, well put together, and seemed completely credible." I don't mention that in retrospect I realize that she was too smart, too put together, too articulate, and altogether too credible.

"And do you think she is married to Jack Cedar?" he asks, taking me by surprise.

This question I don't know how to answer. I really have come to suspect that Aimee is the liar here, not Jack. But if I say so, I will be directing suspicion at myself, either for being in some kind of complicity with her or, maybe even worse for a female lawyer, being just plain stupid. But I will not help them build suspicion around Jack, whom I have begun to like and, at this point at least, find trustworthy.

"I can't tell you that, gentlemen. I really have no idea."

After an hour and a half, they have exhausted questions that are reasonably relevant. They are investigating a missing plane, after all, and don't know if Jack's failure to board the plane has anything whatsoever to do with what caused it. They provide their contact information and ask that I let them know immediately if I am able to locate my client. They tell me that I will hear from them if they have further questions as the investigation proceeds and instruct me to notify them if I want to leave the New York metropolitan area.

They depart my office. I am distraught.

"Jack," I say into my phone, not quite controlling the tremor in my voice. "They just left and it's obvious that I—probably you and I—are suspected of having some kind of connection to this plane." I start to cry and try to do it silently so Jack will not realize it. We hardly know each other, I have unwittingly interrupted his plan to board a plane that has gone missing, and I am not at all sure what he is up to. I am going purely on instinct to conclude that he really is just an earth science professor who was supposed to deliver a talk on environmental protection and not a crazed airplane bomber or involved with one maybe named Aimee.

He is silent and then says in his professional, instructive tone, "Same place, twenty minutes." I am puzzling out this change in demeanor and realize that he thinks his, or my, phone may be tapped and wants to talk in person.

"OK," I reply. We hang up, and when I have composed myself sufficiently, I exit the conference room. Marsha is sitting at her desk typing, looking like she expects the worst to happen at any moment. I reassure her by telling her that the meeting went well, although I don't actually think it did, and ask her what happened with the building engineer.

"I figured out the dates and approximate times that Aimee was here and gave him a description of her appearance and clothing as best as I could remember. He's reviewing the security tapes and will let us know if he finds anything that could be a match."

I tell her I will be back in about two hours and ignore her testy look as I walk out of the office.

Jack is standing in the parking lot of John's Eggery when I pull in. He opens the passenger door and slides in before I can say a word. I know I should be suspicious of him and exercise due caution, but I am unraveling and feel only relief at seeing him calmly sitting there.

"Oh, Jack," I blurt out. "What is going on?" He stares at me, and I burst out crying. "I don't even know you. What have you gotten me into?"

His expression instantly morphs from sympathetic to angry, and I recognize the man who thundered at me when he showed up at my office last Friday, which feels like it was a year ago. "What did I get you into?" he growls. "I'd say you have that backward. You served me with court papers based on bullshit—"

I shout back, "And saved your life by doing so, or didn't that fact occur to you?" and pull a tissue from my bag.

Unexpectedly he reaches across the seat and puts his hand on my shoulder in a comforting way. "Look, Aruba," he says in an almost warm tone, "I should be blaming you for what's happened and be furious, but I actually believe that you were duped by this woman.

We just need to work together and figure out why this has happened. We can't even figure out any connection between us."

He stares at me directly without flinching or even blinking, and, right or wrong, I am confident that his story is true and his compassion for my position is real.

CHAPTER 13

We take our separate cars, and Jack follows me to my house, which on this sparkling autumn day looks particularly inviting. He follows me inside, and I go straight to my liquor collection in a dining room buffet and pull out a bottle.

"Bourbon?" I say. I don't usually drink during the day, but I am on stress overload. My hands are trembling, and my voice sounds tinny and unnatural. I hand Jack a glass, and we sip in silence for a few minutes. No matter how I parse what has happened, I cannot come up with a clue as to what is going on.

From Jack's expression, he is having similar thoughts. Neither of us now has any doubt that we are involved in something more significant than mistaken identity in a divorce case but can come up with no context in which the events that have tied us together make sense.

Finally Jack says, "Do you do any other kind of work? Besides divorce, I mean?" I tell him no, and he adds, "Have you represented anyone in the field of science?" No again. "How about professors, teachers, anyone like that?"

"No, this is the first time I have a case involving a professor," I tell him. The bourbon and the sea air wafting in the open windows are helping to quell my panicky feeling. "How could we be connected?" I ask, but before he can answer, I continue. "How about prior relationships? Could there be a person we have in common?"

He stares at me and says, "That's ridiculous. Even if there was a connection in that way, we would never figure it out. We need a better avenue of research," he says, the science investigator in him speaking with authority, as if to a student.

"I don't agree," I say with my own firm tone, my confidence returning. "Of course we could figure it out," I say. "We need to find the link."

"Oh please," he fires back in a snide tone. "You want us to sit here and have a chat about our social lives? What a waste of time when what the FBI guys are figuring out is how to tie us to a fatal terrorist attack. Cute idea, but we don't have time for this, Aruba," he says.

"Will you stop calling me that!" I blurt out.

He looks at me in surprise. "I thought that was your name. Would you prefer Ms. Jones?" he asks with sarcasm.

"Friends call me Ruby," I say, completely serious and feeling the bourbon coursing through me. Jack just stares at me.

"My parents were—are, actually—crazy and thought it was romantic to name me after their honeymoon destination. So anyone who hasn't met me in person expects a Caribbean guy, just like you did." With this admission, I have now classified Jack as a "friend," which, of course, is questionable. "You should see some of the expressions I get, especially in court," I continue, even as I know I should stop talking.

He fixes his eyes on me and then unexpectedly starts to laugh, a rich, warm sound. "Wow," he says. "Your parents really are crazy!" He retrieves the bourbon bottle and tops off both of our glasses.

I win about how our discussion should proceed, and we spend awhile trading information about our lives. As Jack predicted, we find no connection to explain the immediate events, but I do learn that Jack is a son of an affluent farmer in the Midwest and that, after attending the University of Virginia and then earning his master's and PhD in chemistry at Columbia, he chose the more exciting and diverse atmosphere of New York City in which to build his own life. He had a serious relationship with a female professor of English that lasted six years, but they decided not to marry and parted company.

I reveal that I grew up on Long Island with my now aging hippie parents and younger brother, founder of a tech startup that is doing fairly well and that I attended Tulane University and then NYU Law, a school that really was beyond my academic background but to which I probably was admitted because my unusual name implied that I would be a more exotic addition to their student roster than I actually was. I married an investment banker, very smart, handsome in a TV model kind of way, and making a fortune, who, after four years, announced that he had fallen in love with a man he met on the Long Island Rail Road.

Jack is also on his third drink, and to my relief, he displays no reaction to this revelation, which normally elicits either shock, not that my husband was gay but that I failed to recognize it; sympathy, not that my husband was gay but that I failed to recognize it; or, worst of all, suspicion that I am so deficient in womanly allure that I actually drove my former husband away from the entire female sex.

He says nothing, so after a few moments I ask him to tell me about the talk he had been scheduled to deliver in Ireland, more so I can stop talking and avoid revealing additional personal details that I will later regret than because I have any great interest in the science.

Jack apparently is feeling the bourbon less than I am because without hesitation or moving from his position on my favorite chair, he begins.

He summarizes what he has already told me about rare earth elements and adds that because in the last ten or fifteen years tech items have become "essentials" and the demand to develop renewable energy sources has exploded, the need for REEs has skyrocketed.

Jack looks at me to confirm that he has captured the interest of his audience, which he has.

He stands up and begins to pace around my living room. He tells me that in the late twentieth century China correctly predicted that the demand for REEs was about to explode and embarked on a plan to corner the market. They located and developed REE deposits on the Chinese mainland in Inner Mongolia, and these mines are now the richest source of REEs in the world. "In fact," he says, "having acquired only about a third of the world supply in the 1980s, by 2009 China controlled ninety percent of it."

To my surprise, I actually do find this interesting. I recall news clips of Elon Musk imploring the world to mine more of the elements needed for the manufacture of his Tesla automobiles.

Jack continues. "But there is a dark underside to this great environmental and technological revolution. The refining process needed to render REEs usable generates radioactive and other toxic, even poisonous, waste products that cause some of the worst pollution known to the planet. Problems, serious problems, deadly problems, have occurred near REE mines, which is the focus of the first segment of my talk. I have charts, statistics, et cetera, detailing some of the deadly results, particularly in the western Perak region of Malaysia," he says.

I comment that it sounds like a not unusual dilemma of trade-offs between advanced products and negative impacts caused by them. "Like pollution from fossil fuels versus environmentally friendly but less reliable renewable energy. Is that it?" I ask.

"Well, you're on the right track," Jack says. "But the issue is far more problematic because there just is no substitute for REEs; there is no known alternative that is environmentally superior. So it isn't a question of 'pick your poison'; it's 'have your cake or have no dessert at all.'"

He sits down and adds, "And the deadly damage, some of it anyway, from REEs is immediate and measurable. It's not like the amorphous threat of climate change at some undetermined time in the future."

I ponder this information for a few moments, and it crosses my mind that the topic of rare earth elements, and maybe even Jack's lecture about it, might touch some hot-button issues of interest to certain fanatics: Save-the-world Green New Dealers? Big-money manufacturers desperate to increase supplies of REE? Mining interests hampered by the demands of environmentalists? I am stumped.

"So, what happened in Malaysia?" I ask.

Jack tells me that in the 1980s a Japanese controlled mining company called Asia Rare Earth developed a major site, the Bukit Merah mine, on the west coast of Malaysia in the Perak region. It went fine at first, but then people living in the surrounding towns claimed that illnesses began to appear that were caused by pollution from the mine.

"Asia Rare Earth said the stories had been planted by China to undermine the Malaysian production, which was competing with its own mines. The Malaysian government, well known for corruption, was reputed to be making a fortune on the deal with Asia Rare Earth and was not too interested in disrupting it."

Jack sits back down in my favorite chair, looking right at home. "So?" I ask. "What happened?"

"Well," he says, "competing experts, including scientists sent by the UN and the World Health Organization were brought in to investigate, and they each reached different conclusions. Some said the mine was safe; some said it was an environmental and human disaster. Protest groups from other countries picked up the cause and began to flood into Perak."

He tells me that the protests became more and more disruptive, sometimes violent, and eventually the mine was shut down. But it took about a decade to close it and more than another decade until the site was remediated. By that time, he says, eleven people had died from leukemia in a population that should have had one case every thirty years or so, not to mention the devastating birth defects and elevated rates of other cancers in the area.

I think about this sequence. "So the mine caused the cancer? And birth defects? And you are saying that the only option is to forget about tech products unless we can come up with a way to produce them that does not require rare earth?"

"Aruba—Ruby," he corrects himself, "I'm a chemist, not a physician. I have no idea if the mine directly caused the cancer or any other medical problem. But I can assure you that the waste products from the mine caused catastrophic pollution and environmental damage."

I consider this. I am not an environmentalist, but I am hoping to continue using Earth as my home for a while longer. I ask him what has been done about it.

"Well," he begins, obviously glad to be asked, "the cure was even worse than the disease. Just get this: As the final step in the cleanup, the Japanese team loaded radioactive waste into about 80,000 drums, blasted off the top of one of the limestone mountains in the area, and packed the poison drums into the mountain crater the explosives had dug out. They covered the whole mess with soil and clay, and that was that. No more radioactive waste."

I naively ask if he thinks the remediation succeeded, although his tone of voice already has told me that he does not.

"Of course it didn't work!" Jack jumps out of his seat, throwing his arms up in the air. "Radioactive material lasts for generations depending on various factors and leaches into soil and water. The only thing the so-called cleanup did was get the toxic material out of sight. Sweep it into the mountain instead of under the rug.

"Furthermore," he says, "it was an open secret that after the Japanese were driven out, the Chinese surreptitiously took over and worked the supposedly closed mine for years. It was done under the table, so to speak, and China reportedly paid the Malay government handsomely to look the other way."

I make no comment, and Jack moves on to a more optimistic aspect of his topic. He tells me that the second part of his lecture is a comparison of procedures used in Bukit Merah with new, improved refining approaches. He says they have not yet found a way to eliminate entirely the environmental and health hazards of REE mining, but that new techniques potentially could reduce it significantly. Unfortunately, the processes are expensive and time consuming, so China opposes implementing any changes.

"In 2012 an Australian firm opened an REE refinery in Malaysia that ramped up to full production in 2014. The controversy is still raging, years later, about whether it is safe, with special interest groups protesting and bringing legal action. There are even lawsuits involving the World Health Organization claiming that China pressured the group into issuing a benign opinion because it didn't want its own Inner Mongolia facility to get drawn into the environmental fray."

Jack sits back down, and I conclude that he is finished talking about rare earth mining and his aborted lecture.

We sit in comfortable silence for a few minutes, and I am surprised to note that it is almost six o'clock. "Let's go into town and get some dinner," I say, and Jack flashes me a great smile. He nods in the direction of the door.

At the casual waterfront tavern I choose, we have easy conversation over the grilled mahi and then share a slice of pecan pie.

I am nobody's fool, and while a tiny alarm bell lingers at the edge of my thinking, I am now pretty confident that Jack is, indeed, an innocent victim of Aimee Cedar and that he is mystified by what has transpired.

"I don't think my lecture has anything to do with the plane catastrophe, Ruby," he says easily, and I note that the sneer in his voice has disappeared at least for the moment. "The problems at the Bukit mine in Perak have been well known to environmentalists for thirty years. It's all over the internet for anyone who is interested. Any scientist with a mining concentration knows all about it."

"Then why give an important lecture about it now?" I ask. Jack tells me that, because of the exponentially increased demand for technology and green products, the mining of rare earth elements is suddenly of international interest. And the improved refining methods now possible may enable production to begin in environmentally conscious countries, perhaps even the US, he says, instead of being limited to places like China and Malaysia where environmental protection is not taken seriously.

We next discuss the restraining order that sealed Jack's safe deposit box, which is still in force, and agree that it would be best to leave it alone for the moment rather than draw more attention to the bizarre way in which it came about. He has been instructed by the FBI to not leave the area anyway, so the restraint is moot for now.

I drive Jack back to my house to get his car, and we arrange to speak tomorrow to decide how to proceed. He heads back to his Soho apartment in Manhattan, and I head up to the roof to check out tonight's ships and scan for the logo of Harry Shaw's company as I always do. Coming out on the deck, I am facing the street in front of the house before turning to the ocean view on the other side. I see Jack's Jeep pull away from the curb, and then, a couple of houses down my short street, the headlamps of a parked car illuminate, and a black car I don't recognize slowly pulls into the street and follows him around the corner.

CHAPTER 14

Two hours later I am watching the coronavirus report on TV and fiddling with pieces of a jigsaw puzzle of the Grand Canyon, which has been spread out on my coffee table for weeks. It is the sixth in the series of puzzles I have used to help fill the time at home since lockdowns were imposed to slow the spread of the disease.

It is now well over a year since the pandemic swept out of China at the start of 2020, killing more than 1.5 million people worldwide, almost one-third of them in the United States, and the daily numbers of new cases and new deaths remains the most watched five minutes of every nightly news show. Each of the networks has designed a catchy format to remind us that life remains at unusual risk and that we cannot comfortably return to activities that used to be "normal." Some channels display graphs, some show photos of hospitals and sick people, some have a somber background and tone, but they all let us know where the most people tested positive and which schools, factories, shopping malls, and other places where people congregate have been ordered to close due to an uptick in cases. They also let us know the status of vaccines being administered and potential new vaccines under development, none of which have yet succeeded in creating the holy grail of "herd immunity." Like everyone else, I am now used to it, and, like everyone else, I will never get used to it.

My phone buzzes, and I see it is Jack calling. I am not sure whether to be pleased or concerned, but the moment I hear his voice I know it is the latter.

"Ruby," he says, "my apartment was broken into and ransacked. The place is torn apart, every drawer emptied, everything pulled out of the closets, even the kitchen cabinets." His voice is weary, really weary.

He tells me that the police have just left but told him that burglaries have skyrocketed in New York since the riots began during the lockdown and that they are swamped with similar incidents of theft and looting every day. They have little expectation of finding the perpetrator.

"Jack," I say, "I know this sounds really creepy, but when you left my house, I thought I saw a car follow you down the street."

He hesitates, and I expect him to make a snide comment about my becoming paranoid, but instead he says, "My apartment was already trashed when I arrived at home, so it can't be connected to someone following me." This response completely alarms me. He has not rejected the possibility that someone in a car actually was waiting outside my house to follow him.

"What's missing?" I finally ask, and when he tells me that so far the only items he has identified as being gone are in a red well file containing his lecture notes and his briefcase, neither of us needs to say another word. We silently share the chilling implications of this.

"Why don't you come back out here to sleep?" I say. I have decided I don't want to be alone, and I also am disheartened by the defeated sound of Jack's voice. "I have a nice guest room," I quickly add, although under the circumstances I doubt that he has mistaken my invitation for romance.

"Thanks," he says quickly, to my surprise. "That would be great. I can't start cleaning this up now. Be there in an hour."

When he arrives, we go up to the roof without turning on the lights and scan the street to see if it looks like anyone has followed him. It is after 11:00 p.m., and the houses are mostly dark. There is no activity on the street, no vehicles moving at all, and we go back inside.

Too tense to relax comfortably on the sofa, we sit down at my kitchen table. I offer Jack something to drink, but he declines. I note that he looks terrible.

"There's more to the story," he says. "Before I tell you the rest, do you still consider that you represent this Aimee Cedar, whoever she really is? Because if you do, I can't trust you to be forthright with me. You made it clear that you consider her to be your client and are bound by privacy and other legal ethics requirements. I need to know where you stand before we go further."

He's right, of course. Why should he confide in me if my first loyalty is to a woman who is his adversary, if not in a divorce as she said, then certainly in some way that neither he nor I have figured out? I look at my hands resting on the table and consider: I know beyond any doubt that Aimee has lied to me about her address and her phone number. In addition, I am pretty sure, but couldn't prove it if called upon to do so, that she lied about the whole story. This alone should invalidate our attorney-client privilege, but I know it doesn't. Criminal defendants notoriously lie to their attorneys all the time, yet the client's right to the privilege remains. Similarly, I think my own client, Luis, is lying about the circumstances of his arrest that led to his deportation, but I would protect his confidentiality at all costs.

I know all this, but I say to Jack, "I believe I was duped by Aimee, whoever she is, and do not consider her to be my client. We need to work on figuring this out together, and I assure you that you can trust me." I decide to go all in on Jack Cedar, who, smart or not smart, I have come to like and to trust.

Jack cuts in, looks squarely into my eyes, and says firmly, "You're not making a mistake, Ruby." He says nothing further, and after a moment I nod.

"So," he says, "when I arrived at my apartment, which is on the second floor of a townhouse, no doorman, I knew immediately that something was wrong because the dead bolt was unlocked. With everything that's happened in the last three days, I thought I must have forgotten to lock it, but really I know that I never forget to. I opened the door; the lights were all on, and a man was standing in the middle of my living room, leaning over the stuff that had been thrown on the floor and rifling through a stack of papers from my desk."

My hand goes to my mouth, and I say, "Oh no. . ."

"He didn't look scary, Ruby. The opposite, a slim, dorky-looking guy dressed in neat jeans and a blue button-down shirt. He looked more surprised to see me than I was to see him. Not at all like a thief caught in the act, more like someone really surprised that I was there at all. He stared at me with a look of disbelief and said, 'Professor Cedar?' in an almost respectful tone of voice.

"I barked back at him, 'What are you doing? Exactly what are you doing in my apartment?' The guy looked embarrassed, actually embarrassed, and muttered that he was sorry. Then he grabbed the red file and my briefcase and ran past me out the door. I got to the street-side window in time to see him sprinting away, carrying the things he took."

"Did you tell the police?" I ask, and Jack tells me that he did not. He can't explain why he decided to withhold the thief's description except that he instinctively felt it would be better to let the break-in have the hallmarks of a common burglary. But he confides to me that the prickles on his neck tell him it is something else entirely.

"He thought you were on the plane, Jack. That's why he was so surprised to see you alive and well."

Jack nods. He already has concluded the same thing. "The guy in my apartment believed I had died on that plane," he says quietly. "But Ruby, whoever followed me when I left your house earlier knew that I was alive, so the two incidents cannot be connected."

We stare at each other and silently acknowledge that events have taken on a whole new dimension. Whatever is happening is still happening. It did not end with the plane disaster.

I get up from the table and turn on the house alarm.

CHAPTER 15

As usual I am wide awake before six o'clock, but this morning I am too jittery to remain in bed long enough to review my messages. Instead I just scan the news and see that there are no new headlines about the missing plane, dress in my running clothes, and go out into the hall. Jack's door is closed, and, hearing no sound, I assume he is still asleep. I drink a glass of grapefruit juice and leave a note telling him that I have gone for a run on the beach. He should help himself to breakfast.

I fast-walk down the block to the beach and pick up speed as I head west. At this hour there are only a handful of people on the sand, taking photos of the red sunrise that is underway or walking their dogs, ignoring numerous large signs advising that dogs are prohibited at all times.

As usual, I jog along the elevated boardwalk in Long Beach for about two miles, reverse direction, and then head back. When I reach the sand again, I slow down to a walk and amble along, watching a few surfers in black wet suits floating on the waves and a couple of fishermen casting their lines out into the surf. One of them is wrestling in a nice-size fish, maybe a foot or so, that is thrashing wildly as he pulls it toward shore.

When I am almost back home, I hear Harry Shaw call my name, and I head over to greet him. "What are you doing out here so early?" I ask. I often take this route at about the same hour and have never encountered Harry so early in the morning.

"We have our newest container ship, the *Geneva Star*, heading into New York this morning, and I came out to watch her," he says, smiling broadly, and hands me the binoculars he has hanging around his neck. "She's fourth in line for the docks, so she'll be floating on the horizon for a while. A beautiful sight, isn't she?"

I spot the gleaming ship with Harry's bright red Shaw Global logo emblazoned on the side and see dozens of brightly colored containers stacked on its deck, sparkling in the sunlight as it waits to head west into the port of New York and New Jersey.

"It's a beautiful sight, Harry, on a morning like this. So, what's it carrying?" I ask, happy to discuss something other than the present disaster in which I find myself.

"It's carrying dry bulk from Asia. Mostly salt and other food products from Thailand and garments commissioned by US companies to be made in Vietnam. Also fabrics produced in Taiwan. We now have a logistics company in the US and use our own trucks to pick up the goods from the docks and deliver them all over the States. Very profitable." He smiles and gives me a wink.

The events of the last few days have made me less constrained by manners, and I say, "Profitable enough for you to need that concrete barrier you've erected around your house? You couldn't really call it a fence." I give him my own wink.

He doesn't answer for a few moments, but then he says, "Oh, Aruba, would you like to hear a shipping story today?" But now there is no wink or even a smile, and Harry actually seems wistful. "Stay with me for a few minutes," he continues and gestures for us to sit down on the sand, which we do.

He begins in a somber tone. "In 2014 Muslim fundamentalists, they were never sure which group exactly, boarded our ship, the

Renata, after it discharged its cargo in Cyprus and was supposed to be heading to Italy. The eight terrorists demanded that the ship take them to Tel Aviv, where they intended to use the approach by sea to destroy the Israeli harbor. We refused, called in UN negotiators to help, which was worthless, and finally offered a huge bribe for them to leave the ship, which they declined." He pauses and, tracing shapes in the sand with a finger, says, "This went on for four days. My uncle, the founder and CEO of the company, was recovering from heart surgery, and my cousin, his son, was on his honeymoon in French Polynesia with limited communications. That left me in charge."

He takes a deep breath and continues. "On the fifth day of the standoff, Israel asked to have Mossad agents take over the negotiations. I agreed, but the terrorists overheard us advising our captain that this was our plan. They dragged him to the deck, forty-two years old, tied his arms and legs, and threw him into the sea. It was like the *Achille Lauro* in 1985, when they pushed a wheelchair-bound tourist overboard." Harry looks at me, and I nod to acknowledge that I remember the *Achille Lauro* tragedy very well.

He continues. "The Mossad immediately moved in, and the terrorists fled in life rafts they took from the *Renata*. But as they pulled away, they discharged explosives in the engine room, causing an extensive fire on board. Another crewman and one of the Mossad agents were killed as they attempted to control the fire. Everyone else on the ship was picked up by Israeli helicopters and brought to safety." Harry pauses for a few moments, and I wait silently.

"The terrorists were never caught or even positively identified, although there were rumors that Israeli agents knew who they were and hunted them down and killed them. I hope so, I hope so," he said. He stared down at the sand for a moment and then looked up at me. "But that, Aruba, is why I have an impenetrable, alarmed enclosure around my house, and other places as well."

I was speechless, particularly in light of my personal connection to the plane disappearance only a few days ago, which, according to news reports, increasingly looked like terrorism. "How did you get over it, Harry?" I ask, thinking of my own situation and hoping to get some insight that might be helpful.

"Oh, we revised all our protocols after that. Even though we are cargo ships and have no involvement whatsoever with political activity, we now have at least two crew members on every sailing who have weapons and are trained and licensed to use them if necessary. We have other safety measures installed as well. And for myself, it took me a long time to be at peace with it. It is why I asked my uncle if I could lead our North America division and move to New York. I knew I needed a different perspective, a new start to shake it off. And, of course, I still have, probably will always have, those impenetrable enclosures," he says. In a moment he recovers his smile.

I stand up and say with warmth, "I have to get to the office, Harry. See you soon." As I head down the beach toward my house, I look back at him over my shoulder and say, "Call me Ruby." He touches two fingers to his forehead in a casual salute, a gesture I have seen him make before, and nods.

CHAPTER 16

I find Jack sitting at my kitchen table drinking coffee from my favorite mug, the remains of scrambled eggs and toast spread out in front of him. He had made himself at home in the living room yesterday, and he now seems to have planted his flag in the kitchen as well.

"Hi," he says pleasantly. "I made eggs and toast for you. I hope that's all right?" Surprised, I smile and nod as Jack indicates a chair for me to sit. I note it is the "guest" chair at my own table since he already has taken my own usual seat for himself, but I say nothing and sit down where he indicates.

Without flourish or preamble, he whips a plate of food out of the oven where he has kept it warm and pours hot coffee into a floral mug he chooses from one of several I keep on the window ledge. He looks at my place setting for a moment and rummages in the cabinets to find salt and pepper shakers and a napkin. He has no expression as he does this; he is not looking proud of himself, waiting for praise or anything at all, and obviously thinks it is nothing unusual for a man to cook for and serve a woman. This is unlike most of the men I meet locally, and I think briefly that perhaps growing up on a Midwestern farm confers some benefits I have not considered.

"Get ready for the next disturbing thing," he says as he sits down with his coffee. "I called Ellen Hong, George Hong's wife, to offer some support and was transferred to George's office staff who know me well. The admin said the university—Columbia, that is—told her that Ellen and their teenage children left New York yesterday. That's two days after the plane goes missing. Pretty fast, don't you think?"

"Well, what do you mean 'left'? Maybe she's visiting family or friends to help get through this—"

"No, I mean left. Left *the country*," he says. "Permanently. Moving vans came and took their furniture to storage, and she and the kids flew to China last night. George's admin told me that Ellen wanted to take the kids 'home' to Beijing to be with her and George's families. I didn't even know they were from China! How is that possible? He's been my associate and friend for almost ten years, and I thought they were from San Francisco. George told me about growing up in California: his parents, where they lived, schools he went to, and that Ellen grew up in the same neighborhood. None of this makes sense, Ruby. And don't forget Ellen said George told her I was with him at the airport! I don't know what to make of any of this."

I put down my fork and push the half-eaten breakfast away. I feel like my throat is closing, and my heart has started to race. I concentrate on breathing evenly as I think through this latest news, which is getting worse by the minute. I force myself to focus on the facts and try to connect them. "Jack," I am able to say calmly after a few moments, "at this point we need to assume this has something to do with you, specifically with you. And we can't sit and wait to see what happens next. We'd better start trying to figure out what's going on. Now," I say and marshal all of my courtroom bravado to look squarely at him with confidence I do not feel.

"I agree," he says evenly. "I've been going over the sequence of events since I got off the phone with George's admin and reached the same conclusion. And the theft of my paperwork coupled with the situation surrounding George Hong leads me to consider that my presentation may actually be the possible nexus."

I realize that he does not sound panicked like I feel, but is projecting the analytical demeanor of a researcher tackling a tough problem. I say, "OK, let's think about that. I don't know much about your topic, but what about it could be important enough for this to happen?"

"I've been trying to break it down because nothing about the conference and certainly not my presentation seems to me to be worthy of an international incident or worse. So let's outline it," he says and assumes his lecturer's voice.

"First, consider the global subject of environmental protection. Certainly important enough to some people, actually many people, to become unhinged, but too amorphous to single out my topic for violence. Not likely," he says.

"So drill down: The area of interest could be the broad subject of all mining. Or it could be a specific material being extracted from certain mines, and my talk is limited to rare earth elements and related environmental damage. Both topics could possibly cause flash points, but it's very farfetched to think that environmentalists would have the wherewithal to do this. And if it were crazed 'save the earth' groupies, wouldn't they claim responsibility? If not, what would they even have accomplished?

"Then there are the products that the REEs enable us to produce, such as electric cars that could undermine gasoline-powered vehicles, possibly destroying a huge economic force in Saudi Arabia, Russia, and other countries, or wind turbines that could adversely impact oil-producing nations in the Middle East and even Venezuela, some of which are well known for shocking acts of violence. My focus on improved REE refining techniques would make the green products more attractive to produce, potentially even further undermining the old ones." Jack gets up and starts to pace back and forth in front of my kitchen table, obviously deep in thought as he speaks.

He looks at me and says, "But perhaps it has nothing to do with those issues. The problem could be the *location* of the mines I focus on, which are primarily in Malaysia, where the government's preference for cash over protection of the health of its people has on occasion caused serious unrest and violence. And a corrupt government could conceivably have both the will and the means to perpetrate what's happened. But, that said, I find it so implausible as to reject it out of hand. It would be a lot easier for a government to just deny, deny, deny."

He takes a sip of his now cold coffee. "And then there is REE mining in China, which is terrible, actually shocking, for its environmental destruction. The negative impact there cannot even be calculated since they only permit carefully orchestrated monitoring and access, and I do mention all of that in my presentation. However, would China realistically give two hoots about what an NYU earth and environmental science professor has to say about their mine? Not likely," he concludes.

Two hoots? I think. Really? Is that what they say when they're seriously pissed off on the farm these days?

He sits back down, cups his coffee mug in both hands, and says, "And that's all I've got, Ruby. Nothing too compelling."

"Then Jack, there's something entirely different that we haven't thought of. If it was obvious, you would realize it, so it's way out there, something we have not even considered. Let's take a different tack," I say after thinking it over. "We need to get more information." Now I stand up and start to tick off our tasks on my fingers. "Let's focus on identifying Aimee Cedar. And who followed you from my house last night. And who broke into your apartment. And what's up with George Hong."

He nods. "That's good, really good. Let's work out a plan."

CHAPTER 17

We sit at my kitchen table for the next hour and agree on the best way to find more information about the things we do know, which, we think, may lead us to the things we don't know. We divide up areas to investigate along obvious lines.

Jack will head back to New York and search his apartment for clues about the robbery and pin down the specific items that were taken. We have decided to deconstruct his aborted lecture line by line looking for some unrealized significance, so he intends to use his office files and computer hard drive to put together a duplicate. Jack also will try to find some explanation for the seemingly inexplicable conduct of George Hong and his wife.

I will work on the mystery of Aimee Cedar, review any new information I can find about the plane disappearance and also the GCAC conference, which now is underway in Ireland with a hastily substituted keynote presentation. The science association members are aware that, tragically, an attendee appears to have been aboard the vanished plane and that Jack Cedar, having missed the flight for unknown reasons, is remaining in New York at this time. However, Jack has agreed to reschedule his presentation for next month, to be streamed to the federation members in a special broadcast.

They already have announced it to the attendees in Dublin, who are stunned by the connection of the group to the plane, and Jack's lecture is generating significant interest.

I have all but forgotten that it is a workday until Marsha calls to remind me that I have a client coming in shortly to prepare for the hearing on her application to increase child support. Thinking that the FBI may be watching me, I suppress my impulse to have Marsha advise the client that I have a conflict and adjourn the matter. I feel a shiver run up my arms as I realize that I actually am planning how to best handle surveillance by federal authorities. I wonder if I should consult a criminal lawyer for guidance but decide to hold off for now.

Jack leaves, and I hastily shower and head to the office.

After almost two hours, I am seriously tired of my client, an impressively attired and articulate suburban housewife who self-righteously insists that her former husband, an executive at a financial firm in Manhattan, must provide enough financial support so that she does not need to work and can remain at home full time with their children, ages eight and ten, for the next thirteen years until the youngest is twenty-one years old. My client herself is a CPA but has never considered working, choosing instead to devote her time to spending her former husband's considerable earnings on every conceivable lifestyle enrichment, including anything that she can possibly frame as a benefit for their kids.

Recently she and her boyfriend took the kids on a "Covid-safe" vacation, the bill for which totaled about $20,000 for a week at national parks. They rented the costliest luxury RV on the market at about $1,000 a night, searched out the top-rated restaurants at every stop, even including one Michelin-starred dinner, and hired the most expensive private guides. She now insists that the full cost of the vacation be included in her expense calculations being used to establish a basis for the court to order an increase in the support she receives from her ex-husband. I try to convince her that the judge will likely view this as overreaching, and it could negatively impact his opinion of her entire case.

"Barbara," I say to her, trying to sound sympathetic, "I know that when you were married you went on luxury vacations, but the costs you are using now include your boyfriend's expenses. That entails a second room, all his luxury meals, park admissions, et cetera. I think this will turn the judge off, and we should subtract his share of the costs—"

She abruptly cuts in and says in an exasperated tone, "What was I supposed to do, Aruba, drive the RV myself? If I had hired a driver, it would have cost more than asking Joe to come with us to help out. The driver would have needed a separate room and meals, just the same. And the trip enabled me to keep up the kids' cultural advancement in spite of the pandemic. Any judge will see the importance of that."

I have my doubts about that. But I am too spent to argue and say, "OK, Barbara, it's your decision. Let's wrap up for now, but I need you back here tomorrow afternoon. I'm free at three to go over the remaining details of your testimony."

"I'll be here, Aruba," she says smugly, gathers her notes from my desk, and leaves. I hear her give a cheerful goodbye to Marsha, who almost immediately steps into my office.

"The building engineer was here," she says and holds out what looks like a compact disc to me. "He found Aimee on the second visit."

I am instantly energized and take the disc. "How do we view this?" I ask her, and she tells me to put it in the CD slot of my desktop computer. We both stare at the screen expectantly, and in a few moments the picture comes to life.

There she is: Aimee Cedar, dressed in gorgeous, brown silk, pulling open the front door of the office building. She is wearing large, dark sunglasses that obscure her face, but as she tugs on the door with one hand, she pulls the glasses away from her face with the other. For a moment, one glorious moment, there is a perfect view of her face.

Next I telephone my neighbor who lives three houses down the block from me and ask if she would mind checking the videos made by her Ring camera on Sunday evening at about 9:00 p.m. to see if there were any unusual cars outside. I tell her I am trying to identify a car that may have clipped my friend's SUV, which was parked in front of my house. A widow who lives alone, my neighbor is happy to help.

I hold on while she logs on to her saved Ring videos, and before long she tells me that, yes, there was an unfamiliar car that drove past her house at that time. I accept her offer to email the video to me and assure her that I will let her know if it turns out to be anything important.

My brother is a technology geek who eschewed a formal education in favor of launching his own internet firm. Our parents, never interested in practicalities or making money, were appalled that he preferred the pursuit of commercial success over studying, say, philosophy in college, but he ignored their objections and forged ahead.

So far it has not made him a rising star of the tech world, but the specialty search engine he designed that can be customized to zero in on specific areas of information needed by the clients who hire him is well regarded, and his firm is impressively profitable by any measure. Our parents eventually forgave him for his success and in recent years have been happy to accept from him financial assistance that helps to offset their own failure to prepare for advancing age.

At my request, he swings by my office in the late afternoon, and I hand him the CD from the building engineer and a copy of my neighbor's Ring video clip, which he slips into his pocket.

"So, what exactly are we looking for here?" Steve asks. Lucky for him, our parents had abandoned their penchant for weird child naming by the time he came along.

I tell him only that a client has given me false contact information and I need to get to the bottom of it. "Well," I say, "you're the one who is always telling me about how brilliant your internet searches are and the amazing feats of facial recognition software, so I want a demonstration."

I understand next to nothing about this subject and pretty much tune out when he regularly regales me with the wonders of the internet, but he has never disappointed me when I needed help in his area of expertise. Of course, I do the same for him when he requires legal advice, and we maintain a mutual loyalty and protectiveness of each other that being the children of childish parents can build.

"Obviously you're not planning to fill me in." He smirks as he rises from his chair in my office. "I'll let you know if I get a hit," he says, kisses me on the cheek, and strolls out the door.

CHAPTER 18

I feel at loose ends but force myself to focus on work. I call Luis to discuss with him how we are going to proceed. We are directed to appear in court in a few days, and I tell him that we are out of time to come up with a game plan.

We have only three options and must decide either to appear in court so the judge can resolve the custody issue; try to make an out-of-court agreement with Jazmin's mother; or drop the request for a change of custody entirely. I tell Luis, who becomes increasingly glum, that at this point, since Jazmin's plight already has been brought to the court's attention, the judge may very well insist that he meet everyone in person even if there is an agreement between Luis and Jazmin's mother. If the judge is not convinced that the resolution is in Jazmin's best interests, he has the authority to scrap the whole thing and do whatever he thinks will best meet her needs. He can even take her away from both parents and order her placed in foster care.

"So you told me maybe I can pay off her mother, but how can this come down to money?" he says. "We're talking about my daughter here and how to protect her. Her mother isn't taking care of her!"

"Luis," I say, trying to be patient, "the problem here is not money. It's that you snuck into the country illegally and are afraid of getting caught. We're talking about money only because it is a possible way of helping your daughter without risking going to court because you're afraid to go to court."

He is silent. Finally he mutters, "Try to make a deal with her mother," and hangs up.

A few minutes after five o'clock, Marsha appears at my door and asks if I need anything before she leaves. Pretending to be deep in thought about the file on my desk so I don't have to engage in conversation with her, I shake my head no and wave good night.

I get home at about six thirty and find that I am exhausted. I realize that the stress of the last few days is wearing me out, and I determine to have a relaxing and hopefully uneventful evening. Anxious to share my progress with Jack, I leave two messages on his cell phone but get no response. I had half expected to find his car in my driveway when I got home and can't help but feel somewhat disappointed that he seems less interested in comparing notes than I am.

Wanting to establish some semblance of normal routine, I light the barbeque and grill a steak for myself. I pour a glass of Montepulciano, settle on my small patio with today's *Wall Street Journal*, and eat with the fine sea air wafting around me, just the right temperature. I keep my cell phone next to me, hoping to hear from Jack, but there are no calls. I decide it would be too aggressive for me to call him yet again and decide that I will just wait to hear from him.

When the light fades and it becomes too cool to sit outside, I move to the living room and switch on *Game of Thrones*, which I am in the middle of watching for a second time. Like everyone else, I have viewed endless TV series since the pandemic struck, shutting down movie theaters, concerts, sporting events, and just about any enjoyable entertainment outside the home.

At this point the networks are unable to produce new content as fast as it is demanded, and like many people, I have exhausted the programs that are remotely interesting to me. The current craze seems to be for game shows in which contestants try to complete ludicrous physical feats, such as crossing a swimming pool by jumping from one inflated, plastic pillow to the next without ending up in the drink. Every contestant has some poignant backstory, like Great-Grandma slowly dying of rare cancer at ninety-eight or their brother unable to get out of Honduras because of gangs chasing him. Viewers get to see these poignant cheerleaders: Great-Grandma in bed, head swathed in scarves, gamely shaking her fist in support; the brother, surrounded by South American jungle with gunfire audible in the distance, yet somehow streaming the contest to a laptop he has perched on a massive fern.

I stick with *Game of Thrones* but find that I am no better able to figure out what is going on than I was the first time I watched the series. I am admiring the hair and makeup of the Mother of Dragons when my phone finally rings. I hope it is Jack but see from the caller ID that it is my brother, which is not a bad second choice under the circumstances.

Without preamble he says, "I haven't gotten a hit on the woman yet. But I did find the car without too much difficulty. Ruby, what are you into here?"

I am not ready to share details, but I sit up straight and say, "Well, it's not me who is into anything, Steve. It's my client who we haven't been able to find—"

He cuts in. "Aruba, the car is registered to the FBI. Not hard to find at all. So, why would the FBI be sitting outside your house?"

I am astounded by this information. It has never occurred to me that the FBI might find me or Jack of sufficient interest to use surreptitious means to track us. I immediately wonder if it could have been the FBI searching Jack's apartment, but I reject this notion as I assume they would have obtained a search warrant and advised Jack of that fact rather than run off into the night when he confronted them.

When I say nothing, Steve continues. "Look, Aruba, I need to know if there's something dangerous going on here. I'm not going to help you get yourself in some kind of trouble."

My mind is clearing, and I reply, "Steve, they're not following me," although I am not at all sure this is true. "It's the client, the woman whose photo I gave you. She lied to me about her identity, and they must be looking for *her*." I say nothing about the connection with the missing plane. "Try to find her for me," I continue. "She is the person they're looking for."

"You think I can find her when the FBI can't?" he says, annoyed.

"Well, they don't know what she looks like," I tell him. "I didn't give them her photo, and without my help, which they haven't asked for, they wouldn't know how to identify her on the building security tapes."

"Why don't you give them the photo?" he asks quite sensibly, and I don't know how to reply. Perhaps it is just the habit of client confidentiality, but I instinctively feel that it would be premature to lead the authorities on this path before I know more about it myself.

"She's still my client," I say, "and I can't just give information about her to authorities without her permission, which I can't get because I can't locate her, or without getting an order by a court to do so." This is all true, strictly speaking, but it really has nothing to do with my actual reason, which is called a hunch. "You've got to try to identify her for me."

Steve thinks for a moment and then says, "OK, if I can't find a hit within forty-eight hours, I will most likely never find one. I'll keep running the photo for you, but you have to agree that if I have nothing in two days you'll let me know what's going on and be sure there's no danger to you." I agree, and we say goodbye.

My brother is a great guy.

And where the hell is Jack? I decide to forget about how it may look and call him again. Again no answer.

———

About eleven o'clock I am still sitting on the sofa flipping through channels and keeping one eye on my phone, which remains silent. The doorbell rings, startling me, and for a moment I am paralyzed with anxiety. The house seems dark and quiet, a Halloween house even though the holiday is still weeks away.

I force myself to go to the door and look through the peephole as I ask, "Yes? Who is it?" I see only the midsection of a man's dark suit, but his face is above my field of vision. I have not seen Jack in business attire, but I doubt that it is him. My heart is pounding, and I wait for a reply.

I see an ID card encased in plastic thrust at the peephole of the door, and a man says loudly, "FBI, Ms. Jones." I do not expect this, and after a moment I crack the door open a bit. I need to look up in order to see the face of a very tall agent. Peter Drost is standing there, and he is not smiling.

"May I step in?" he asks.

"What is this about, Agent Drost? It's after eleven at night," I say with an edge to my voice. I don't even know if "agent" is the correct way to address him and hope I haven't offended him by sounding sarcastic, which I did not intend.

He looks at me squarely and says, "Jack Cedar has been involved in an incident and has been injured."

Involuntarily my hand goes to my mouth, and I barely say in a hollow voice, "Oh. . ." I am surprised by my own reaction, as if a close friend had been injured, not someone I met only days ago and who has brought with him all of this trouble.

My reaction is not lost on Drost, who is, after all, an FBI agent. He studies me for a moment, obviously considering that my relationship with Jack may be more complicated than he had thought. He says briskly, "He'll be all right. My partner is bringing him here when he leaves the emergency room. We need more information about your and Mr. Cedar's relationship with George Hong. We need it immediately."

"George Hong?" I say, mystified and irritated that I am being pulled into this further and further. I say angrily, "I don't know a thing about George Hong, and I certainly have no relationship with him. The only time I have ever even heard his name was when Jack Cedar," I say, consciously including Jack's surname to sound less personal, "told me he was supposed to travel with Mr. Hong to Ireland and that Hong had called his wife from the airport." I leave out the rest of what Mrs. Hong said her husband told her in that call.

"Yeah," Drost says. "That part is true. George Hong was scheduled to fly on that plane, but that's about the only part that's true."

PART FOUR
JANUARY
2020

Asia

CHAPTER 19
Beijing

Pao Den Chin stared out the window of his Beijing office in Government Building No. 7, surveying the small square below. Opposite him was Government Building No. 6, and on the two perpendicular streets of the square were a noodle shop, a dumpling restaurant favored by tourists since it had been written up in a popular guidebook, and several shops selling cheap clothing and housewares. Unusual for Beijing, there were three bronze sculptures in the center, each surrounded by a small garden, which probably accounted for the complimentary review in the travel guide. It was one of the few relatively smog-free days, and, Den Chin thought, the square actually looked attractive.

He had returned from Taiwan a week before, three days after Mai's funeral. She had spent her last few days with him in the apartment in which she had lived her entire life, attended by the loyal health care aide whom Den Chin had employed for almost seven years. As she had lived, Mai quietly drifted into the next world without anything to say to her son, making no fuss. She had simply squeezed his hand affectionately and closed her eyes for the last time. After her modest funeral, Den Chin took care of emptying the apartment, keeping a few personal items to remind him of his childhood in Taiwan. He gave the aide a handsome severance payment and returned to Beijing.

But he had been melancholy and found himself preoccupied with existential questions of life and death. Compared to the drab atmosphere in Beijing, Taipei had seemed colorful and full of life. People strolled the streets talking animatedly and laughing, the restaurants and bars were full, and the shops overflowed with all types of merchandise made locally as well as in the West. It was vastly different from the days of his youth when Chiang Kai-shek's violent regime had terrorized the masses and catered only to the wealthy and well connected. In contrast to the Taiwan of today, Beijing was gray, the people were glum as they walked the gray streets, and the only merchandise available to buy was utilitarian. Shanghai, he knew, was quite different from Beijing, booming with capitalist-style businesses and retail shops and enthusiastic people. But he also knew it was only a matter of time until the party clamped its fist around Shanghai to bring it into line, just as it had done in Hong Kong.

Den Chin considered the future of Taiwan. The party continued to claim that the island was part of Communist China, but Taiwan itself insisted it remained an independent country, the Republic of China, just as it had been when Chiang Kai-shek set up his government there in 1949. In recent years, the liberal elected leaders had forged strong alliances with western countries, making it problematic for Beijing to exert authority. The United States had even directly challenged the PRC on the matter and adopted the Taiwan Relations Act of 1979, which recognized Taiwan as a free and democratic nation, even declaring US support to help the nation resist coercion that might jeopardize its freedom.

Maintaining a carefully orchestrated policy of stating its control but not exercising it in ways that would inflame the West, Beijing made good use of Den Chin's Taiwanese connections to surreptitiously obtain information and communicate with its agents on the island. As a result, Den Chin was able to travel back and forth with minimal red tape or advance planning. He was recognized by many in Taipei and considered an esteemed physician rather than an unwelcome official of the Communist party. He was treated without suspicion when he moved about the city; he had sometimes walked slowly with his mother on his arm until she became too frail to do so.

Most mainland Chinese, even those with respected positions within the party, were required to apply for permission to travel to Taiwan well in advance and to provide detailed itineraries and reasons for their trip. Those who were permitted to go were treated by the Taiwanese with condescension, if not outright contempt, and were unable to move about without attracting attention, which was always negative. But that was not so for Den Chin, who had been able to observe firsthand the evolution of the island from the White Terror days of the 1950s to its present, forward-looking free society.

Really, he knew, his loyalty to the committee had begun to ebb when he returned from Malaysia in 2014. He had been badly shaken when the Malaysia Air flight vanished and with it all evidence of what had happened in Perak. The mystery of the plane's disappearance had never been solved, and after years of searching by governments as well as private salvage companies from all over the world, there still was no reliable explanation of the events. It was not even known whether the plane had crashed into the Indian Ocean or flown, literally below the radar, to an unknown location.

Upon his return to Beijing immediately after the 2014 airplane disaster, Den Chin had arranged a meeting with the two committee members with whom he had planned the mass evacuation from Kuala Lumpur. They had agreed that the loss of the plane was a terrible and disturbing incident and that the coincidence of it carrying the teams departing from Perak was tragic, but when Den Chin pressed them further, even stating that he could not view the event merely as a coincidence, the member for environmental options had turned to face him directly and stared at him pointedly with a somber expression. He waited a few moments, drawing gravity to his words, and then said with no inflection in his voice at all, "Perhaps you are too disturbed by the event to continue in your position as head of Foreign Actions in Environmental Epidemiology."

The silence in the room deepened. Den Chin was sufficiently experienced to understand the full import of the committee member's words and was careful to show no expression as he considered his response. While he had achieved an important and respected position in the party, his authority did not even approach the power of the committee members. He knew that pressing for continued discussion would lead to his being demoted to a minor functionary at best, a dead or vanished one at worst. Like the plane, he thought.

"Of course not," he managed to say in an almost affable way. "I was focusing on whether we could devise a different method to study the illness in Perak. . ."

"No, no," said the member for developing export strategies, with a tight smile. "We have fumigated the caves, and that should be the end of it."

And it was the end of it. Except that Den Chin could not forget that at the last minute the committee had arranged for him to go to Taiwan, and that was the only reason he had not been on the doomed plane.

A scientist, a practical man, Den Chin resumed his laser-like focus on his work, which, as always, provided him with purpose and satisfaction. He believed that inadequate supplies of potable water would be the scourge of the twenty-first century and developed a complex protocol to study the issue. He dispatched teams to Africa and South America, the areas already most afflicted by the problem, to identify sources of waterborne contamination that routinely caused hepatitis-like illnesses of the liver that shortened the lives of countless people.

But the Malaysian disaster of the rare earth mines of Perak never completely left his thoughts. The disappearance of the plane, and with it all scientific evidence of the calamity, had deprived him of the opportunity to study the matter and arrive at scientific conclusions for future mining and refining of REE products. He felt certain that there was some connection between the mines and the bizarre illness that had first appeared in bats, then apparently infected other species and finally eight people who probably had come in direct contact with the infected animals. He was, after all, a renowned expert in infectious diseases.

Could it be the rare earth elements themselves, he pondered, that were the problem, or was it something in the refining process? Or could it have been the ridiculous "cleanup" method used by the Japanese, which not only failed to remediate the area but also caused greater seepage of chemical waste into the water supply? Water supply was now his primary focus, and he wondered if rare earth elements, even if in the ground and undisturbed, could leach into water supplies and contribute to clusters of illness in those locations. Was the illness in Malaysia the result of a chaotic system where some change in habitat or process of a particular mine, even if seemingly insignificant, had caused a deadly result that might never reoccur?

The mystery haunted Den Chin when he woke in the night or when his focus on the water project flagged. He recognized that events had precluded him from developing scientific evidence to support his theory, reducing his suspicions to mere hunches, but they would not leave him.

On two occasions he tried to develop a research agenda for rare earth mining at meetings of the scientific investigations committee that planned and arranged financing for scientific and medical projects supported by the party. He emphasized that, since the Malaysian mines had been shut down, the huge mainland Chinese mine and refinery in Baotou, Inner Mongolia, was now the supplier of more than 80 percent of worldwide demand for REEs. Accordingly, he argued, understanding the chemical and health aspects of the mining process was essential to China. He quickly recognized that the general health of workers and ecological concerns in a remote region of Inner Mongolia were not priorities for the party, so he tried framing the issue as important to economic benefits, stating that maintaining a safe environment would boost production and profits.

It was all to no avail. He was politely but pointedly advised that these were interesting topics that might be investigated only if there came a time when more pressing scientific concerns did not demand attention. It was made clear that he was not to bring the matter up again.

He focused his energy on water, but he studied rare earth. He read about the history of every mining operation since REEs were first identified; he studied complaints that had been lodged against the projects of cancer deaths and birth defects in Perak, of polluted water and soil around the Mountain Pass Mine in California, about radioactive waste products, of foul smells from the mine shafts and standing water, and on and on. He found nothing at all, anywhere, about infectious disease associated with the mines, not in bats or other animals or people. Still his hunch lingered on.

In 2019 he came across a series of articles published in British tabloids and repeated on the BBC that had been prepared by a private English scientific mission. The essays, complete with photographs, purported to describe the great Chinese rare earth refinery in Baotou, Inner Mongolia.

It was a bleak and chilling portrait of China's relentless drive to supply the commodities needed to satisfy the burgeoning worldwide appetite for tech and other gadgetry, even at the cost of destroying the land, air, and water around the mines and refineries. Even worse, the conditions reflected a total lack of regard for the human beings living in those areas, let alone those working deep in the ground to extract the elements.

Negative interest in the Chinese REE mine caught on, and articles followed in several Asian and Western newspapers and other venues, even including a well-publicized segment on a US television network that concluded that China was, indeed, a "very poor citizen of the world." Den Chin scoured the articles, watched the news reports, but saw nothing about an infectious illness.

On a pleasant day in January 2020, Den Chin was summoned from his lab in Beijing to meet with the member for environmental issues who had appeared unannounced and was waiting in Den Chin's office.

"We need to address the clamor over Inner Mongolia," the member said placidly. "We have arranged for the World Health Organization to send a delegation to observe and investigate the mines and refinery in Baotou and submit a report. They are well respected, and it should put an end to the upsetting rumors about Inner Mongolia, which are being spread by our competition."

Den Chin was silent. Finally, he said, "But what if the report is not flattering and confirms the description given by the British?"

"We expect you to host the WHO tour of the facilities and ensure that they do not agree with the British group," the member replied, staring squarely at Den Chin. "It has all been arranged. We will plan the exact route through the facilities that the delegation is to follow, and you will escort them and direct their attention to the correct activities."

Den Chin was shocked. He was dedicated to the party as a physician and a scientist, brilliant at research in the field of infectious disease and environmental hazards, but he knew his own shortcomings. He was like his mother in many ways, poor at cordial conversation, serious to the point of seeming dour, and hardly qualified to be the promoter of a good image for something in which he did not even believe.

Seeing his discomfort, the member said, "Don't worry, Pao Den Chin," surprising Den Chin with the inclusion of his first name, which, he realized, he had hardly heard spoken aloud in months. "Everything has been arranged, and you will be an impressive and prestigious guide. The tour will be effective if you stick to the itinerary we prepare. The delegation will arrive in Baotou next

Wednesday afternoon and depart on Friday morning to enjoy a special, top-echelon curated tour of the Great Wall that we have arranged specially for these most 'honored guests,'" he said, his tone sarcastic. "You mainly need to impress them with your scientific credentials and flatter their belief that we consider them to be high-level dignitaries. They will be gone before you know it."

Den Chin said quietly, "With due respect, I am concerned that I am not the best choice for this job."

The member's voice hardened, and he leaned forward. "To the contrary, we have decided that you are the perfect person for this assignment. After all, you have made yourself quite knowledgeable about the subject of rare earth mining, investigating and studying the subject at length. And, of course, you have asked us to fund a full scientific study of the Baotou mines on more than one occasion." He sat back in his chair and stared placidly at Pao.

"Of course," Den Chin said, concealing his shock that the member was aware of his interest in REEs. His reading had been conducted on his own time, at his residence, not in the office. "Of course," he repeated, "I will use my research to impress the WHO."

CHAPTER 20
Inner Mongolia, China

Den Chin climbed atop the berm so he could better view the scene unfolding before him. From here, with no trees, no buildings, no obstructions at all, he surveyed the huge man-made lake filled with black, oozing sludge that stretched for more than five miles into the distance. It was so large he was told it could be seen from space.

The perimeter surrounding it looked to be clay and dust of a filthy, gray-brown color tracked with shiny rivulets of black slime slowly wending into the main body of heaving waste material. The entire scene was devoid of vegetation or any other indication of life, devoid of any color whatsoever. It is like a ring of hell in Dante's *Inferno*, Den Chin thought, and the black lake is the River Styx.

In the distance to his right a seemingly endless row of black chutes six feet apart arched high over the berm, spewing constant streams of dark muck into the lake. On his left, a small battalion of trucks dug out and carried away earth to enlarge the lake, which was inching toward full capacity as more and more slime tumbled into it from the chutes.

On the far side of the lake, in the gray, smog-filled distance, Den Chin could make out the massive refining complex with its warren of smokestacks and a stream of trucks delivering material from the nearby mines into the factory. The complex created, he thought, an assault on the senses, with the noxious smell of chemicals rising from the lake and the roar of equipment creating a constant din that made it impossible to think clearly. He was revolted.

He thought to himself that it was fortunate he had left his driver and small security detail in the parking area so they would not see his reaction. By the time he strode back to the three black SUVs that comprised his escort, he had recovered his usual serious demeanor and inscrutable expression and gave no hint of his response to the site.

He climbed into the back seat of the middle SUV and instructed his driver to take him back to Baotou, the closest city to the rare earth mines of Inner Mongolia that he had just inspected. He was dismayed to see gray muck clinging to his shoes and a film of filthy dust lining the creases of his clothing. As he usually did, he had chosen a hotel with Western-style services and would have the shoes polished and his garments cleaned as soon as he returned to his room.

He was hosting the delegation from the World Health Organization at dinner this evening and would need time to formulate the explanations he would provide to them for the obvious problems existing at the mines and the refinery complex.

Fortunately the member for developing export strategies, who Den Chin thought was a genius, had carefully arranged the WHO itinerary to exclude the worst areas. Avoiding any panoramic views of the lake, the group had been shepherded directly into small production buildings where healthy-looking workers sat comfortably at individual stations assembling items for export; then to the buildings dedicated to the final packaging of manufacture-ready REEs for shipment all over the globe. These products were pristine and gave no hint of the poisonous refining process that had brought the materials to this point.

Den Chin had marveled at the foresight of the committee when it determined to corner the world market in rare earth elements twenty years before, in anticipation of the boom in technology products that would require REEs for their manufacture. And then, since the Green Movement had surprisingly become a rallying cry in the West, the demand for REEs to produce green products had skyrocketed to almost unimaginable levels. The requirements for electric car batteries alone could occupy a new production building twenty-four hours a day, Den Chin calculated, and here in Inner Mongolia was the most prolific mining and refinery facility in the world. The only serious competition, Den Chin thought, had been in Malaysia.

Of course, the WHO tour of the area had not been without problems. At one point en route to the refinery, protesters had blocked the bus carrying the delegation, hoisting signs crudely lettered in English reading, "Give us back our Land" or "Our Health is not worth your Piles of Gold." The security guards accompanying the tour had removed the protesters from the road, fortunately without resorting to violence, and the bus had rolled ahead in short order. But then, when they ventured into the cerium processing plant, the workers had looked glum and even afraid. One of them even had pulled at the sleeve of a WHO member in an attempt to start a conversation before the production floor supervisor stepped forcefully in between them with a broad smile and steered the delegate away from the row of workers.

Den Chin followed behind the group as he had done for the entire itinerary, which now was almost completed. He had only the dinner this evening with which to contend. The tour had gone relatively smoothly with no significant issues, but now he watched the delegate whose arm had been tugged by a worker and felt a frisson of concern. She was an attractive Asian woman, probably in her forties, who obviously was not impressed by the pristine sights being pointed out and carefully described by the guide. As a senior refinery manager, the guide had projected efficiency and concern for both workers and the environment throughout the tour.

The Asian delegate, however, stared at the huge production floor that was the final stop, appearing to study the exhaust piping and machinery, which idled today so the delegates could proceed without the usual din, which, when operational, was so overwhelming that it provided a hazard for workers subjected to it for eight-hour daily shifts.

Den Chin quickened his pace and moved through the group of about twenty-five people until he was beside the delegate who had attracted his attention. "Very impressive, isn't it?" he said to her, glancing at the name tag affixed to her black jacket, which read "Hana Chang, MD, Work Environment Hazards." "The cleanliness of the setting, I mean," he said, extending his arm toward the expansive, shining floors and huge machinery that looked to be either brand new or recently polished. "And the design of the area, with twenty-five-foot ceilings sloped to direct natural air flow toward the giant ceiling fans, which are vented directly to the outside."

"Yes," she answered without enthusiasm. "It looks quite impressive, but where are the workers? And why is the machinery idle? How can we possibly draw accurate conclusions without seeing the facility as it actually operates?" She looked at his name tag and added, "Dr. Den Chin."

He tried to formulate a plausible explanation, but in a moment Dr. Chang raised her arm dismissively and said, "That was not a rhetorical question, but I suppose, as usual, there won't be an answer." She looked at him with disdain.

"Dr. Chang," he said in a firm voice, recovering his authority, "if the production facilities were operational, you would hardly be able to view the machinery in close detail as we are doing or listen to the extensive scientific narrative being provided to you by our experts. Certainly there would be no opportunity to have conversational exchanges with those experts or with the actual production supervisors who have accompanied us throughout the tour and have provided firsthand information about the work environment and atmosphere at each step of the mining and refining process." He paused and decided that a strong response would likely be more effective than an attempt at flattery, for which he had dismal skills in any event.

"Contrary to your . . . desire"—he hesitated on the word—"for superficial content, we designed this itinerary specifically to give the delegation—you are all science and medical professionals, after all—a complex and expert-level view of our mining of rare earth. We did not deem that a tour of the facility appropriate for tourists who merely want to snap photos of 'real' Chinese workers would be suitable for the WHO."

She appeared to be considering Den Chin's explanation but said nothing. He looked around at the other WHO participants, all of whom were casually asking questions of the experts and making notes on the program literature that had been distributed to them at the start of the tour. From appearances, Hana Chang was the only problematic link.

"Dr. Chang," he said, "won't you join me at my table at the closing ceremony this evening? I will do my utmost to answer any questions you have." He spoke pleasantly, suppressing the authoritative demeanor he had displayed moments before, but did not smile.

Hana Chang stared at him, considering, and nodded. "Thank you," she said, turned away, and rejoined the discussions among her colleagues.

The dinner went well, and Den Chin was satisfied and relieved when the last of the delegates departed for their hotel rooms at about nine o'clock. He had managed to visit each of the four tables and have a personal word with each WHO member and now felt an introvert's exhaustion from the effort of prolonged socializing. He felt he had executed his instructions from the party well, even though the environment engendered natural discomfort for him.

He had saved the seat next to his own for Hana Chang and was concerned when she failed to appear until about ten minutes after the first course had already been placed at each table setting. He noted, though, that once seated she gave no sign of the skepticism or irritation that she had shown earlier in the day. While not overly talkative, she made easy conversation with the other delegates at the table and contributed well-reasoned observations to discussions about the mine and refinery.

The dinner was a Chinese banquet consisting of eleven courses, mostly famous Mandarin dishes that were commonly served around the world in poorly prepared imitation of the Chinese originals. The committee had spared no expense to impress the WHO, Den Chin noted, and each course was exquisite. He thought that the highlight was his own favorite, Peking duck, carved tableside, with a delicately crisped skin that was delectable.

"Dr. Chang," Den Chin said when the duck was cleared, turning to face her. "I promised to answer your questions, and I am prepared to do so. Please let me know any areas of concern so I can address them."

She smiled back at him, very different from her glare that afternoon. "Thank you, Dr. Den Chin, for being so direct. During the break I reviewed the handouts and also my own notes made during the tour. I have no specific questions at the moment, just a general concern about the environmental and health problems reported at rare earth mining sites over the past twenty years or so." She paused and then looked at him directly and said, "It seems to me that there has been a disturbing trail of problems that has never been disproved or even properly investigated."

"Or proved," interjected Den Chin in a confident voice. "I can assure you that we have taken every known precaution to protect our workers as well as the environment of beautiful Inner Mongolia." He suppressed his impulse, an impossible urge really, to share with her his own suspicions about the strange, infectious-type illness that had appeared in Perak.

"This area of China is the location of a number of exceptional historical and natural sites. It would be an offense to the earth to treat them carelessly with industry that might damage them," he said with such seriousness that Chang replied with mirth in her eyes.

"Tell me about one of them, Dr. Den Chin."

Hiding his embarrassment, Den Chin said, "Pao." She looked perplexed and raised her arms in a questioning gesture. "My name," he said, "it's Pao," and she nodded at him.

He settled more comfortably in his chair and continued. "Resonant Sand Bay, for example. It is a scientifically unexplained phenomenon, unknown anyplace else in the world. When the dunes of sand are disturbed by a vehicle or sufficient pressure from anything, even just walking upon them, strange sounds arise from the depths of the dunes that mimic well-known sounds."

"Such as?" she asked.

"Such as a jet engine. Or a motorcycle. Or even a musical instrument." He allowed himself a small smile in response to her obvious surprise at this explanation. "It's true," he said. "I assure you."

"I'd like to see it," she replied. "How can I get there? Tomorrow," she said. "The rest of the group is departing tomorrow for the grand tour of the Great Wall, but I have a commitment in Switzerland the next morning and had to decline."

"I will take you," he said and quickly added, "if you would like, of course."

She said she would be pleased to go with him and agreed to meet in the hotel lobby at 10:00 a.m.

CHAPTER 21
Inner Mongolia, China

Almost immediately Den Chin began to question his decision to make
the trip to Resonant Sand Bay with only his driver and a single
security agent seated in the front passenger seat of the black SUV.
He had wanted to emphasize his status as a physician rather than a
high-ranking member of the party, which he thought would be less
intimidating to the WHO delegate sitting next to him on the back
seat. But no matter how he tried, Den Chin found he could not
project the demeanor of an approachable scientist, and the absence
of his usual trappings of political influence just made him even more
ill at ease than usual. He had inherited his mother's natural reserve
and would never shake it, he thought.

Hana Chang was quiet as well but gave no appearance of being
uncomfortable with the silence. She stared out the window as
the high-rise buildings of Baotou vanished behind them and the
structures became smaller and smaller until, on the very edge of the
populated suburbs, there were only small, earthen houses with goats
strolling around them. Then came the sand, endless rolling hills of
golden sand stretching ahead as far as they could see.

"It's the Kubuqi Desert," Den Chin said, "not the Gobi as many tourists think."

"Ah," Hana added pleasantly. Although they were driving on a well-paved road, she saw that they created a billowing cloud of yellow sand behind them. "Is it the same in the Gobi?" she gestured out the window.

"Oh yes," Den Chin replied. "But the singing sounds of Resonant Bay, and the strange sounds from the sand dunes that we will experience, are unique to this desert. Unique in the world actually."

"Quite a diverse topography," Hana commented. "To have the rare earth mines and an endless desert with singing sands within an hour of each other," she said, trying to make conversation with her reserved host. "In Switzerland, of course, we have neither. We have green mountains and rushing water everyplace."

They passed a caravan of camels being guided along the side of the road by traditionally dressed Mongolian herdsmen. "I am not too familiar with high mountain ranges like the Alps, but I know quite well the type of green and lush terrain you describe. It is predominant in Taiwan," Den Chin said. "I grew up there and only moved to Beijing as a young man. I still sometimes long for the green hills and go to Taiwan to visit."

"Oh, I like Taiwan myself," Hana said. "Have you been to the National Palace Museum? The collection of Chinese art is magnificent."

Den Chin felt a momentary sadness as he recalled his father's role in preserving the museum's collection even after his demeaning treatment by the nationalists.

"Yes, I have been there many times. In fact," Den Chin said, "my father played a part in bringing the art collections from the Forbidden City to Taiwan in 1949. He was an expert in Chinese ink painting."

Hana Chang thought this over. "And yet you are a Communist," she said. "An important one, I gather. That's surprising."

"Yes," said Den Chin. "Sometimes the path to one's correct place in life is surprising. And you? Did you grow up in Switzerland?"

"No, I grew up in Hong Kong," Hana said. "My father was a wealthy banker with strong business connections in Western Europe. We had a beautiful home on Victoria Peak, and I attended the most exclusive private schools." She smiled. "When China gained control of the island in 1997, my father's business associates urged him to relocate to Europe, but he loved our life in Hong Kong and would not leave. By the time he realized that the Hong Kong we loved was in the process of being murdered by the Chinese," she said, risking insulting her host, "it was too late to leave with his wealth intact. But his friends helped us to move to Geneva with sufficient resources to live a comfortable life. I went to medical school there and have come to love Switzerland, especially the Alps."

To her relief, Den Chin did not appear offended by her statement. "You see," he said placidly. "The route of one's life is complex and cannot be predicted."

They rode in silence for a while. Passing miles of uninterrupted sand dunes, Den Chin noticed subtle changes in the vista, the angles of the slopes and small gradations in the color of the sand depending on shadows created by the surrounding dunes. He was entranced by the landscape and thought he would study artwork of the desert when he returned to Beijing.

They passed a cluster of bright white tents arranged in concentric circles, and Den Chin explained that it was the Grain of Sand Resort, which marked the entrance to Xiangshawan Port and Resonant Sound Bay. Their car stopped at a small, white building marked "Tourist Center," and his security agent vanished inside for several minutes. When he returned, he held a blue plastic ID of some kind in the windshield, and they were waved along a narrow road by the guards, driving past the parking areas, past an area where tourists appeared to be renting what looked like surfboards at a small hut, and past a group of families boarding a multicar sightseeing tram.

At the end of the road, the driver pulled their car onto a small, paved area and came to a stop.

They exited the car, and Den Chin waved his guest to the other side of the parking area where an ark-like vehicle was waiting for them. Sitting on eight wide wheels with deep treads was an open compartment containing eight rows of upholstered red velvet seats divided by a center aisle. Everything was trimmed with ornate gold braid. The front sloped down and had a full, clear windshield in front of a driver's seat, and the carved wooden rear of the vehicle rose into the air and was topped by a sand screen decorated with intricate carvings.

The driver of the tram, dressed in colorful Mongol clothing, climbed down four steps to the sand and smiled broadly. He was deeply tanned with furrows at the sides of his eyes and yellow teeth with large gaps at the front.

He opened a storage area in the side of the arch and pulled out two pairs of bright red, oversize socks with rows of fringe and handed them to Den Chin and Hana, explaining in Mandarin that they were to go over their shoes to protect them from being soiled by the sand, which would be stirred up during the ride.

Designed to hold about thirty people, the ark had been reserved just for them, and they settled into their own row of seats, opposite each other across the center aisle. The driver started up the vehicle, silent and apparently powered by electricity, and drove off onto the sand. The heavy wheels pulled them slowly onto a packed sand track leading up the side of a dune, and Den Chin translated to Hana the driver's proud announcement that conditions were perfect: there had been no rain for two weeks, and they would have a very good ride.

When the path had climbed to a height of about twenty-five feet above the parking area, the driver pulled off the track and started across the sand, running parallel to the parking area for fifty or sixty yards. As the tram accelerated, yellow sand created a cloud behind them, and a humming sound began to rise from within the sand around them. It grew louder as they moved faster, enveloping the ark in a weird, all-encompassing noise that could not be traced to any direction or location.

The driver looked back to confirm that his passengers were comfortable, which they appeared to be, and he gradually began to accelerate across the sand. The sound rising around them became louder and higher in pitch, and when the driver abruptly swung the tram into a curve, kicking up a huge cloud of yellow sand that obscured their view to the effect of looking through yellow gauze, the sound turned into the deep and resonant clanging of a huge bell, holding its trembling note as they sped through the sand.

Hana began to laugh out loud.

They rode on, and the driver, seeing his passengers' delight, executed a series of intricate twists and turns that caused the sounds from the sand to alternately sound musical or like the engine of a plane or, at one point, like a bugle wailing a plaintive melody.

When the driver returned them to the parking area after an hour, he extended his arm to Hana to assist her down the steps and then bowed deeply to them. Den Chin thanked him in Mandarin and said something to his security agent who pulled bills from his pocket and handed them to the ark driver, who smiled broadly and raised his hand in thanks.

Unaccustomed to casual social interaction, Den Chin was nonetheless put at ease by Hana's high spirits on the ride back to the hotel.

"My former husband would enjoy this adventure immensely," she said, "and he is the only person I know who would actually travel around the world to Inner Mongolia just for the experience. I must tell him about it."

"Where would he travel from?" asked Den Chin. "It is less than a three-hour plane ride from Beijing to Baotou, not bad at all."

"He's not Chinese, and he lives in New York now, not exactly convenient to Inner Mongolia. He's Swiss, a wealthy businessman, but he had a terrible, life-changing experience a number of years back and needed to remake his entire routine to move past it. That's why we were divorced and why he left Europe. I could not leave Switzerland with him; my family, my career are all in Europe. And there is a big age difference between us, twenty years, and he had grown bored with Europeans, and I still like them." She chuckled. "He and I are still great friends. He is my best friend actually." Den Chin nodded but made no reply. "Are you married, Pao?"

"No," he said. "The party has formed the great relationship of my life, and my work as a physician and scientist is very satisfying." He was quiet and then, not wanting her to think him lacking in human connections, he added, "I do have friends in Taiwan, though. Men and women I have known since childhood, whom I visit several times each year."

When the car delivered them back to the hotel, Hana handed Pao her business card and asked that he contact her if he thought of any information about the mine and refinery that might be relevant to the WHO evaluation. She told him that the investigation schedule required them to submit their written report and conclusions within thirty days.

She thanked him for the wonderful tour of Inner Mongolia and said she would like to reciprocate and take him on a cog rail train ride to the peaks of the Alps should he come to Switzerland.

They shook hands cordially and said goodbye.

CHAPTER 22
Inner Mongolia, China

Den Chin told his driver that he would not be needed for the balance of the afternoon and permitted him to take the SUV into Baotou for a bit of sightseeing before they were to depart together on the 9:00 p.m. flight back to Beijing. He then stopped at the front desk and confirmed that the members of the Chinese host committee had departed the hotel together with the WHO delegation to begin their VIP tour of the Great Wall while he had still been at Resonant Sand Bay with Hana Chang.

Back in his hotel room, Den Chin engaged the chain lock on the door, pulled his suitcase from the closet, and took out two oversize leather briefcases, one black and one brown. He inventoried the contents of each and, satisfied that they were correct, placed the bags near the door of the suite.

He called the hotel desk and requested that a car be engaged for him. He would need it for one to two hours and would be downstairs in five minutes. He took both briefcases and rode the elevator down to the lobby. To his relief, he saw no one that he knew, and no one greeted him until he found the driver waiting for him outside.

The driver pulled away from the hotel and followed Den Chin's directions to the REE refinery and the parking area at the perimeter of the sludge-filled lake where his escort had waited for him two days before. He instructed the driver to wait for him there and said that he would return within a half hour. Den Chin took the two cases and set out on the same path over the berm that he had walked previously.

When he reached the top of the hill, he visually confirmed that he was in the same location; the endless row of black chutes spilling out sludge was at the same distance he remembered on his right, and trucks moved about like industrious automatons on his left. He walked three paces to the left and at the base of the berm on the lake side found the small boulder he sought. He looked behind it and, lodged in the sludge exactly as he had pushed them with his shoe on his previous visit, were four dead bats.

He opened the cases on a small, waterproof tarp he had brought with him and removed the biological collection equipment inside. He snapped on plastic gloves and looked around to confirm that he was alone on the berm. He kneeled and set to work carefully sealing the carcasses in the sanitary units he had brought, which he then divided between the two cases.

In fifteen minutes he had completed the collection of the specimens and resealed the cases, which, this time, he locked. He stowed the dirty tarp and dirty gloves behind the boulder and headed back to the waiting car.

When he deplaned in Beijing, despite the late hour, Den Chin instructed the driver to take him to his laboratory complex before going to his apartment. Without comment, Den Chin declined help from the guards at the door of the sprawling facility and carried the two briefcases he had brought from Inner Mongolia directly to the secure refrigeration unit. He entered his classified credentials to unlock the steel doors to a large room ringed with a series of metal doors opening onto separate refrigeration compartments maintained at different temperatures deemed optimal for preserving the different specimens stored within. The unit was empty of people at this late hour.

He went to the door marked "Reserved for the Director," entered another string of numbers into the lock and the door popped open. Den Chin removed the samples from the first briefcase, wrapped them in a dry ice pack that concealed the contents, and applied a label to the exterior marked "Director Den Chin, Control Samples."

He closed the secure unit and went to another set of doors that indicated "Samples Awaiting Transport." He carefully packaged the contents of his second case in a dry ice pack, which he then placed in an insulated shipping container. He labeled it "Dr. Keiji Takama" with tomorrow's date and resealed the refrigeration unit. He had contacted Keiji before leaving Taipei and arranged for the younger doctor to appear at Den Chin's lab sometime tomorrow to retrieve the sample marked with his name.

He did not share the details of his unease with Keiji but merely asked him to analyze the bat carcass for known or unknown viral agents, saying he had concerns that doing the research at his own facility in Beijing could result in excessive attention being paid to a matter that most likely was innocuous. They agreed that Keiji would report his findings directly and only to Den Chin on the Taiwanese cell phone that he had started to carry with him for communications that he did not want to risk being shared with the party.

Keiji would have no direct contact with Den Chin, and the handoff of the specimens would be treated as a routine matter that each lab worker assumed had been arranged by someone else.

Even so, Den Chin knew that he was exposing his friend to some risk by asking him to conduct the analysis of the detritus, really a clandestine investigation, at the facility the younger man supervised in central China, but he decided to do it anyway. Assigning the analysis to another facility was, after all, well within Den Chin's authority and should not arouse any suspicions.

Years earlier, Keiji Takama had been the person to notify Den Chin about a Chinese tourist in Malaysia with an unknown respiratory illness possibly linked to bats. That revelation had set in motion the chain of events that culminated in the disappearance of the Malaysia Air flight. It had haunted Den Chin ever since.

Keiji, of course, had no suspicion that the plane disappearance had been anything other than an unfortunate coincidence and was unaware that it had been filled with people involved with the rare earth catastrophe in Malaysia. Still, when he learned that the pneumonia patient had been on board the doomed plane, he had called Den Chin to express his frustration that the woman's illness now could not be investigated or diagnosed.

In that first contact with Keiji years earlier, Den Chin knew that he had been abrupt to the point of rudeness despite Keiji's earnest scientific intentions. Den Chin was impressed that Dr. Takama had had the self-assurance to contact him again immediately after the plane tragedy to express his commitment as a virologist to investigating the source of all potential viral illnesses.

Thereafter the two doctors had remained in touch, speaking a few times a year about scientific matters. On one occasion, when Den Chin had been in central China in connection with his clean water project, he made a surprise appearance at Keiji's facility, causing excitement to ripple through the scientists and doctors under Keiji's supervision. In front of the assembled group, Den Chin had lauded Dr. Takama's leadership and the excellence of his central China facility. He knew that he had cemented his relationship with a loyal colleague.

The next day, Den Chin casually checked the transport records of the lab and confirmed that at 11:42 a.m. a cold pack parcel had been picked up by Dr. Keiji Takama.

Den Chin prepared to wait.

CHAPTER 23
Beijing

On the third day after Keiji retrieved the specimen, Den Chin began to check his Taiwan phone every few hours, but there was no activity. By the fourth day, his anxiety over what he had set in motion began to mount.

What if Keiji had been discovered conducting a suspicious evaluation? Den Chin had not encountered it personally, but it was generally believed that the party had well-placed spies who enabled them to have current information on virtually everything happening. Or what if the analysis had yielded results so important or surprising that Keiji had felt compelled to share it with the party hierarchy? In that case, Den Chin himself could now be under suspicion for initiating an investigation without consulting the members for authorization. He vividly recalled the clear threat made by party members when he suggested pursuing the circumstances behind the plane catastrophe in Malaysia.

By the fifth day, Den Chin found himself unable to focus on his current lab work, an unusual occurrence that had happened only two or three times in his long career. His usual laser-like concentration, usually undisturbed by emotions or personal concerns, had been a major factor in his rise within his profession as well as the party, and he felt alarmed by its sudden disappearance.

Late afternoon of the fifth day, his Taiwan phone vibrated in his pocket. He closed his office door and greeted Keiji.

"I was growing concerned since I hadn't heard from you, Dr. Takama," he said. Although he sometimes called his colleague "Keiji" and had invited him to use the casual "Pao," they still maintained a formal manner of speaking during laboratory hours.

"Yes, I am sorry for the delay, Dr. Den Chin," Keiji responded. "I was perplexed by the initial results and decided to rerun the samples before reporting to you. I regret that I did not think to update you on the delay."

Consistent with Chinese manners, Keiji waited to be invited by his superior to continue. Den Chin, not wanting to appear overly concerned with the matter, forced himself to delay for a few moments before saying in a neutral tone, "And what are the results, Dr. Takama?"

"Well, as you suspected, there is a viral pathogen present. On examination it appeared to have caused an unusual breakdown of cell structure leading to significant deterioration of molecular integrity. This is not consistent with viral agents typically found in bats or other small mammals." Keiji paused, allowing Den Chin time to process this information and ask questions, but he said nothing, so Keiji continued. "Moreover, I was able to isolate the organism and could not match it to any viral agent known to our lab." He paused again, and again Den Chin was silent.

"So I reran the specimens, even took fresh cuts to use besides the original ones so I could isolate the error if there was one. The results were identical. The same unusual breakdown of biologic function, no identifiable microorganism."

"Did you then look for bacterial agents?" asked Den Chin.

"Yes, I did," came the quick reply. "In fact I checked for bacterium, parasites, even environmental agents. I could identify nothing. No clues." When Den Chin did not say anything, Keiji felt compelled to continue. "And, Pao, the deterioration of the biologic material was pernicious. Total destruction of the cell boundaries and structure. The disease appears to be particularly virulent."

Den Chin felt a tingle at the back of his neck. "But is the destruction consistent with viral agents?"

"I would say it was worse than I would expect. Is it possible that something other than an infecting organism, or in addition to it, affected the specimen? I don't know anything about the sample collection, but could it possibly have caused contamination? Or additional damage?"

Having collected and packaged the material personally, Den Chin knew that this was not the case. "Dr. Takama," he said in a commanding voice, his equilibrium recovered, "do not ask additional questions or discuss your findings with anyone. This is very important." He paused for effect. "Repack the specimen in a new cold pack and enclose your written results within the cylinder. Do not keep any record of your findings and mark the pack clearly for personal delivery to me only and in person. I will have it retrieved by a lab assistant tomorrow." He let his instructions settle on the younger doctor. "Do you understand me, Dr. Takama?" he asked. "These instructions must be followed exactly."

"Yes, Director Chin, I understand, but don't you think we should evaluate what this might be? I have no idea where the specimen was located or the circumstances that may have resulted in isolating a previously unknown viral agent."

"Dr. Takama," Den Chin said harshly, adopting the impatient and commanding tone with which he had spoken to Keiji in their first conversation years before, "are my instructions to you clear? Is there some part of what I said that is causing you confusion?"

Seeming to barely contain his indignation, Dr. Takama said in a cold tone, "Certainly, Dr. Den Chin, your instructions are perfectly clear and of course will be followed exactly."

They hung up, and Keiji returned to the lab to prepare his report and package the sample for transfer back to Beijing.

Den Chin sat at his desk, considering a course of action for quite some time. Keiji's analysis supported his own suspicion that, in addition to the sample from Inner Mongolia, the dead bats observed in Perak years before had most likely died from a viral agent, one that as of now remained unidentified. Proximity to the mines in both instances could be purely coincidental, he thought. It might well be entirely different causes of death in bats found more than six years apart and separated by thousands of miles.

Moreover, he knew that the ill Chinese tourist had been in the area of Perak, but Den Chin had no information suggesting that she had actually been near the Bukit mine. In fact, the only confirmation of his suspicion that her illness was somehow related to the bats, if you could even call it a confirmation, was her statement to authorities that "it must have been the bats." And that, Den Chin silently acknowledged, could mean absolutely anything, even that she had indeed been high on drugs as the police had believed. Still, Keiji had informed him that the hospital where the woman had been treated could find no known viral agent or other infectious agent to explain her illness or evidence of drug use. Was this a stronger confirmation than he'd originally thought?

Den Chin was well aware of the pernicious environmental hazards of rare earth mining, as every informed scientist was, but the acid-washed runoff from radioactive material would cause damage to earth and water supplies and was implicated in cancer and other long-term health effects such as kidney and liver illness. He had not seen a single study, or even an implication, that an environmental hazard could somehow translate to a contagious viral pathogen.

Or, he thought, perhaps the infection had nothing at all to do with the obvious environmental issues of rare earth but instead arose from an infective agent buried deep in the earth, dormant for decades or even centuries, inadvertently released by the mining operations.

He had only questions, no answers. He knew that only the limitless resources of the party would enable a proper investigation, but accepted that he could not call upon them. After all, the committee members had flatly refused to permit analysis of a similar crisis after the Malaysian plane disappearance in 2014. Den Chin felt compelled to find the cause of the seemingly similar events in Inner Mongolia.

The WHO report would be released in only a few weeks and might yield new insights on the Inner Mongolia mine. He decided to obtain as much information about the mine as he could while he waited for the report. After conducting an online search, he selected half a dozen articles from scientific journals and ordered hard copies, which, as opposed to online versions, he could read in any private place. This time he had the material sent to his apartment rather than the lab and charged the cost to his Taiwanese credit card.

The next day he dispatched one of his young research assistants to the lab in central China to retrieve the cold pack that he had instructed Keiji to prepare. When it was handed to him late in the day, he removed all markings that would indicate its origin and placed the unopened cylinder in his private refrigeration unit beside the other sample that had been there since his return from Inner Mongolia. He now knew the specimens contained some form of novel infectious agent, but until he could formulate a theory of origin, he would keep the matter in the sealed containers in his private storage area. He would not risk the party again shutting down an investigation.

PART FIVE
2021
Long Island, New York

CHAPTER 24

Drost clearly does not intend to leave. He has taken me by surprise showing up at my home at eleven o'clock at night with news that Jack has had an "incident." I walk away from him and slump onto the sofa. He looms in front of me, his great height making him look like a monolith blocking out the lamplight coming from behind him. When I recover myself sufficiently to speak, I ask him what happened to Jack.

"We were tailing Cedar when he left his apartment and he was jumped by three guys," he says. "Lucky for him, we were pretty close and they only landed a couple of blows before we scared them off. But they hit him with something metal, so he needed the emergency room. My partner took him for treatment, and I came directly here to see if you had any problems. So have you? Had any problems, I mean?"

I stare at him, mystified. "Why would I have problems because Jack Cedar was mugged, Officer Drost?" I ask, the blood returning to my brain, clearing my mental stupor. "Even if you think the attack was something other than a random robbery, what possible connection could it have with me? I only met the man last Friday and know nothing about him except what a woman claiming to be his wife told me," I say indignantly. "And," thinking of what my brother has told me, I raise my voice and add, "I'd really like to know why there was an FBI car sitting outside my house a couple of nights ago. Am I under surveillance or something?"

In a sharp tone, threatening actually, that I have not heard from him before, he says, "I need to know about your relationship with George Hong, and I need to know it right now, Ms. Jones." I realize he is not the affable sidekick to Hamilton that I initially judged him to be.

"I would like a drink," I respond, needing time to think this over. "Will you have something?"

"I can't drink liquor. I'm on duty," he says. "But a bottle of water would be fine."

I get one for him and then pour a small amount of scotch into the tumbler with ice that I have brought for myself from the kitchen. "Why don't you sit down, Officer Drost? I am uncomfortable with you towering over me."

He sits down on the armchair, and I return to my position on the sofa. "Look," I say, trying to sound sincere and convincing since what I am saying is, after all, the truth, "I do not know *any* of these people! Aimee Cedar appeared at my office a few weeks ago, paid me very well to do what I do for a living, and then vanished. I had never met her before and haven't been able to find her since. I met Jack Cedar for the first time when he stormed into my office last Friday and told me that Aimee is not his wife. And I most certainly do not know anything whatsoever about George Hong, whom I have never met or even heard of until now!" Drost stares at me and waits, but I say no more. I am learning from him to let silence sit heavily without feeling a need to fill the void.

"You said Mrs. Cedar paid you twenty-five thousand dollars in cash. Where is it?" His pleasant manner is restored, but now I know it is just an interrogation technique, and I remain wary.

This is a tough question for me to answer. I don't want to acknowledge that I have placed the cash in my safe deposit box as this might be construed as an intent to commit tax fraud.

"What does this have to do with anything?" I say with bravado. "The finances of my law firm have nothing to do with anything here—"

Drost cuts in and says, "Oh, you would be dead wrong about that, Ms. Jones. Investigating cash payments in connection with terrorist acts is not uncommon actually. Ever hear the expression 'follow the money'?" He leans forward and stares at me, his eyebrows raised in a question. "Twenty-five thousand dollars in green could certainly buy information or convince someone to look the other way. . . or maybe even pay an attorney to create an ironclad alibi for someone by getting their passport sealed in a bank vault." He stares at me and waits.

I am horrified by the implication he is making. I consider if it is actually possible that I have been duped into complicity with a terrorist act.

"If you prefer," Drost continues, "we can go to court for a warrant and give a judge about ten, maybe a dozen, solid reasons for us to gain access to everything, and I mean everything, about your law firm. And about you, by the way. Personally, I mean." He stares directly at me, the shadow of a smirk on his face.

I stare back and say evenly, "The money is in my safe deposit box at my bank," realizing that whether I plan to pay taxes on the money is laughably trivial in the new context of his questions. "I put it there and planned to deposit it into my law firm account on Monday. I never got there, though, because of. . . what happened," I say and look away, suddenly overwhelmed by the tragedy and the mystery of the last few days. "Excuse me, I'm going to the bathroom," I say, turning my back on him just as my eyes begin to well over.

I delay in the powder room, breathing deeply to try to quell the panic that is overtaking me. I hear talking from the direction of the living room and realize that Jack and Hamilton have arrived. When

I return to the living room, I find Jack seated on the sofa and the two FBI agents talking quietly to each other on the other side of the room.

"Oh, Jack," I say, taking in the battered condition of the left side of his face, which is swollen and lined with purple streaks surrounding a three-inch bandage across his cheekbone. With Hamilton and Drost huddled in the corner, I restrain my instinct to touch Jack's arm, but I sit down on the other end of the sofa and ask in a voice that clearly reflects my distress at his condition, "What happened? How did this happen?" He looks at me for a moment, and he notes my agitated state.

Before he can say anything to me, the FBI agents approach us, and Hamilton takes over. "Right now I need to know about George Hong," he says in the onerous manner that he used when we first met in my conference room. Jack and I stare at him blankly. I, at least, have no idea why he is interested in George Hong. I am thinking about how to handle this when Jack speaks up.

"Agents, I have explained this to you several times already," he says in a tight voice, seeming to be in pain. "I have known George as a co-professional for years, maybe five or six years, and we have attended seminars and meetings together, he representing Columbia and I, NYU. On a few occasions we attended the same multiday science conferences and got to know each other somewhat, and twice, I think three times actually, we went to science-related dinners that included spouses, or in my case, a date." He sits back and rubs his forehead. "That is it!" he says firmly. "I know the man only in that capacity and no more. I met his wife at the few professional dinners, and she told me all about their life in San Francisco before moving to New York when George took up his position at Columbia."

"Who was your date at those dinners?" Hamilton demands without preamble.

"Oh my God," says Jack in a weary voice. "No one! No one with any connection to anything! An English professor I went with for a while and haven't seen in about two years." He sits back on the sofa and closes his eyes.

He looks so spent that I am moved to intervene. I muster up my attorney tone of voice and say, "Look, agents, I think Professor Cedar has had it for today. It appears he was seriously injured in this mugging and should be permitted to rest. Anything else you want to know can wait until tomorrow." Jack does not even open his eyes, which causes me some concern.

They both stare at me, and I assume they are considering whether continuing the questioning under these circumstances might taint the reliability or legal use of any information they obtain.

Finally Drost says, "A last question, Mr. Cedar—for now, that is. Do you have any idea who attacked you? Or why?"

Jack still doesn't open his eyes or appear even to have heard the question. But then he suddenly and angrily says, "No, I do not. But I note that since the plane disaster, my apartment has been broken into, and I have now been mugged and seriously injured. And George Hong, in whom you seem to have a great deal of interest, may or may not have been on that plane, but his family has definitely departed the country in a very abrupt and peculiar way. Oh, and don't forget that some woman, who now seems to have vanished, claims to be my wife. This cannot be coincidence, agents," he says, raising his voice and sitting forward on the sofa. "Particularly since up until last week I led a routine life as an earth science professor!" He winces and puts his hand to his injured cheek.

Jack turns to me, ignoring the two FBI agents as if they are not sitting opposite us in my living room with threatening demeanors, and says, "Aruba, I really am not feeling well enough to head back to the city. May I please impose on you to use your guest room for the night?" I am too nonplussed to speak and simply nod.

Hamilton and Drost sit silently for a moment, and then Hamilton stands, his decision made, and says, "We will resume questioning you tomorrow at 10:00 a.m. We require that you both remain here, and I will post a car outside to insure that." Drost follows his lead and stands up. As they near the front door, Hamilton turns back to us and says, "And of course the agents outside will also protect you from any danger."

Actually he means "protect his own ass," I think, since he is claiming to have an official capacity to confine us without a warrant or official order of any kind.

They close the door behind them, and Jack and I sit, silent, on the sofa.

In a few moments Jack goes to the front door and watches through the sidelight as the two black cars pull away and roll down the street. The agent they have requisitioned to sit outside overnight apparently has not yet arrived.

"Ruby," he says gravely. "They think George Hong is a Chinese spy. I can't believe it. This is a guy I have spent time with, spoken to for years, traveled with to conferences; I know his wife. I can't even fathom what this means."

I would actually think he is joking except that the overall circumstances are yielding one astonishing possibility after another. "They told you that?" I ask, incredulous, thinking that on the FBI shows on TV, which are my only frame of reference for the FBI, the agents would be far too cagy to reveal this suspicion to a suspect.

"No," Jack says. "My friend at Columbia told me. I spent a couple of hours there this afternoon trying to get information on what happened to George's family—you know, Ellen and the kids just picking up and going to China. I'm good friends with Dean Sittah of the science school over there, and he told me that the FBI showed up this morning and were all over George's office, carting off the contents of every file cabinet, his desk, everything. Then they questioned George's admin, his student interns, and the professors in his department."

"And that means they think he's a spy?" I ask, doubtful.

"They told Dean Sittah that! He initially refused to let the agents enter George's office, but they whipped out a federal warrant directing that they be granted access to any information relevant to George Hong's scientific research and his contacts with officials in the Chinese government. They had even asked the court for access to material documenting George's contact with Chinese nationals in the US who are not US citizens, but the judge crossed that out. Otherwise, Sittah would have been required to let them have phone records and notes about George's interfacing with Chinese professionals in his department. That includes professors, teaching assistants, students, administrative personnel. You know how many Chinese citizens there are in the science departments of our universities?"

"And you never noticed anything strange about George?" I ask, finding this hard to accept.

"No," Jack says. "Believe me, since I left my meeting with the dean, I have mentally reviewed everything I can remember about every contact I ever had with George. I can't think of a single thing that should have triggered suspicion. He was a typical science guy in every respect. He seemed to be happy with his wife, his kids, and his job and loved to discuss research like all the other professors."

"Well, I guess the Chinese wouldn't kill their own spy, so that would eliminate them from suspicion about the plane," I say.

"Guess again," interjects Jack with an ominous tone. "The agents told the dean that George never got on that plane. In fact, he never even went through security at the airport. So they asked Sittah to contact them immediately if George shows up at Columbia or if they hear from him. And that would focus more suspicion on the Chinese, not less."

I am too exhausted to puzzle out the implications of this news, and it is obvious that Jack also is unable to continue our conversation. I hand him a bottle of Advil Extra Strength and urge him to go to bed. I reiterate that he should help himself to anything he needs in the bathroom or in the kitchen.

I sit out on the patio for a while and then go to bed myself. I, too, am drained of energy, but still I toss and turn, unable to let sleep overtake me. How is it possible that Jack noticed nothing unusual about George Hong? I wonder, and I cannot shake the thought that perhaps I have been too trusting. Jack's good looks and easy charm are valuable assets for a man trying to put one over on someone; I think of my ex-husband and how that had worked out.

Also useful talents for a spy, I realize.

In the morning Jack looks remarkably improved. The swelling has just about disappeared, and the purple streaks on his cheek have faded to a less shocking shade of pink. Owing to his injuries, though, this time I cook breakfast, and we sit down to eat scrambled eggs and croissants I have dug out of the back of the freezer. Both of us are on aggravation overload, so we try to find topics that are pleasant. This proves to be exceedingly difficult: the Covid vaccines licensed last year have inoculated hundreds of thousands, but there are constant media explosions revealing that the affluent and privileged have jumped the line ahead of the impoverished, leading to more claims of racial injustice and rioting in many cities; although the death rate has dropped significantly, Covid infections continue to spread, and experts say it will take two to three more years until the number of cases falls to the level of a typical infectious disease that does not disrupt normal life; and political rancor continues, endlessly it seems, so that as soon as one scandal or complaint is resolved, another is revealed.

Jack says he would like some fresh air, so I take him to the backyard and show him the private beach path that leads directly to the sand without ever emerging on the street in front of the house. I and three of my neighbors maintain the narrow walk, keeping it shielded from view with thick beach grass. Jack and I assume that the FBI agent stationed at my house until Hamilton and Drost arrive at ten is out there, but he will not see us leaving the house through the back. We decide a stroll on the beach is not a violation of the agents' instruction to stay put since the beach itself is a part of the real estate of the community. The deed to my property actually says that my zoned lot comes with "rights to the Atlantic Ocean included."

We leave our shoes at the edge of the path where it meets the sand and start to walk. Jack takes some deep breaths, and natural color starts to return to his face. "This is amazing," he says, admiring the sparkling water rolling into the shore in low waves. We see only a few isolated walkers in the distance and pretty much have the beachfront to ourselves.

"I never get tired of it," I say, smiling, forgetting for the moment that Jack may be a Communist spy. "It's different every day, different waves, different birds, some days with tide pools, some days without, crabs on the sand or not, ships on the horizon or not."

At the mention of ships, Harry Shaw emerges from his path over the dunes and calls out to me. I wave at him but pretend to not understand his gestures beckoning me to come to him. He begins walking toward us, and short of being outright rude, there is nothing I can do to avoid him.

Jack, however, seems perfectly comfortable with the intrusion and holds out his hand as soon as Harry is close enough to shake it. "Jack Cedar," he says pleasantly. Harry returns the greeting and extends his own hand.

We exchange pleasantries about the beach and the weather, and then Harry points at the horizon and says to Jack, "See that long, gray ship with the orange and blue containers on deck? Can you make out the writing on its side? It says Shaw Global." The ship is close enough for us to read the words and also see the familiar red logo, the top line of the S extended into a thick horizontal line above the entire name and ending in a bold, red arrow point. I have always thought it to be a great design, conveying speed and reliability. "My family business,"

Harry says. His pride is low-key so that what might have come across as a boast instead seems a friendly sharing of personal information.

Jack is delighted with this news and despite his facial injury manages to flash his brilliant smile at Harry. "How exciting it must be to see your ship, your name, chugging into the harbor of New York City with all kinds of stuff loaded on it."

"Yes. It actually is exciting, even for a wizened old guy like me," Harry says with his self-effacing charm. Standing there on the beach, he looks handsome and rich, I think. He is wearing perfectly tailored khaki pants and a pale blue linen shirt. His elegantly styled gray hair blows gently in the sea breeze. Harry looks at me, hoping for a clue as to who this guy is that I am walking with first thing in the morning, but I give away nothing. He is almost openly appraising Jack, I notice, and then he says, "So, do you live around here, Mr. Cedar?"

"No, actually not. I'm a professor at NYU, earth and environmental science, and I live in Soho. Ruby and I have a"—he hesitates—"a business matter that we're reviewing together."

"Oh, I see," says Harry, noting that Jack, like himself, has apparently been invited to use my nickname. "Well, I won't delay you then. A pleasure to meet you, Mr. Cedar." Harry seems quite interested in Jack and continues to study him intently. I fleetingly wonder if Harry's friendship toward me is more than neighborly.

"And you as well, Mr. Shaw. I will be on the lookout for that red arrow from now on and will think of your ships with a whole new interest."

Jack and I walk on.

We make sure we are back in my living room by nine thirty, where there is no indication that anyone, including FBI agents, has noticed our absence. I make us coffee, and we sit down at the kitchen table to wait for our friends Hamilton and Drost.

"So, how much do you know about Harry Shaw?" he asks. "If I recall correctly, Shaw Global is a Swiss company. What's he doing in a beach house on Long Island?"

I tell him that Harry is the nephew of the founder of Shaw Global and that he runs the North American division out of Manhattan. Last year at the height of the pandemic, he wanted to get out of the city where he lives in a duplex apartment on the posh Upper East Side, so he bought the beach house. "As you could see, he's still renovating it," I say, chuckling.

"I couldn't even see the house," Jack says, "but the fence—I should say the cement wall—encircling his property makes it look like some kind of a fortress."

"I know." I laugh lightly even as I notice that Jack's observation reveals an interest in stealth. "I commented on that too. Harry told me he had a terrible experience with a terrorist attack on one of his ships that has made him very conscious of security." I tell Jack an abridged version of Harry's story and add, "Harry was—still is, I guess—so traumatized by the event that he actually left his wife in Switzerland and moved to the US for a new start."

Jack does not respond for a few moments but appears to be thinking this over. "So he's divorced?" is his response, and he makes no comment at all about the shocking part of the story, which is, of course, the terrorist attack. I am taken aback that he says nothing about a horrific incident that happened to someone he just met.

I cannot figure out Jack's reaction, or lack of reaction, but neither can I handle another unfathomable question at the moment. "I think he's divorced," I say to Jack lightly and then change the subject. "Did you think of anything else about George Hong that might be helpful?" to which he shakes his head no.

At 9:55 a.m., the doorbell rings, and right on schedule Hamilton and Drost come in and take up their positions to continue questioning us.

"So, when did you two first meet?" Drost says pleasantly enough, and Jack jumps right on it.

"When I went to her office on Friday afternoon because the court papers I already provided to you indicate that Aruba Jones is the attorney for a woman claiming to be my wife. That's the first time I ever heard of Ms. Jones."

"So today is Wednesday," Drost continues, "which means you have known each other, let's see, that would be five days, correct?"

Jack and I both nod at him and simultaneously realize where he is going with this.

"And, Professor Cedar, you've slept here at Ms. Jones's house twice, right? That would be two of the five nights that you have ever known each other."

"Yes, Agent Drost, that is exactly right. Your math is excellent," Jack says angrily, using the same condescending tone I recall from my office when he first burst into it. "I'm promoting you to third grade."

Drost does not let Jack bait him and continues in the same matter-of-fact way. "How did you manage to get over your anger so fast after being mistaken for someone else and having your travel plans and an important meeting all bollixed up?"

"Oh, that's really an easy one, gentlemen," Jack says, glaring at them, one, then the other. "Just have the plane you were supposed to be on vanish into thin air. That'll do it right away! Poof, no more being pissed off about mistaken identity having kept you at home," he says and then looks away, disturbed at himself for having referenced the possible deaths of innocent people in this cavalier manner. "I'm sorry I said that," he practically whispers.

They hammer away at Jack for a while, and I sit silently, watching, listening. He seems so sincere and consistent in all respects that I find it almost impossible to contemplate that he may actually be a secret colleague of George Hong, who may secretly be in the Chinese spy business. But still, I myself have noted some surprising conduct and statements from Jack, and a sliver of doubt remains.

Finally, Hamilton and Drost turn to me. "How many clients have you represented of the Muslim faith?" Hamilton asks.

"What kind of a question is that?" I ask indignantly. "Are you actually implying that every Muslim would have a terrorist connection?" He doesn't even flinch, let alone back down at my blatant accusation of political incorrectness. Instead he placidly, silently stares at me until I finally say, "None."

He nods and continues. "How about Chinese clients. How many have you have represented?"

"A few—Asians, that is. I have no idea if they were of Chinese descent."

"And how many clients, or adversaries of clients like Jack here is, have you invited back to your house for a sleepover?" I don't answer, and he follows up. "Is that typical conduct for you, Ms. Jones?"

Drost has not read me properly, and after a few more questions of this nature, I am inflated with anger rather than unnerved as he had expected. "This interview is over, gentlemen. Professor Cedar and I have cooperated with you in an effort to be helpful in view of the tragedy that has occurred. However, I am not comfortable with the direction this is taking and conclude that Professor Cedar and I each need our own separate counsel if you intend to continue." I am amazed at my own moxie in announcing this since I never have handled a single criminal case and have zero experience in this area. Jack sits silently.

I stand up, gesture toward the front door, and say, "Let me know if you intend to continue, and we will make appropriate arrangements."

Hamilton and Drost are surprised to be brazenly challenged, but they rise and start toward the door. "Certainly, Ms. Jones," Hamilton says with no apparent rancor. "We'll let you know," and they leave without another word.

CHAPTER 25

When the door closes behind them, Jack actually starts to laugh, cupping his hand to his injured cheek, which apparently is hurting him. "Bravo, Ruby," he says cheerfully. "That was really impressive. I can see why Aimee Cedar chose you for her attorney. I wouldn't stand a chance."

His gaiety is shocking under the circumstances, which are pretty grim and deteriorating by the moment. "Jack, I don't think you realize how serious this is—" I start, but he cuts me off.

"Oh, I realize it perfectly, Aruba," he says. "But I, and probably you as well, are victims here, not perpetrators. Let's just keep that in perspective, OK? Because I am not ready to let the absurd and insulting innuendos those guys are leveling at us control my life." I don't respond, so he continues. "Look, they can suggest I'm some kind of terrorist or spy or whatever ludicrous thing they can come up with, but I just can't take it too seriously. In fact, the whole thought is so totally absurd that I cannot even position it in the serious part of my brain. And I can't grasp, really, what they are saying about George Hong either since he seemed a completely regular professor guy to me!"

He sits down, holding his face, and says, "I am a science professor for Christ's sake, and now I'm accused of being a Chinese spy? Right! I can picture it, me hunched over an oil lamp translating my chemistry notations into Chinese in my closet in lower Manhattan."

"And you!" he goes on, gathering steam. "Aruba Jones, American attorney for a Chinese spy ring, camouflaged as a mainstream Long Island divorce lawyer but actually conspiring to. . .what? Overthrow? Undermine? Host a coup d'état against the US government?" he says without missing a beat. He turns one eye, the uninjured side of his face, up at me to gauge my reaction, and I am, by now, smiling.

"OK," I say, "you make a valid point," and I think to myself this man cannot possibly be a spy. He cannot be anything other than an earth and environmental science professor from NYU.

It is Wednesday, and I am due in court at two o'clock with Luis. I have Marsha call him to confirm the time and where he will meet me, but she reports back that she is not at all confident that he is going to appear.

I rush Jack out of the house, shower, and get to the office at about twelve thirty, in time to review the file and jot down a few notes in support of a change of custody to Luis before I head to the courthouse. I haven't been in my office since the meeting with Hamilton and Drost in my conference room on Monday, and there is a pile of message slips and mail on my desk that I ignore for the moment.

The atmosphere of the office, rich leather seats in the waiting room, my walnut desk that I purchased at an antique shop in Vermont and had refinished, the well-oiled machinery, computers, copy machine, phone systems, all restore my feeling of order and competence. The plane disappearance, the FBI, even Jack Cedar and Aimee Cedar, recede to the back row of my consciousness.

When I get to the hallway outside the courtroom where we are scheduled to appear, I see a group of people surrounding the court-appointed lawyer who is representing Jazmin's mother because she is indigent. I have worked with him on several occasions and consider him to be fair-minded and fine to deal with. In his late fifties and well experienced, he will zealously pursue his client's interest, but I have not found him to be underhanded or nasty as many of the matrimonial attorneys tend to be.

Next to him is a young, Hispanic-appearing woman whom I take to be Jazmin's mother. She looks unkempt, with messy, unwashed hair, and is wearing pants and blouse that are mismatched, wrinkled, and have obvious stains.

Jazmin is clinging to her legs, attempting to hide her face in her mother's clothing. Next to Jazmin is a tall woman wearing a navy blue suit and holding a clipboard whom I assume is the court-appointed lawyer for Jazmin, her law guardian. I have never met her and did not even recognize her name when she was appointed, but I have spoken to her several times in an effort to resolve the case, and she seems sensible and truly interested in the welfare of her child client.

My own client is nowhere to be seen, and at 2:15 p.m., the judge orders us all into the courtroom. We take our places, but I am alone at the plaintiff's table while the defendant's table is crowded with chairs for the two lawyers and their two clients.

We make our formal statements of appearance for the court reporter, and I say that my client has been unavoidably delayed and is on his way. Maybe it is true, I hope. The judge is skeptical but directs a thirty-minute recess, ordering us to reappear at three o'clock. Before we file out of the courtroom, he says sternly, "Ms. Jones, if your client is not in this courtroom when we return, I am dismissing his petition. You may wish to contact him, wherever he may be, and let him know that."

In the hall I call Marsha and tell her to try every number at which she might find Luis. And I tell her to call his mother and his sister and let them know the consequences to Jazmin if her father does not appear. I am too keyed up to sit down and do some work while I wait in the hall outside the courtroom, so I just pace around and say hello to a few attorneys I know who are milling around waiting for their own cases to be called.

At 2:55 p.m., I am mentally formulating my argument to try to convince the judge to put the matter over until tomorrow when the elevator doors open and Luis, his mother, and his sister appear. He is squeezed tightly between the two women who see me and steer him in my direction.

We are directed into the courtroom before I have any opportunity to speak with Luis. Now, while the others return to their previous positions, I am joined at the counsel table by my client. His mother and sister take seats directly behind us. The judge takes the bench and gives all of the assembled parties the once-over. He has been around and is a sharp guy, and it is apparent to me that he has actually read the report of the law guardian and correctly sizes up the situation in a few moments.

"Ms. Jones," he begins, and I can almost feel Luis quaking with fear beside me. "Where do the parties stand on this application? I have reviewed the report submitted by the child's attorney, and it seems that a change of custody to the father warrants serious consideration by the court." He looks at me squarely, nodding to let me know he is aware of all of the issues here. "Of course if we have a full hearing we will need to put on the record"—he pauses, maybe searching for the best wording or maybe just going for emphasis—"details about the parents' lives, their employment, living arrangements, immigration status." He has just dropped a few bombs for both Luis and his daughter's mother to consider. He gives it a minute to sink in and then looks first at Luis and then at Jazmin's mother. "And that record will remain on file for future reference should it become necessary." He nods at me, inviting me to speak.

"Your Honor," I begin, "I believe we have a good chance of resolving this dispute amicably if we have a little time for discussion and the assistance of Jazmin's attorney to insure that Jazmin's needs will be met in the best way possible. My client's mother and sister are

in the courtroom"—I half turn and point them out to the judge—
"and are ready to commit to also assisting with Jazmin's care."

The judge looks at the group at both tables again. He sees that
the child's mother appears dissipated, with hollow cheeks and eyes
ringed with dark, puffy swelling, staring at her dirty shoes and
hardly exhibiting maternal promise. On the other hand, the judge
is well aware of Luis's tenuous immigration status and that he may
not even be a resident of the United States much longer. For a judge
with earnest intentions like this one, it is a difficult position in which
to be.

"That is a fine idea, Ms. Jones, to have some settlement
discussions," he says. "My bailiff will assign you a room and you
have until four thirty to put something together. But I am warning
you all," he says as he looks sternly among the adults, "that with the
serious allegations being made in this case, I will not put the matter
over. At four thirty you either report back to me that you have an
agreement that is satisfactory to the law guardian, which we will
put on the record at that time, or the plaintiff will begin testimony
today, and the case will continue tomorrow morning until we are
finished. Is that clear to everyone?" He does not wait for an answer
but instructs the bailiff to open a large conference room down the
hall that we can use for discussions. We file out of the courtroom
and ask Luis's sister to stay in the hall with Jazmin.

Luis does not want to proceed with a hearing because he is
terrified of being deported. His former girlfriend's attorney explains
to her that if she proceeds with a hearing she may be arrested for
drug use or, maybe even worse, prostitution. And then, he says to his
client, there is the matter of child neglect and endangerment since she
has left Jazmin alone in the apartment overnight several times while
she was working. With the law guardian solidly behind a change of
custody to Luis so long as his mother and sister will help to care for
Jazmin during the day, the child's mother realizes she has little choice
at this point but to agree.

Her attorney insists on visitation one day each weekend, which the law guardian agrees to on a trial basis for one month, but I am adamant that Luis will not pay her any support since he will be providing for Jazmin's care on a full time basis. I tell the mother she will have plenty of time to work and support herself, although I realize this will probably come from a string of men whom she now will be able to bring to her apartment without being hampered by Jazmin's presence. At my direction, Luis hardly says a word and looks downcast and worried for the entire time we are in the conference room.

He nods his agreement and makes the deal. I jot down the points that I will dictate into the court record when we return at four thirty. Luis looks so glum that in the hall I steer him to one side and whisper harshly, "Luis, this is what you want, right?"

I am relieved that he bursts into a broad smile and says, "Aruba, how could you even ask me that? I am so happy. I just can't be sure it's OK until we get outta here. This building, the whole thing being here, makes me feel sick like you can't even think about."

I smile back at him, knowing I have achieved the best result possible for Jazmin, and we proceed into the courtroom. The judge says he is pleased with the agreement, that all custody matters are better settled between the members of the family than by the court. Of course, I know the agreement has let the judge off the difficult hook of deciding whether to hold a hearing that might get Luis deported and Jazmin's mother incarcerated. It takes only fifteen minutes to conclude the matter, putting the agreement on the record of the court so it will have the full force of an order of custody.

Luis and his family are ecstatic when we exit the courthouse, hugging and kissing me a bit more than I would prefer but with such good humor that it is hard to resist. Even Jazmin shyly hugs my legs and smiles after she tells her mother that she will see her on Saturday and kisses her goodbye.

It has been a good afternoon, and I am feeling confident and cheerful as I swing my car onto the Meadowbrook. But then my phone rings. It is my brother calling to tell me that he has gotten a facial recognition match for Aimee Cedar, and I am abruptly returned to the disaster.

CHAPTER 26

Steve's loud voice booms over my car speakers, and he obviously is looking forward to imparting some interesting news. "Are you ready to hear where we picked up the likeness of your missing client?"

"From the sound of your voice, I would say probably not," I say, meaning it, since I have just had my first few hours not dominated by anxiety since I laid eyes on Jack Cedar last Friday. "Well, I guess you might as well tell me."

"Ta-da!" he trumpets, announcing his grand disclosure. "Geneva. Switzerland, I mean, the airport, last Wednesday." He waits for my applause.

"She had just arrived there?" I ask, incredulous, goggling at the fact that after she duped me into restraining her husband, or whatever Jack is in relation to her, from leaving the country, she herself got on a plane and went to Switzerland.

But Steve does not know any of this back story, only that my client has vanished and now he has found her for me.

"Can you tell where she had come from?" I ask him, and I realize that I have failed to provide kudos for his technology feat, which really is pretty impressive, maybe even amazing.

"Actually she was in the departures area going through security, not arrivals. And I can't tell where she was going or anything else about her except that the facial recognition match says there is a ninety-seven percent certainty that the woman in the Geneva airport is the same woman who entered your office building. I'll email you the photo of the match so you can look at it yourself."

"Steve, you are a wonder!" I laud him. "Thank goodness our parents failed in their effort to force you to become a flower child!" We both laugh, and I say, "Really, Steve, I can't thank you enough. Unfortunately this raises a whole new bunch of questions, but there it is."

"Let me know if there is anything else I can help you with, Ruby," he says. We hang up, and I decide to go straight home instead of stopping at the office. I really have had it and need a break. I hope there is no one at my house, especially the FBI, and perhaps I will have a few minutes to think straight.

I switch on the radio news as I drive and learn that there still are no clues to the whereabouts of the Emerald Air plane that vanished last week, no sightings of it either intact or as wreckage; no witnesses have come forward from other planes in the area or ships traveling in the sea below the route, and no reports have come in from the closest land masses, which are the southern regions of Greenland or possibly Iceland. Mercifully for me, the story has dropped to second place, now trailing after an unexplained surge in coronavirus cases in South America where vaccine doses have been notoriously hard to come by, leading to new condemnations of global discrimination against Latinos.

I arrive at my home and am relieved to see that the only cars parked on the street are owned by my neighbors. The weather is glorious, and I am almost ecstatic with the anticipation of not talking about Aimee or Jack Cedar or the airplane tragedy for a while. I change into leggings and a hoodie, grab a bottle of Albariño from the fridge, a plastic wine flute, and a towel, and head out the back door to the private path to the beach before anything can happen to disturb my tranquility.

My hopes are rewarded when I cross over the dunes onto the sand just in time to see an array of pink and gleaming silver wisps of cloud float in front of the lowering sun, now an orange globe still well above the horizon. I sit down on my towel and pour a glass of wine that I sip as I survey the scene before me. Two fishermen are a bit west of my spot, wearing dark, rubber waders as they stand in the surf and cast out. Farther west is a family with three young children tossing a colorful beach ball around on the sand, laughing. I count four couples of various ages strolling or sitting. I notice six ships spaced out on the horizon, one of which clearly bears the Shaw Global logo.

I enjoy the tranquility and the wine and think that perhaps I should just stay here on the sand until the weather gets too cold to remain in a month or so. After a while I see Harry in the distance, heading back toward his house from the west. I am surprised to see that a woman is on his arm. They are too far away for me to make out details, but they are leaning into each other and appear to be laughing. Then Harry points toward the horizon at his ship that seems to be suspended there and hands the woman the binoculars that always hang around his neck. They gesture back and forth to each other, talking, and then head toward the dunes at Harry's house, his arm wrapped around her shoulders and their hips lightly touching as they walk.

So much for my thought that Harry might have a romantic interest in me, I think with a chuckle. He has never mentioned a woman friend, and I am surprised by the obvious body language of a couple that is comfortable with each other, who know each other. This is not a new date, I think, but he has kept it close to the vest. Harry is a surprising man.

PART SIX
2021

Asia

CHAPTER 27

After an absence of almost a year and a half, Den Chin thought of the sweet air of Taiwan, and it kindled a tiny spark of joy in his heart. He had been captive on the mainland for more than sixteen months as the Covid-19 pandemic swept through China and then the world. The approval of travel to and from Taipei and several other Asian cities had just been granted by the committee. Until now, the party had directed that all medical and scientific resources be marshaled toward the singular goal of controlling the spread of the disease domestically. There had been no interest in suppressing the epidemic beyond China's borders, so Den Chin's Foreign Actions in Environmental Epidemiology became virtually dormant. His water project and other studies underway had been summarily curtailed, and all of his personnel were reassigned to their best use fighting the infectious disease on the mainland.

For the entire period, most domestic travel and all international travel, which included Taiwan, even though China technically considered the island to be its own province, was prohibited. The party's obsession with maintaining secrecy about the illness and its source had made it impossible even to speak to people in other locations, and Den Chin was convinced that he and other mainland professionals had been intentionally deprived of accurate information about the spread of the deadly virus throughout the world.

He had, of course, had access to domestic developments and was troubled by videos of people being forcibly carried from their homes, sometimes hysterically screaming and flailing as they were carted away by workers covered from head to toe in protective gear. The dispossessed were told that the actions were necessary to prevent transmission of the virus in crowded areas, and perhaps this was true, Den Chin thought. Clearly the affected people believed they were being permanently, callously separated from their families and communities for no good reason, which, he knew, might also be true.

Limitations on even the most mundane and basic activities imposed by officials in the interest of national secrecy closed in like a clamp on the mainland. The Chinese people were long accustomed to a lack of personal freedom and being subjected to the quixotic demands of the ever powerful party, and they adjusted as necessary. But Den Chin, used to relatively free communication throughout China and also with the outside world, and accustomed to traveling to Taiwan at least two or three times a year without restriction, and often to more distant places, began to feel that his life force was being strangled.

It was bad enough that his investigation into the Inner Mongolian mines, which he thought was likely to be the most important scientific study of his entire life, had become impossible to pursue, but the suspension of all scientific inquiry, including his global clean water initiative, which was needed now more than ever, was almost too much to bear.

For a long period he had managed reasonably well, fulfilling his need for intellectual challenge with reading and planning protocols to commence when the restrictions of the virus were lifted. But then Keiji had called.

The younger doctor had been offended by Den Chin's abrupt treatment of him when he reported his findings of an unknown illness in the specimens from Inner Mongolia, and he felt he had been dismissed in a disrespectful manner by the superior he had come to consider a friend. The two men still kept in touch, but their communications had been less frequent and now had a cool edge.

Den Chin knew he had wounded Keiji but still chose not to reveal that his abruptness arose from dangerous political implications surrounding the analysis. Keiji was unaware that the committee had unequivocally instructed Den Chin to discontinue his study, an order he had blatantly disregarded. He believed it would endanger Keiji to know more about the matter.

There were few people whom Den Chin considered with any degree of friendship, and Keiji was one of them. He missed the easy warmth that had grown between them but still remained silent, deeming it safer for the younger man.

"Don't you think the findings on the bat carcass might be related to the epidemic and should be disclosed?" Keiji said to Den Chin coolly. "It is possible that it is the very same pathogen involved, and if so, we may have knowledge of the source."

Den Chin was silent, considering how much to tell Keiji. "It's not the same agent," he lied. "I've seen the studies on Covid-19, and it is not possible to be the same viral agent."

"Then why not provide it to the researchers working on this?" Keiji said, sounding exasperated. "What can it hurt? And how can you be so certain that there is no connection?"

"Keiji," Den Chin said with warmth in his voice that had been long absent, as if he were speaking to a younger brother who could not accept a difficult truth. "You surely remember my instruction that you not disclose the study of the bats or discuss the matter with anyone. I ask that you trust that I have very good reasons for this, and I repeat that same instruction to you now." Keiji was silent. "There is to be no more said about it," Den Chin continued, now using an authoritarian tone to emphasize that this was a command from a superior, not the suggestion of a friend.

Keiji said nothing for a few moments. The silence hung heavily between them, and then he said, "I would never have thought you to be callous toward the suffering of people, to remain silent when you possibly could help them. It is a deep disappointment to me, Pao Den Chin," he said and hung up.

The exchange awakened a gnawing pain in Den Chin. He longed to tell Keiji that Keiji's own safety meant more to him than the slim possibility that disclosure of the bat analysis could in some unlikely way help to conquer the virus sweeping across the world.

Den Chin's mood darkened more each day. He was engulfed in despair that he had not felt since he had held Mai's arm, trying to give comfort in the way of a child as his father died before their eyes almost fifty years before. Now he longed for Taiwan, the lush, green countryside, the fine ink painting collection in the museum, but he was locked in Beijing.

Three weeks later Den Chin received a call from the senior medical doctor at the Central china research facility where Keiji was director. He related that three days earlier Keiji had failed to appear for work with no explanation. Keiji's wife said that he had left for the lab that morning as usual but never returned home. She had not heard from him or been able to obtain any information about his whereabouts. She and their two young children were heartbroken but held out hope for his return.

Numerous people at the lab, the senior doctor said, reported that in the days before Keiji's disappearance he told them he had personally performed tests on a bat carcass, which confirmed that it had died from an unknown viral agent. Keiji suspected it might be the Covid-19 pathogen but had no proof of a match and no longer had access to the specimen. He told his colleagues that the sample had been discarded and refused to give any information about how he had obtained it or where it came from and would not say if he had reported the results to anyone else or shared information about the analysis.

The senior medical doctor said he was aware of Keiji's relationship with Den Chin and was calling to see if he had any information that might help to locate Keiji or explain his absence.

Den Chin was stunned. He could not formulate a response, and after a long silence, the senior medical doctor said, "Dr. Den Chin? Are we still connected?"

Den Chin cleared his throat and said, "Yes, yes. I was thinking about when I last spoke with Dr. Takama." He said he had had no contact with Keiji for at least several weeks and had no information that might be helpful. He asked that the senior medical doctor let him know of any further developments and hung up.

Den Chin slumped at his desk. He rested his head in his hands and found it difficult to breathe. If only Keiji had followed his instructions, he thought. It was his fault that this young, dedicated doctor, a kind and serious man, was now surely dead, eliminated by the party because he posed a threat to their mission to maintain secrecy. If only he had explained to Keiji the reason he had asked that the information about the novel pathogen be kept between the two of them, they could have developed a plan together. They were likeminded.

Den Chin was overwhelmed with regret for his actions that had led to this fate for his friend. He advised his lab that he had taken a wrong step and twisted his ankle, and he would remain at home to rest it for three days. For the first time in his life, he remained in bed, barely eating, and planned what he would do.

CHAPTER 28
Beijing

When Den Chin returned to the lab, his colleagues were accustomed
to his cool, unemotional demeanor, and no one seemed to notice that
he had undergone a transformation that would irrevocably change
his life. He went about his work, still limited since most resources
continued to be allocated to the pandemic, with his usual quiet and
serious concentration and drew no attention.

A week later he requisitioned from the committee the report that
George Hong had recently filed, alerting them that an American
professor of earth and environmental science was to give the keynote
address at the upcoming GCAC international conference in Dublin.
The presentation was titled "Twentieth Century Disasters in Mining
Rare Earth Elements."

The lecture, Hong reported, would include the well-documented
history of extensive damage caused by REE mining itself as well as by
the refining process, and would focus on the disaster at Bukit Merah
in Malaysia. The talk would also explain China's success at cornering
the world market in REEs and that the mines in Inner Mongolia
had been expanded and were now the greatest REE producer in

the world, reportedly causing significant environmental and human devastation.

Den Chin had never met George Hong, but he was legendary in the foreign actions section. Supported and guided by the party, he had earned his doctoral degree in earth sciences at Harvard almost twenty years before and then accepted a teaching position at University of California at Berkeley, all the while clandestinely reporting back to his superiors in Beijing. He was a natural master at building relationships with the American professors and scientists engaged in research and maintained a steady stream of reports to the party providing details of projects underway at the great American research centers at Berkeley and Stanford. His summaries were detailed, always proved to be accurate and complete, and even included sufficient ancillary notes about personalities and locations to provide context. George had an uncanny ability to sense which research would be of particular interest to the party and could fluidly cultivate his unwitting sources.

In 2011, with diversity among teaching staffs a major source of status for universities, George had emphasized his Chinese ethnicity along with his Harvard education to snag a full professorship at Columbia University. Beijing was impressed and considered George's move to a prestigious East Coast university to demonstrate exceptional talent as well as commitment. He was extremely well regarded, and his reports were routinely made available to the party's senior science directors on the mainland, including Dr. Den Chin. They all knew the name George Hong.

Den Chin received Hong's full communiqué about REE mining in a secure email the next day, and he spent two evenings reading and digesting it. According to Hong, who said he had personally reviewed notes on the planned lecture, Professor Jack Cedar of New York University would commence his talk by reviewing the products fueling the exponentially increasing demand for REEs, most of which were manufactured in China. He would segue to the history of REE mining, focusing on Malaysia because of its substantial rare earth deposits and lax regulations. Cedar intended to review statistics for deadly illnesses found in villages surrounding the Bukit Merah mines and studies of water and soil, which confirmed the presence of radioactive material and other pollutants, including acid wash. He would state that the subsequent cleanup of the area took more than two decades and had not, in fact, reversed the environmental destruction. Indeed, recent but unconfirmed reports had emerged describing human illness as well as animal and plant destruction that were likely related to the shuttered Bukit mine.

Cedar would summarize the recent uproar about the Chinese Inner Mongolia facility that had been ignited by devastating reports by British journalists, as well as his belief that the benign conclusions reached by the WHO team sent in to investigate were unreliable, the product of political pressure by China.

Cedar would describe new mining and refining techniques that held promise to eliminate, or at least significantly reduce, the human and environmental destruction caused by methods of REE mining currently in use. There were ways to do it safely, he contended, but they would be costly and reduce efficiency. Since the primary producing mine is deep inside of China, he would say, there is little chance of effecting these changes.

George Hong quoted verbatim the conclusion Cedar had set forth in his lecture notes, which Hong had been able to copy:

> As long as the human and ecological destruction associated with REE mines is confined to the geographic area in which the mining is performed, currently a remote area of Inner Mongolia that has no impact on the western world, you may say why is this issue of dire importance? Well, what if that damage, which is poorly understood, spread beyond Inner Mongolia? What if the REEs themselves, or

pollutants released from the mines, somehow carried their devastating effects around the world? We all are aware of theories about cell phones causing cancer for example. Or consider whether mutations in animal life originating in the mines might spread a deadly effect far beyond China. Or what about contaminated water flowing to the sea, delivering that contamination to other continents? I leave you, fellow professionals, with these questions to ponder. There is no group with more collective knowledge of environmental problems borne in the earth than this esteemed body, and I challenge you to consider these questions.

CHAPTER 29
Beijing

Den Chin considered Professor Cedar's upcoming lecture for a few minutes. A course of action snapped into focus with stunning clarity. He pulled out his Taiwan cell phone, which had sat in his desk unused for many months, and placed a call to Hana Chang in Switzerland. She answered on the second ring.

"Dr. Chang," he said in a neutral tone, "this is Pao Den Chin from Beijing. You may not remember me, but I was your host at the WHO tour of the rare earth mining facilities in Inner Mongolia."

"Oh, Pao," she replied. "Of course I remember you. In particular, I have a special memory of the afternoon we spent together at Resonant Sand Bay. It was a special experience that I will not forget," she said with warmth that surprised and pleased Pao. "I notice that the phone from which you are calling is listed in Taiwan, where I believe you told me you have special ties. Is that where you are now?"

"No," he said. "But I am planning to travel to Taipei next week and would like to propose that you meet me there, as I have a matter of some importance I would like to discuss with you." Hana made no reply, and the moments ticked on in silence. Den Chin began to grow embarrassed, feeling that his idea had been foolish and that he was ignorant in the ways of the world outside of China. He could think of nothing further to say to ease his discomfort.

Finally Hana said, "Pao, that's quite a serious request, having had no communication with each other for quite some time. Is it more than a year? Are things all right with you?"

"Oh yes, oh yes," he said, relieved that her hesitation had not translated to an immediate refusal of his request. "Please forgive my lack of social courtesies, Dr. Chang. The party does not favor conversation for the sake of amiability, and it is only when I am in Taiwan that I have had experience with the manners of the West. Because of the pandemic I have not been able to leave the mainland since I last saw you, and I am afraid my Western graces have been unused. Yes, I am healthy and have not had personal experience with the virus. And please allow me to inquire about your personal health and your family?"

"Yes, Pao, I am healthy, and my family is as well, thank goodness. Although I must say that the atmosphere here in Geneva has been difficult, as it has been all over the West. Just about all resources of the WHO have been directed to issues related to the virus—getting the vaccines to third-world countries and impoverished communities, reducing contagion, education about personal hygiene and distancing, distributing masks, et cetera. Of course, it is the most important issue of the day, but infectious disease is not really my area, and it has been very disheartening to be forced to abandon my projects in other areas of study that were underway."

Den Chin immediately warmed to her easy conversation as he had when they spent time together in Inner Mongolia. "I have had the same experience," he said. "I had a clean water initiative in progress that I have been most sorry to cease working on." He knew that the conversation was now on a better footing.

"So, what is the nature of your request that I meet you in Taiwan? As you must be aware, travel is returning but still quite difficult, and

Taipei is about a fifteen-hour flight from Geneva. Is it connected with the WHO in some way?"

Den Chin chose his words with great care. Although he was on his private Taiwanese phone, he still considered that his conversations might not be secure.

"Dr. Chang," he said, maintaining a formal veneer, "there is no connection to the WHO. However, in the course of our professional meeting in central China, you and I engaged in several stimulating scientific discussions on unrelated medical topics that we planned to investigate." He paused and then said, "I feel that the public health may be served by two esteemed professionals, if I may be forgiven for including myself in that category, exchanging knowledge on matters of regulation of the well-being of urban populations, such as we touched upon previously."

They had never said anything whatsoever relating to urban populations, and he could only hope that Hana realized that he was trying to communicate to her that he could not provide her with details of his true intent over the phone. He waited silently.

After a long pause, in a formal tone, she said, "Yes, Dr. Den Chin," letting him know by her reversion to his formal appellation that she understood his meaning. "I recall our conversations. I certainly can see your point and the advantage to us meeting. When exactly do you have in mind?"

They spoke for another five minutes primarily about medical topics related to the coronavirus and then agreed on a date eleven days hence to meet in Taipei. Den Chin summoned his assistant and instructed her to book a flight for him to Taiwan in eight days, to return eight days after that. He requested that she reserve his usual suite at the Taipei Marriott.

Then he sat back at his desk, tented his fingers in front of his face, and smiled for the first time in months.

地行不識名和尚
姓大以口遊高陽一
酒店一毛彷彿葛仙宴
罷淋漓襟袖尚糊塗

CHAPTER 30
Taipei, Taiwan

Den Chin steered Hana through the gallery of the National Palace Museum of Taipei until they stood before *Immortal in Splashed Ink.* They gazed at the framed paper scroll, which Den Chin told Hana depicted a mighty, ancient deity. It exuded power although it was rendered mainly in splashes of ink.

Den Chin gestured at the painting and explained, "For centuries, Chinese artists used only fine ink lines drawn on parchment, but this painting illustrates what was a new style in the seventh century, in which the artist could 'splash' ink onto the medium to create an impression of his meaning rather than draw actual details."

"It's quite lovely and mysterious," Hana said. "I'm afraid that my education in art, especially Asian art, is regrettably limited, but this figure, this deity, exudes a sense of purpose, of moving forward with strength and commitment. And he looks unstoppable, as though he cannot be deterred."

"Yes, exactly." Den Chin nodded. "It was one of my father's favorites of the entire collection." He told her that the painting was an example of the Chan school of Buddhism, which said that all people have Buddha in their nature and that personal enlightenment will arrive suddenly, at any random moment, and not as the result of a meditation.

"In other words," he said, "one's absolute spirit or central core, the Chan school says, will suddenly engulf you, and you will know the way."

"I think that's a wonderful sentiment, and I shall be hoping for it to descend on me at an unexpected moment to light the path forward," she said smiling, lighthearted but serious at the same time.

"Dr. Chang," Den Chin said, turning to face her. "I would like to explain to you why I felt it was important to ask you to travel halfway around the world to meet with me. Shall we find a table in the café and have some refreshment while we talk?"

They had met an hour earlier in the lobby of the museum, and Den Chin had guided Hana through the galleries, pointing out both his and his father's favorite pieces. The collection of more than 700,000 items representing 8,000 years of Chinese fine art was far too vast to be on display simultaneously, so the galleries were changed several times each year, and Den Chin could find treasures he had never before seen every time he was in Taiwan.

They found a table in the museum café, which had a peaceful tearoom atmosphere and was mostly empty at this midafternoon hour.

"When my father arrived in Taiwan in 1949, he suffered unspeakable mistreatment by the nationalists. In China he had been a museum curator, and he helped to smuggle the very art treasures in this museum from the mainland across the China Sea when the Communists overran the Forbidden City. As a child, I became convinced that my father had chosen the wrong side in the civil war and that the Communists had a better ethic and would have respected him more than the nationalists did."

The waitress brought their tea and a platter of small cakes that Den Chin had ordered and carefully placed the items around the table in a pleasing layout.

"That is why I joined the Communist party as a young person," he continued after the server moved away, "out of my belief that the Communist party was on the right side and would faithfully take care of the needs of its members. And that did seem to me to be true for quite some time. The party put me through school, the best medical education, placed me in the most advanced research facilities, and did take care of me." He prepared his tea and took a sip. "I have had a fulfilling life, able to complete meaningful research and projects that are important to humanity. I have lived in comfort and been treated with respect and dignity."

"And has there been some change, Pao?" Hana asked. "It was apparent when you called me to arrange to meet that you did not feel at liberty to speak freely."

"Yes," he said. "There has been a change, and I myself have changed. I have come to realize, finally now in my sixties, that in fact there is not a right side. There never was one, not when my father thought he had chosen the right side with loyalty to the nationalists and not when I thought I had done so by joining the Communists."

He paused and after a few moments said, "Hana, I have learned there is only a right time for a certain idea, which eventually yields to the right time for a different idea."

He chose a small tea cake from the platter and took a bite. "They have wonderful sweets here," he said. To his own surprise, verbalizing his decision to repudiate the beliefs and loyalties of a lifetime was not causing him doubt or distress. He felt calm and at peace with the course of action he was executing.

Hana chose a cake for herself. "I believe it is most admirable to have personal growth at all stages of life," she said. She had come to like this serious and introspective man and looked at him with warmth. "This new insight you describe sounds like the meaning you attributed to *Immortal in Splashed Ink*," she said, smiling.

"Yes," Pao replied, mirroring her smile. "I think that figure could be me, striding forward without clearly defined features. But just a man, hardly a deity."

They enjoyed their tea in comfortable silence for a few minutes, and then he said, "I would like to tell you my plan and my request."

She nodded and said, "Yes, please go on."

He told her that in the course of his work he had unexpectedly come upon critical scientific evidence of a previously unknown pathogen that may or may not be related to the origins and spread of the coronavirus pandemic. In either case, he told her, it was an important discovery that required full scientific evaluation. For a variety of reasons, he said, he was unable to draw upon the resources of the party to continue the research.

"It is not feasible, or even safe, for me to work on my own," he said. "I therefore have concluded that I may serve humanity by providing my information to scientists in the West who will have limitless resources to move the research forward."

Hana stared at him, processing the magnitude of the confidence he had just casually imparted to her. "May I know what is the nature of this scientific evidence? And in what way is it connected to me? You told me that your request has nothing to do with my role with the WHO."

"That is correct," he said. He told her that he now asked for her assistance because when they became acquainted in Inner Mongolia he had sensed that she would share his goal of providing the world with information that might help unravel and conquer threats to the environment and public health.

"And also that you are a trustworthy and competent person," he said, staring at her, serious and intent. "Hana," he said, switching to her first name, "if you have hesitation about being involved with this matter, please tell me that right now, and we shall not speak of it again. I already have lost a good man, a young and dedicated doctor who failed to heed my warning about using utmost discretion in this matter."

"What do you mean 'lost'?"

"He has vanished without a trace. That is not uncommon with the 'right' side I chose, you know. It was this man's disappearance that confirmed for me the need to take action." He took a sip from the delicate porcelain cup and studied her. "Please think very carefully if you wish to join me in this effort, which could result in personal danger to you."

Hana did not hesitate. "Yes, Pao. I have no doubt that you are a brilliant scientist and a serious and principled man. I would like to help with your plan. If there is even a chance that your information will help to conquer the virus, it must be taken."

Den Chin did not smile, but his shoulders relaxed; he breathed deeply, and the sharp angles of his face softened. "Then please meet me at my hotel, the Taipei Marriott, tomorrow morning at ten o'clock. I will reserve a private room in the business center where we can speak in confidence so I can tell you the details of my intentions. I also will give you a letter that is to be delivered to a person in the United States." They agreed on the plan and said a cordial goodbye in the tearoom, going separately to their respective hotels.

PART SEVEN
2021
Long Island, New York

CHAPTER 31

When I return to the house, I consider the deteriorating state of affairs. Switzerland, I think. In the time since I last saw her, Aimee Cedar has been to Geneva and is leaving for someplace else, and I still don't have the faintest idea what her connection is to me or to Jack Cedar. Maybe that is not really a sign of deterioration, I reconsider; maybe it's actually a sign of improvement. Whatever she originally wanted, she's now gone, in another country, across the ocean and on the move. Perhaps I will never know what brought her into my life, but she has made her exit and good riddance.

I text Jack her picture and let him know it was taken at the Geneva airport's departures terminal. In about two minutes, he writes back that she looks no more familiar to him than she did in the prior photo and asks if I know what she was doing in Switzerland, which I don't. We exchange non-information for a few minutes and then I remind him that I need to appear in court about the restraining order on his safe deposit box tomorrow morning at nine thirty. I tell him he should be there and ready to state that he has never been married and so on. We will meet outside the courtroom at 9:00 a.m.

Amazingly the evening is peaceful and relaxing. No phone calls, no late night knocks on the door, just insipid TV shows and a dish of peanut butter chocolate ice cream. I go to bed about eleven o'clock and have a great night's sleep.

I am surprised at the warm pleasure I feel when I see Jack step off the elevator in the courthouse and come striding down the hall directly toward me. He still has a large bandage running across his cheek, but the swelling and discoloration have largely subsided, and his good looks are restored. The bandage even adds a somewhat rakish air, I think as I watch him approach.

"Hey, Aruba," he says with relatively good cheer, all things considered. "So, what's the routine here? What do I need to do?"

"As you know, the restraining order was obtained without you having had an opportunity to tell your side to the judge. Because you were not able to state your own case, the restraining order is good only for a few days, and today the judge hears what you have to say about it and decides if the order should continue." Jack just stares at me but says nothing, so I continue. "So you should explain why you think the order should be lifted." He still says nothing.

Finally I ask, "Any questions?"

"Well, just one, I guess. Aren't you going to tell the judge that the order should be removed, or however you say it? I don't have to convince anyone of anything," he says, and his face starts to flush with anger as he thinks about the injustice done to him, which, of course, happens to include the fact that he has not vanished along with the plane he was supposed to have been on. But of course the circumstances of that remain obscure.

I am thinking about what to reply, or whether to reply at all, when the court officer steps into the hall and calls out, "Cedar versus Cedar." I wave my arm to let him know we are here and head toward the courtroom, Jack trailing behind me.

I stand at the plaintiff's table and direct Jack to the defendant's side, and we remain standing as Judge John Simon takes the bench.

The court reporter is seated and types into the court record the full name of the case. I state my name and that I am appearing for the plaintiff, Aimee Cedar. After being prompted to do so, Jack states his own name and that he is appearing in court without an attorney.

"Your Honor," I begin, "I was retained by my client about three weeks ago for the purpose of restraining her husband from removing their two minor children from the jurisdiction without her consent. Mrs. Cedar convinced me that she had valid reasons to fear for the safety of the children, and I succeeded in obtaining the temporary restraining order on which we appear today. It was served on Jack Cedar last Friday, and a restraint also was served on his bank to prevent him from gaining access to his safe deposit box in which his wife stated their children's passports were kept."

The judge, an impatient type, cuts me off abruptly and turns his attention to Jack.

"Mr. Cedar," he says, "have you retained legal counsel in this matter?"

"No, I have not," Jack begins in his professorial tone, clearly gearing up to present a full lecture, but the judge cuts him off also with an annoyed wave of his arm.

"Mr. Cedar, these are serious matters that your wife has brought before this court, and they involve not only you but the welfare of your children. I will put this matter over for two days to enable you to retain an attorney to represent you in this case." He turns to his clerk seated next to the judge's bench, and says, "Put this on for the day after tomorrow."

Jack, an impatient type himself, does not remain quiet.

He says loudly, annoyed, "Judge, this has to be removed now! There's more to this, or maybe I should say less to this, than you are aware."

Judge Simon turns around and stares hard at Jack.

"Mr. Cedar," he says, drawing out the 'mister' to drive home his annoyance. "I see from the motion papers that you are a professor at NYU, a fairly prestigious professor, it appears, and I surmise that you are accustomed to holding the stage. However, in this room, I hold the stage. *Only I* hold the stage, and you do not interrupt me." He pauses for effect and then says, "Is that crystal clear, Mr. Cedar?"

"Yes, perfectly," says Jack, not in the least hesitant or subdued. I just watch. Jack actually speaks louder than before. "But I really thought you would be interested in knowing that I have never been married, let alone had children, and I have absolutely no idea who this woman claiming to be my wife might be. Therefore, the restraining order should be removed, taken away, or whatever the terminology is, today. Not in two days, but today."

This statement definitely does capture the judge's interest. He stares at Jack for a few moments and then turns his attention to me, and unlike Jack, I am hesitant and subdued.

Judge Simon puts his elbows on the bench in front of him and leans forward, glaring at me. "Ms. Jones, I wonder if you might like to comment on that little bit of news."

"Yes, Your Honor," I begin gamely, "that's exactly what I would like to do, was planning to do as soon as I was recognized to continue speaking. I met with Mrs. Cedar at my office twice, once to take her information and be retained and once for her to sign the moving papers. She provided contact information in the form of a local address and cell phone number, which my staff used to successfully contact her. However, since the order to show cause was served on Mr. Cedar and I became aware of his claim of mistaken identity, I have been unable to locate my client."

The judge starts to speak over me. "What do you mean, unable to locate your client? Has she left the jurisdiction without advising you of her whereabouts? That would be a serious, in fact, a very serious infraction since she has convinced this court to bar her husband from doing exactly that," he says in a loud voice. His snarky manner is starting to blossom into all-out anger. I know I am about to add

Nassau County Supreme Court to the list of entities that are taking shots at me since I met Aimee Cedar.

"No, that actually is not what I mean," I say, trying to sound respectful. "The phone number Mrs. Cedar provided is no longer in service, and the address I have on file apparently is occupied by someone else entirely, who knows nothing about the Cedar family, has never heard of them."

Judge Simon appears to be speechless. Finally he says, "Well, what do you think is the situation here, Ms. Jones?"

"I don't know what to think, Your Honor, except that there has been an irretrievable breakdown in my relationship with my client, and I would like to make a formal motion to be relieved as her counsel." The judge actually snickers out loud at that, and he and I go back and forth debating the multitude of problems with this, starting with the reality that there is no way to know whether Mrs. Cedar disappeared because she has come to some harm and moving on to if there are actually any little Cedar children to worry about. Jack watches the colloquy in silence.

"The major problem I see is that this Mrs. Cedar provided you with correct details about this man's address, occupation, and even a photo of him. So we rule out mistaken identity," the judge says.

As he is speaking, out of the corner of my eye, I notice a very tall man leaning over the law clerk's desk at the front of the courtroom, deep in conversation. Even from the back, I instantly know who it is, and my heart begins to pound. I am sure my face is turning red as I realize that Drost is about to tell the court that I am somehow involved in the disappearance of the plane to Ireland last week. I am well known in the matrimonial court and pretty well respected by the judges and court personnel, not to mention the other lawyers of the family law bar. This is devastating to me, very different from being harassed by the FBI, with which there is no real connection to my actual life.

Jack follows my gaze and recognizes Drost as well. We exchange a look that is not lost on the judge, who now is staring frankly at the tableau in front of him. In a moment, his law clerk approaches the bench, extending a business card as he speaks quietly to the judge.

"I want everyone in my chambers, including Mr. Drost over there. We will be on the record, so I need you, Susan, as well," Simon says to the court reporter, who nods. "Ten minutes, all of you," he snaps as he rises and strides out the rear door of the courtroom, giving no hint of what is going on to the lawyers and clients milling about the courtroom waiting for their own cases to be called. To a person, they have been watching the action unfold with rapt attention.

When we assemble in the judge's large conference room, the court reporter enters the full name and role of each person on the record and then nods to the judge. The first thing he does is ask Jack if he wants time to retain an attorney to appear with him. If so, he says, he will adjourn until two o'clock. I try to signal Jack that he should accept this proposal, but he is having none of it.

"Absolutely not, judge," he says. "I have done nothing wrong, I have no idea who this woman, Aimee Cedar, is, and I do not wish to inflate this bizarre situation any further. I simply want to document that I have nothing whatsoever to do with any of this and be released, or whatever it is, from this lawsuit."

Next, Judge Simon questions Drost about what the FBI has to do with a matrimonial case. Drost does an impressive job of making Jack and me sound like Bonnie and Clyde, implying that we cooked up this elaborate plan that has some obscure connection to the recent airplane mystery. He does, at least, admit that the investigation is in an early stage and that at this point there is no proof in support of the scenario. But then he lobs his grenade.

"My agency has held off formally curtailing the movements of Mr. Cedar and Ms. Jones because of the pendency of the restraining order issued by this court. We hoped it would provide us about two weeks to investigate and decide if we have enough evidence to take this further. If your restraint is lifted now, judge, I am instructed to immediately commence a proceeding in federal court seeking to restrict Professor Cedar and possibly Ms. Jones from leaving the jurisdiction."

Jack visibly begins to swell with anger, almost catapulting out of his seat. I take one look at him and decide I had better take over the negotiation before he demonstrates to the FBI and the judge that he is, indeed, a dangerous character. I realize we cannot win this one, so I will accept the next best thing rather than risk getting stuck with the worst option.

"Since Agent Drost has indicated his office needs two weeks to investigate all aspects of the airplane event," I say, "it seems like a sensible solution to simply leave this court's order in place for that period rather than commence a whole new proceeding in federal court. I am confident that the authorities will confirm I have no involvement with anything they are investigating and will have no further interest." I am tempted to say the same about Jack but realize that since I only met him six days ago and he is the adversary of my missing client, my confidence in him has no solid foundation and might actually cast more suspicion on both of us. I look over at Jack, silently willing him to say something similar.

He somehow gets my message and, suppressing the fury that is quite obvious to me, he agrees to leave Judge Simon's order in place and expresses certainty that the FBI will put an end to its interest in him before the end of the two weeks.

We hash out the details of a new order, which we then dictate to the court reporter. It continues the existing restraint and also affirms that both Jack and I agree not to leave the New York metropolitan area pending the new return date of the matter seven days from today, at which time extending the order for an additional week will be considered. I state on the record that I will aggressively try to locate my missing client and will report to the court immediately if I make any progress. As a consideration to my and Jack's reputations, the involvement of the FBI is never mentioned and is kept out of the record.

The judge "so orders" what we have dictated, giving it the full force of a court order set forth in writing in the more traditional way, and instructs his clerk to see that Jack and I are each provided a copy. He also has one given to Drost who then says a pleasant goodbye to all of us as if we have just attended a friendly social gathering.

CHAPTER 32

When Drost disappears into the elevator, Jack and I look at each other, and neither of us can muster up the energy to say anything. Finally, Jack murmurs, "Let's go," and I follow him down to the lobby.

"Let's take your car. I'll leave mine here in case our pal Drost is watching it," he says. I still don't say anything, but I lead him to my car, which is at the back of the building where there is an area reserved for attorneys. As I pull out of the lot, we both watch to see if we notice anyone following us. We see nothing.

It's only four o'clock, so rush hour traffic has not yet started to clog the parkway, and we are able to head to Point Lookout with a clear view in the rearview mirror that convinces us no one is coming after us. I hold it together, somehow managing to hide the fact that I am teetering on the brink. But the brink of what, I wonder.

We go inside, and I slip into my favorite chair in the living room, my briefcase and purse heaped on my lap, feeling worn out and drained beyond description. Jack also looks grim and white-faced, but he remains standing near me. He leans over and without asking takes everything off my lap and puts it on the end table.

"I'll get you a drink," he says. "Bourbon?" he asks, and I nod. He seems to have noticed that I am not firing on all cylinders.

When he returns and hands me my drink, tears are slipping down my cheeks, and I don't even care. I mutter, "Thanks," and take a sip but then can't help blurting out, "This is entirely different. This nightmare now involves my workplace, my profession." I can barely contain a sob. "This can destroy my career, my reputation with the court, with the attorneys with whom I work, my entire life." I take another sip and look at him. "I don't even know you. I have no idea who you really are, and you just show up and ruin my life! I saved your life somehow, and you are ruining mine!"

He looks stricken and sits on the sofa opposite me, his own highball glass in hand. "Aruba, Ruby, I am so sorry, so very sorry," he says. "Believe me, I am as mystified as you are. I have no idea, no idea at all what this is about and why it involves me, let alone you." He finds a box of tissues and hands it to me.

"I don't know what we should do, but I think we both need lawyers who specialize in this type of thing," he says.

"This type of thing?" I say, his statement jarring me to life. "What *is* this type of thing? I wouldn't even know how to describe it. I am a matrimonial attorney, and suddenly I'm suspected of being a spy for China, perpetrating some kind of fraud that led to the disappearance of a passenger plane? Who the fuck are you, Jack? What have you brought me into?" I wonder if I am, in fact, sharing my living room with a spy.

Before he can answer, the doorbell rings, and we exchange a look confirming that we both know it will be trouble. I don't move, so he gets up and strides to the front door where he finds Drost.

"What do you want?" Jack snaps at him. "We've had about enough of this, so you can just get out of here and leave us alone." He starts to close the door in the FBI agent's face, but Drost's foot snaps inside and the door bounces open.

Drost sneers at him. "You two are looking pretty cozy here. That was crafty, leaving your car at the court, Mr. Cedar, and sneaking off together. And you two claim you just met the end of last week?" he says, snickering. "You should have perfected your act a little better." I think Jack may actually punch him in the face, but then he abruptly pulls back and walks into the living room, leaving the front door ajar with Drost standing there.

Like he is an invited guest, Drost saunters in, closes the door behind him, and follows Jack to the living room. "So, Ms. Jones, care to explain to me why you snuck this man away from the courthouse and are entertaining him in your home like you're old friends of about five days? Not to mention that he happens to be your adversary in a so-called lawsuit?"

"I did not sneak him away, and I am not 'entertaining him like old friends,' Agent Drost. In fact, Professor Cedar and I have been through an intense experience as you are very well aware. I am exhausted from it mentally and physically, and we are conferring in an effort to figure out what is happening here." I try really hard to muster up my usual bravado but am unable even to achieve a confident manner. My voice cracks, I cannot hold back tears, and I look away in embarrassment.

Jack tries to intercede and says calmly, "Look, Agent Drost, Ms. Jones and I are completely shocked by this entire series of events. We have no idea what has tied us together in this. . . scenario. . . and neither of us has any idea what is even going on."

Drost ignores Jack as if he is not present, makes a beeline for my chair, and leans over me with a hard expression. He turns on the steel-edged voice I have heard from him before and says, "Then it's time to ante up, Jones. You're already implicated in a terrorist act resulting in the disappearance of a commercial jetliner, and if you want things to go a little easier for you, now is the time to cooperate and tell us what you know." He senses that my reserve of strength is exhausted, and he has moved in for the kill.

Can this really be happening to me? "I know nothing about any of this," I manage to croak out, barely louder than a whisper, crying. My hand flies to my face, and I cover my mouth as I try to stifle a sob. I know I am pitiful, reduced from a confident professional to a sniveling weakling.

I see Jack spring forward from his position behind Drost, and before I know it he has wedged himself between the agent and me, his legs spread slightly, holding up both hands, palms making a firm "stop" motion. Instead of weakening him, Drost's bullying has invigorated him. He radiates vitality and stands his ground, implacable.

"That's it, Drost," he says in a deep and resonant voice that I think he must use to make his students listen up. "You are finished here. In fact, Ms. Jones is finished with this. I am not a lawyer, but as far as I can see, you have nothing at all to connect her to the plane mystery, to George Hong, or to any of these events other than some fictional theory. Unless you have a warrant or some other official document, you have no right to be here or to harass her anymore. You got what you wanted by continuing the restraining order, so just get out of here and leave us alone." He takes a breath, and Drost just stares at him. Jack doesn't move; he stays planted firmly between me and Drost.

"That's it, time to go," Jack says. "And I'd better not see a surveillance car on this street either, or I'm going to call in the legal department of NYU to assist me. And let me tell you, Drost, I can promise you that the high-powered legal representation of a very liberal university in a very liberal city like New York is likely to cause a heap of trouble over unauthorized FBI surveillance. I'd call it harassment actually, don't you think?" I watch in shock as Jack actually puts his arm around Drost's shoulder and steers him to the front door, which he opens.

Drost clearly is not even a little intimidated, but he is thinking about the repercussions of what Jack has said. "That will be fine, professor," he says calmly, not even sounding offended. "We'll take it to the federal judge and get authorization for full searches and whatever else we need." He turns on his heel and leaves.

Jack does not pause before slamming the door shut and returning to where I am sitting, observing this whole scene unfold as if it is a movie and I am an unwilling star. "These guys are just too fucking big for their britches," Jack says in the same deep and serious voice, and despite my distraught condition, I have a sudden picture of the Cedar family farm, the corn as high as an elephant's eye, and jack intimidating the tax collector or whoever it is that causes trouble for farmers. I wonder who exactly does cause trouble for farmers but have no clue.

"We need something to eat," Jack says, looking at his watch as if this is any ordinary Thursday and nothing unusual is going on. "Let's go to that place you like down the road. What is it called, the Watch or something?" He takes my elbow and helps me out of my chair. "Do you need anything before we go?" he says, and I tell him I will just be a minute as I head for the bathroom and make a valiant effort to look alluring.

It's still on the early side, so when we get to The Pocket Watch, we are able to get a table on the deck at the water's edge. The sun is lowering in the sky, creating a yellow-and-mauve haze along the horizon, and a half dozen ducks glide peacefully just below us. Without asking my preference, Jack orders drinks and an appetizer of mozzarella sticks and popcorn shrimp.

"This is a great spot," he says as we wait for the food to be delivered. "It's landlocked where I grew up, and I still find being on the edge of the Atlantic Ocean, which can carry you across the world, to be immensely exciting."

"Where did you grow up actually?" I ask, wondering if maybe it was a farm on the outskirts of Beijing.

"Nebraska, the Cornhusker State," he says. "About a hundred miles northwest of Lincoln in the middle of farm country, farm country as far as you can see in every direction. Or as you put it, in the middle of nowhere, nowhere as far as you can see." He laughs. "Not that it doesn't have its charms. The night sky on an August evening, the corn stalks rustling in a breeze that has just a knife edge of cold autumn air riding in, there's nothing like it."

"So did you leave because of the 'nowhere' part?" I ask, believing him, taken by his poetic description and more interested than I had expected to be.

"Well, in part," he says. "But farming is a tough life. You're always fighting things that are way beyond your control. You spend your time trying to outwit nature: too much rain or too little rain, too cold, too hot, a tornado. The list is endless." The server brings our drinks and spreads the food on the table between us. Jack tells him we will order our main courses later, again without asking me.

"Our soil was deficient in phosphorus, a problem with our corn crop every year, weakening the plants and reducing the yield. One summer when I took high school chemistry, I invented a way to distribute phosphorus to the plants in a liquid solution cheaper and faster than anything else we had tried. My father and my grandfather were really impressed and used my system on the entire corn acreage. A week after we applied it, we had torrential rain for three days. It diluted the solution, washed a lot of it away, but we were afraid to apply more because too much can kill the plants. We ended up with the worst crop we had had in a decade. They never blamed me, but I was devastated," he says. "I decided I liked the chemistry part of it much better than the farming part."

He lifts his drink toward me and flashing that amazing smile says, "To us! We will never know anyone who met the way we did, Ruby." We clink our glasses, and I am surprised to realize that I am smiling as well. Maybe the farming background has given him experience dealing with unexpected disasters like our present situation, I think, unless it is just good spy craft.

"That's for sure," I agree. "I guess we should eat, drink, and be merry for tomorrow the FBI gets us."

"They're not going to get us, Ruby. We didn't do anything wrong, so something will happen to prove that. That crop disaster because of my invention, for example? That same year our potato harvest was the strongest on record, so overall the season worked out fine."

"Are your parents still in Nebraska?"

"Yep, still going strong. They're not too happy that I chose to live in the wicked city teaching chemistry and environmental science to people who will never use it to grow food or enhance the land. My father thinks real chemistry is only about soil, nothing else. 'No one knows dirt like farmers!' he says at least once a month." Jack is laughing in a charming way, not insulting his parents but actually sounding affectionate toward them.

"I've already told you what you need to know about my family," I say, the margarita softening my worries. "In case you forgot, I am actually named after a vacation. Who does that to their kid?"

"Actually, I did some research on that very point," Jack says, looking serious. "In fact, there are a total of six people in the US named Aruba, which means that one in every 46.24 million Americans have parents just like yours."

I start to laugh and say, "You're making that up. . ."

"No, I'm not," he says, unable to contain his own laughter. "That is directly from the last US census. We professors know how to conduct research, if you please."

We chat easily until we finish our appetizers, and then I signal for the waiter. "My turn," I say to Jack, turn to the server, and order another round of drinks, a platter of crab cakes and one of grilled lobster tails, plus corn on the cob. "The corn is in honor of your cornhusker background."

"OK," he says. "I can tell you the exact phosphorus content of the corn after two bites," he says.

I immediately ask, "Why not one? Obviously you're an amateur." We both laugh, and Drost and the whole question of Chinese spies may be important to the *Wall Street Journal* but not to us.

By the time we finish the meal, we actually have become old friends and have pushed the whole horrible disaster out of our minds.

It is now dark outside, but the moon creates some great sparkles on the water, and we hear intermittent laughter from a group of cheerful people at the bar. We are both feeling mellow and happy as if this was a normal date.

Jack pays the bill and then comes around to my chair and pulls it back for me. He leans down and with his index finger sweeps my hair away from my ear. He traces the back of my neck. and leaning very close he whispers, "Let's go back to the house, Ruby."

I feel a warm shiver sweep down my spine, and I suddenly know for sure that Jack will never tell me that he has fallen in love with a man he met on the train or anywhere else. "Yes, let's," I whisper.

And we do.

PART EIGHT

2021

Taiwan

CHAPTER 33
Taipei, Taiwan

They met at the hotel business center the next day, and Den Chin told Hana about Jack Cedar's upcoming lecture in Dublin, which had been reported to the committee by one of their spies embedded in a US university. Hana listened intently, seated across from him at the polished mahogany table in the private conference room he had reserved.

Cedar's talk, Den Chin said, would cast negative light on rare earth mining, a subject that the party wanted to suppress. It had huge economic implications to China, and, even more important, Den Chin had discovered, really by serendipity, that REE mining might also have some connection to a new pathogen, possibly even the pandemic. As far as Den Chin could determine, the professor was completely unaware that he would be speaking on a subject of unusual interest to China.

"Professor Jack Cedar is in grave peril right now, as we speak," Den Chin told Hana. "His life is in danger even if he remains in the United States, where the party is most reluctant to use violence against individuals. If he leaves the US, his life will surely be over. He likely will vanish, as my friend Keiji did."

"But why?" Hana asked. "You said Jack Cedar has done nothing and knows nothing about your research at all or even who you are."

"That is correct, Hana, but you fail to understand my country. Deflecting attention from the rare earth mines in Inner Mongolia is of utmost importance for numerous reasons you cannot possibly understand, and Professor Cedar's intention to focus the interest of the world's scientific community on that very subject will not be permitted to happen," he said but could see that she found his statement unconvincing.

"Take note of the WHO, for example," he went on, switching to a topic with which she had more personal familiarity. "You yourself were skeptical of things you noticed in Inner Mongolia. In actuality, the tour provided to your delegation was a meticulously orchestrated showpiece arranged by the party with leadership of the WHO. From the first, it was carefully planned to display only healthy workers and clean conditions, all the while concealing the devastating pollution and human rights violations at the site. I easily noticed that you were unconvinced by the tour and that you guessed that the true conditions were being hidden from your team."

"Yes, that's certainly so," she said. "But reaching around the world to suppress dialogue about a scientific issue, even one that has great financial or environmental implications, seems to me to be farfetched. And you are suggesting that your government would even resort to violence to silence the discussion. I don't know, Pao."

"If anything, I have understated the degree of danger to Jack Cedar. Even though you find this difficult to accept, I ask that you consider my warning with utmost importance and devise a means to ensure his safety. I am not sufficiently familiar with how matters of personal protection are addressed in the West, and I cannot possibly evaluate how to handle it. So you must."

"All right," she said. "I will think about that. Can you tell me more about the research findings you are trying to protect?"

"I will not inform you of the specific nature of the information I am transmitting except, as I told you yesterday, that I have accidentally uncovered scientific evidence that may well be related to the origin and nature of a previously unknown human illness, maybe even the pandemic. The research can only be completed and interpreted in the West. I deeply regret that even telling you this creates some degree of personal danger to you, but, to reduce this, the less information you know, the safer you will be. I will tell you my plan and instructions that I have devised, and then you can tell me if you are able to help. Is that an acceptable procedure?"

"Before you do that, I have one more question. Why not just take your evidence to the United States mission in Taipei and deliver it to the West that way? It would avoid risk to me and to Professor Cedar."

"I already have given that idea careful consideration, Hana, and rejected such a plan. The most important reason is that I have learned that governments, even Western ones, cannot be trusted to use information like this to benefit humanity. The acquisition of power and financial gain intrudes on judgment, and the pure scientific importance of even essential advances is often subjugated to political considerations. I believe that in history this has happened innumerable times, and I cannot risk this evidence being intentionally misused or even destroyed," Den Chin said, recalling the Malaysian plane disaster that continued to haunt him.

He told Hana that he also had a personal reason. "If I were to transmit the material through official channels, my government would know immediately of my act of treason, and I would have no chance of escaping the wrath of the committee," he said.

Hana sat thinking for a few moments. She took a sip of the tea that had been set out before her and then said, "Yes, Pao, I will help you in any way I can. Please tell me your ideas."

They sat together for the next hour as Den Chin provided Hana with the details of his plan. He asked her to hand-carry to New York and somehow personally deliver a letter he had written to Professor

Cedar that explained the overview of the situation. Den Chin placed a white envelope bulging with papers on the table in front of Hana, showing her that it was addressed to Jack Cedar in his own neat handwriting. He turned it over, revealing that he had closed it with a solid bead of gray sealing wax. This would protect her, he explained, since in the event of a problem she could honestly say that she had no idea what the envelope contained, only that a physician she had met in China had asked her to deliver it when she went to New York.

Den Chin then slid two packages across the table, each wrapped in plain brown paper and addressed to Jack Cedar. One was about the size of a shoebox and the other somewhat larger and flatter. He told Hana that the most problematic part of his plan was deciding how to transport these packages to New York. He certainly could not send them by a normal carrier like FedEx, which would subject them to possible loss or seizure and also provide a trail right back to him. He did not think that Hana could bring them with her on a plane to the United States either. They would likely be searched, which would be catastrophic. The best plan he could devise was for her to send them from Taipei to New York by international carrier. He said that if she had access to WHO labelling to put on the parcels, it would significantly minimize the likelihood of them being searched or held up at customs.

He told Hana that he felt it was a weak plan, and it troubled him greatly, but he had not been able to come up with a better one.

"I'm not asking about what specifically is in the boxes, Pao, but what do they contain in a general sense?" Hana asked.

"This one," he said, pointing to the shoebox-size box, "contains specimens in a locked cryogenic canister with a twenty-one-day liquid nitrogen holding time. I personally packed it two days ago and carried it with me from Beijing to Taiwan, so there is at least a nineteen-day window to preserve the sample's integrity in which it must arrive at a facility that is able to take over its preservation. If we cannot meet that deadline, the sample will begin to deteriorate but probably will continue to have some analytical value if placed in the right hands."

He told her that the second parcel contained his research notes, beginning in 2014 and including full detail and photographs. "I have kept the two packages separate so that in the event one of them is intercepted or adulterated, enough of my material may still get through to guide research teams in the direction of my discoveries."

Hana studied the items on the table in front of her and was lost in thought. She said nothing.

"Do you prefer not to participate with me in this project?" Den Chin asked. "If not, I will understand perfectly, and I will try to arrange a different plan." He knew that he had placed Hana in a difficult, even untenable position. He was asking her to expose herself to considerable personal risk without even explaining the importance of his findings, and he was asking her to act in secret, outside normal ethical consideration for her employer, the WHO. "I know that even should you decide to help me there is no possibility of knowing that the plan will succeed. Even the best plan will fail if luck is deficient."

She looked directly at Den Chin, thinking this last fatalistic observation sounded like a Chinese proverb. She said, "I most certainly do wish to participate with you, Pao. And I don't feel it is essential, or even advisable, for me to know the details of your scientific conclusions, as I have developed a great respect for you both as a man and as a scientist. I do not believe you would ask me to do this if you did not think that the benefit to humanity outweighed the personal danger."

Hana sat back in her seat and then appeared to have reached a decision.

"Pao, I have an idea on how to possibly arrange to transport the material, but it will take me a day to see if it can be done. I am going to contact my former husband in New York who I think may be able to help. He is a good man and can be fully trusted with your information. He has great resources, enormous resources, and he is motivated to accomplish something positive for the international community because of the terrible experience he had in his business some years ago, which I believe I mentioned to you when we were visiting Resonant Sands. If he cannot help us, I will proceed with the plan as you and I have discussed it today. Is it acceptable to you that I confer with my former husband?"

Den Chin smiled. The calm resolve with which she spoke and her placid, deliberate manner gave him confidence. He recalled their conversation about her former husband and the high regard she had for him. "That would be fine, Hana," he said. "I fully trust your discretion in this matter. I will hold everything here tonight. What time would you like to meet tomorrow?"

They agreed on 10:00 a.m., and Hana left for her own hotel, filled with purpose and thinking through the details of the plan Pao had mapped out.

She arrived back in her hotel room at 11:30 a.m. In New York it already was quite late, after midnight; nevertheless, she pulled out her cell phone and punched in a number. On the third ring a man answered.

"Hana?" he said in a voice muffled from sleep. "Is everything all right, my love?"

"Yes," she answered, "but Harry, I need your help right now. Wake up."

CHAPTER 34
Taipei, Taiwan

At ten the next morning, Hana sat with Den Chin in the same conference room they had used the day before and told him that in numerous phone calls with her former husband overnight they had arranged a plan that they believed would accomplish their goals. She told Den Chin that, as she had expected, Harry was immediately supportive. Overnight he had marshalled his powerful connections as managing partner and Chairman of North American Operations of one of the world's largest global transport conglomerates and arranged safe transport for the two packages from Taiwan to New York with maximum security and speed.

By relying on her ex-husband's assistance, she could get the packages to New York in about fifteen days, leaving a few days to spare before the cryogenic preservation started to fail. She herself intended to leave Taiwan immediately with the sealed letter for Professor Cedar, hoping to minimize the chance of her somehow being connected to clandestine activities with Den Chin or detained for any reason.

Hana said she would locate Jack Cedar and somehow interrupt his travel plans to Ireland for the meeting. She had not yet figured out how to accomplish it but would confer with her former husband and come up with a plan.

She asked Pao if he thought she should give the letter sealed with wax to Cedar before the specimens arrived or wait until she had everything to provide to him at the same time. Cedar's lecture in Ireland was scheduled for less than a week after the specimens would arrive in New York if all went well.

Den Chin was thoughtful. "First, please extend to your husband my fullest gratitude for his assistance. In China we do not have men with this magnitude of influence and power who are able to call upon personal resources outside of the government's reach. It is truly an amazement to me."

He leaned forward and continued. "As far as the professor is concerned, I emphasize that the most important issue, of paramount importance, is his personal safety in advance of the lecture he is planning to deliver. I realize you do not truly comprehend the methods the party would employ to stop him from drawing attention to this issue, which they have decided to suppress. I have found that Westerners simply cannot accept that the People's Republic of China conforms to an entirely different concept of the individual, which it believes is an insignificant, meaningless speck in the great movement of society. I urge you to consider my warnings about the safety of Professor Cedar with the highest priority."

He stared at Hana for a moment to further emphasize the gravity of what he was about to say. "As I stated yesterday, if Professor Cedar leaves the United States, I am quite certain that he will not arrive at the meeting where he is scheduled to speak. The party strives to avoid incidents that would bring international condemnation, possibly even military repercussions, and therefore would devise an 'elimination' that seems unrelated to international issues or even to the conference he is attending. Perhaps he will simply disappear on his way to the hotel in Dublin or in a random theft when he's exiting the airport that ends in violence, for example."

He paused. "Hana, you must use your best judgment to decide when to provide my letter to Professor Cedar. Since it explains the nature of the material I am entrusting to him, it may help to convince him to remain in the United States. However, before the actual samples arrive, he is likely to be doubtful of the authenticity of the letter and may be resistant to your requests."

Hana stared at Den Chin and then replied, "And what about the future, Pao? Is this man being consigned to danger for the rest of his life? How can we do this to him?"

"No, Hana, no. Once the information in my communiqué is revealed to the world, in the Western style of free speech, the danger to Jack Cedar will be gone. My government will not want to be the obvious suspect should harm befall him, and in any event, once the information is made public, there will be no point in trying to suppress Professor Cedar's lecture."

They reviewed every detail of their plan. When they were satisfied, Pao told Hana that he would remain at his hotel in Taiwan for three days and she could easily reach him should any complications or questions arise. When she rose to leave, Hana resisted her urge to hug Den Chin and instead extended her hand.

He took it in his own and said, "I have been most happy to make your acquaintance, Hana, and will remember you always," surprising himself with warmth in his voice that had come to him without thought. "If our efforts are successful, we may together have given an important gift to humanity."

At noon a courier arrived at the Marriott carrying an empty metal case and a sealed manila packet, which he delivered to Den Chin. About the size of a small suitcase, the metal container was air- and watertight and closed with a locking mechanism. The case was marked in large, black letters "SHAW GLOBAL Personal Property of Chairman, North America." The locking code was provided to Den Chin in a small, white envelope, which he put in his pocket.

He took the container and the manila packet from the courier and left the man waiting in the lobby for about twenty minutes. When he returned, he handed the locked case back to the messenger, who walked out of the hotel and got into a black SUV that had been waiting for him at the entrance. Den Chin watched until it drove off.

Moments later, he stopped at the front desk and confirmed that he would check out of the hotel in five days. He requested that the clerk also confirm his flight to Beijing on that day and be sure of his seat assignment.

Then he left the hotel and headed for the National Palace Museum, an unaccustomed spring in his step and the hint of a smile on his face.

CHAPTER 35

> The cherry blooms are gone;
> In between the trees,
> A temple has appeared.
> —Buson (1716–1784)

The haiku, memorized in childhood, filled Den Chin's thoughts as he stood before the magnificent *Ancient Temple Concealed in Seclusion* displayed in the gallery of the National Palace Museum devoted to the Song Dynasty. After half a century the words still filled him with serenity, and he stood quietly for several moments before moving on. Few party members shared, or even understood, his appreciation for Chinese art, and the absence of colleagues with whom to discuss the evolution of Chinese civilization had been a void in his life.

Following his final meeting with Hana, Den Chin spent three days visiting and revisiting the sites in Taipei that had been his refuge during the lonely years of his childhood. He went to a different gallery of the museum for a few hours each morning and in the afternoon chose a place that had special meaning for him. He spent an hour in the Bao'an Temple, admiring the breathtaking roof carvings; intricate depictions of colorful, intertwined dragons; and other Chinese symbols.

Dozens of burning joss sticks lit by chanting worshippers created a fog of aromatic smoke that enveloped Den Chin in memories of his youth. He visited the majestic National Revolutionary Martyrs' Shrine honoring the Kuomintang war dead and watched as soldiers clad in elegant, red uniforms solemnly completed the changing of the guard.

He walked and walked, trying to commit to memory as many scenes of Taipei as he could absorb, knowing that this would be his last visit to the city that he loved, in the country that he still considered to be a separate nation from the People's Republic of China to which he had devoted his life.

At four o'clock on the third day, he returned to his room at the Marriott. He showered and dressed in fresh clothes and packed his briefcase with a few personal items. He left his clothing, phone, laptop, and other electronics in the room. When he closed the door behind him, he did not look back.

He left the hotel and walked two blocks before hailing a cab. He instructed the driver to take him to Keelung Harbor, and when asked which ship berth he wanted, he indicated that the entry to the port would be fine since he was sightseeing and not meeting a ship.

He watched the cab pull away and then found an information desk and asked where the cargo ship *Alpine Star* was docked. The clerk rifled through pages of a manifest and told Den Chin it was docked at Berth 4. He pointed out the location and said it could be reached on foot in about ten minutes.

When Den Chin arrived at the entrance to Gate 4, he saw the massive ship parked beyond, colorful containers stacked three or four stories high on the deck and smoke curling out of the massive stacks. He noted the familiar Shaw Global logo with its giant, red arrow blazed on the side of the ship.

He approached the security gate with trepidation, uncertain of how to handle it, when a uniformed ship's officer seated behind the metal detector stepped around it and said, "Mr. Kwan? I assume you are the chairman's guest? I was instructed to meet you here and give you the replacement passport that we obtained for you." He extended an envelope to Den Chin, who took it hesitantly.

"I'm the ship's captain, by the way, Tim Lynch," he said, extending his hand to Den Chin. "Glad that we could help with that replacement passport. It can be such a hassle taking care of a lost passport, especially in Asia. My brother was once stranded in Vietnam for six days waiting for his to be prepared by the embassy."

Den Chin hesitantly returned Captain Lynch's smile, a Western gesture that was awkward for him. He opened the envelope, removed the passport, and without checking it handed it to the security guard waiting at the scanner. He placed his briefcase on the conveyor belt and watched it slide through the machine without incident. The guard handed back the passport and said, "Have a good voyage, Mr. Kwan," without so much as a glance.

Lynch guided Den Chin up the gangway and told him that the chairman had instructed that every courtesy be extended to his honored guest. He showed Den Chin to a stateroom that had a brass plaque affixed to the door indicating "Guest Quarters" and said that he was welcome to join the ship's officers in the mess hall for meals or he could call the kitchen and have food delivered to his room. If Den Chin needed anything at all, he should contact Lynch at any time.

"I'll let you get settled now, Mr. Kwan," he said, heading to the door. "We sail in an hour and ten minutes, and it's a beautiful sight exiting from the port of Keelung. You might want to come on deck to watch the sail away." He started to walk down the hall but turned back and said, "On the desk there's a list of ports that don't require us to obtain advance permission to discharge a passenger. The chairman said you would decide where you want to disembark and let me know." He walked away, and Den Chin closed the door.

The room was paneled in dark wood with burgundy carpet and curtains over the window that opened to a view of the harbor. On the desk was a wrapped box marked "Mr. Kwan" that contained a phone and laptop with instructions to log on. There was also an envelope containing $250,000 in US currency and an American Express card in his new name. A small selection of clothing was placed neatly in the bureau and closet.

Den Chin opened the passport that Captain Lynch had handed him and saw that his new name was to be Pao Lin Kwan. He said it aloud a few times, training his ears to respond to it. He pulled his old passport from his pocket, found a scissor in the desk drawer and cut it into pieces, which he placed in his pocket.

He spent some time familiarizing himself with his new electronics and setting up internet access and accounts in his new name. When he heard the first loud blast of the smokestack signaling preparation to sail, he made his way to the deck where a dozen or so of the crew had congregated and were cheerfully talking. They greeted Den Chin in a friendly way, and he did his best to smile and say Western niceties like, "Good weather to sail." He was confident that the social customs of his new society would become easier for him with time, although he knew that he would always be content to be silent, with only himself for company.

In a few minutes he felt the engines of the massive ship power up beneath his feet and the deck begin to vibrate. He politely excused himself and went over to the railing to watch them sail away in solitude.

The engines thundered, and the final blast from the smokestack muffled all other sound as the huge ship slowly slipped away from the berth and began its trip to the sea. Den Chin watched Taipei recede into the distance, the late afternoon sun illuminating the shoreline after the city had disappeared.

The sailors drifted away to work or dinner, and finally Den Chin stood alone on the deck. The *Alpine Star* was leaving the harbor area and about to enter the open sea. He pulled the passport pieces from his pocket and dropped them into the roiling water below. He watched until they vanished into the deep.

Pao Lin Kwan turned to face the vast ocean ahead of him and smiled.

PART NINE

2021

Long Island, New York

CHAPTER 36

I wake up early as usual and study Jack, still sleeping peacefully beside me. He looks like a handsome farmer, I think, not someone involved in international intrigue.

I mentally review our conversations and what I have heard him say to Hamilton and Drost. He became appropriately angry when they harassed him and especially when they crossed the line with me. I don't think he would be protective of me, to the point of inciting the agents against himself, if he were intentionally using me to some nefarious end. And then there is his story about being told by a dean of Columbia University that his friend, George Hong, is suspected of being a Chinese spy. If Jack were hiding his own identity, why even tell me anything about this revelation that he says he finds shocking?

He shifts his position and reaches his arm over to find me in the bed. I touch his shoulder affectionately and whisper, "Sleep some more, it's very early. I'm going for a run."

He doesn't open his eyes, but quietly says, "OK," and adjusts his head on the pillow.

I drink my orange juice as I watch the sun rise higher in a perfect blue sky and realize that I actually feel wonderful. I am standing in my kitchen alone and smiling. I have not been unhappy since my divorce, but it's been awhile since I felt really great. How terrible it would be if I were falling in love with an utterly charming psychopath who works for an unfriendly foreign government and calmly participates in the disappearance of a passenger jet filled with innocent people.

I push the thought aside, refusing to even consider it any further, and go out the back door. I gasp when I see Harry Shaw calmly sitting on my patio.

"Harry!" I say. "What are you doing here? You scared me!"

"I'm so sorry I startled you, Ruby," he says calmly and stands up, "but I have something important to share with you privately. I know you've been having some problems with law enforcement, and I was hoping to catch your attention without catching theirs. Are they still sitting in front of your house?"

I am taken aback. "How could you know that, Harry?" I ask in a sharp tone, suddenly on full alert and knowing, somehow, that this is a serious development, a very serious development. "I didn't tell you that. Actually, I didn't tell you anything at all about what's going on in my life." I stare at him and hope there will be some acceptable explanation, but the pit of my stomach tells me there won't be.

"Aruba, I have a complex story to fill you in on, but we can't do it here where we may be overheard. Let's go down to the beach." He reaches out to touch my arm, but I recoil, partly in anger but also partly out of real fear. What have I missed about Harry? I think, and recall my surprise at his obvious interest in Jack.

"I'm not just walking off with you, Harry, not until you tell me what's going on here." I inch backward toward the door while I wait for his response.

Harry stares at me, weighing his options. He can see that I am actually afraid of him, which he seems to find bewildering. But he is a sharp guy and knows that he will need to provide some explanation if he wants me to do what he has asked. We stand there for a few moments, at an impasse.

"Aruba, how can you be afraid of me?" he says, his voice choked.

I am moved by his obvious emotion but not enough to comply with his request for a private chat. "How? Harry, you just revealed to me that you somehow know about some pretty scary things happening in my life that I never told you! You want to fill me in on how you know about my problem with law enforcement?" I am less fearful now but stand firm.

Harry looks me in the eye and says quietly, "It's about Aimee Cedar. I know who she is."

I am nothing short of flabbergasted. I stand there speechless, gaping at him.

"Ruby," he says quietly, "I need to explain this to you. It is an extremely complicated story, and I want you to hear it before anyone else. Then you can decide what to do. If you want to tell the FBI about it, you can do so. But decide after you hear the full story, please." He waits, and when I still say nothing, he extends his arm to me and says, "Please let me explain. I promise it is nothing you could possibly have expected. Just walk to the beach with me."

I glance back at my house to see if there is any sign of activity and say, "Jack Cedar is inside, and he knows I went to the beach. If I'm not back soon, he'll come looking for me." I lead the way, and Harry and I take the hidden path to the beach.

When we get there, Harry says, "Sit down with me," which we do, and he is careful to keep some distance between us so I will be more comfortable. He begins. "I've thought for hours about the best way to explain to you what has happened, and I'm afraid there is just no way to really soften it, so here it is: As a result of something happening across the world in the Chinese Communist Party, which Jack Cedar knows absolutely nothing about, his life is in imminent danger. Keeping him off that plane, preventing him from leaving the United States, was intended to protect him, which it obviously did. However, no one involved in this ever had even the slightest thought that the Chinese would actually target an entire plane because they were after one man." Harry's voice cracks, and he looks away from me toward the ocean. He cannot speak for a few moments and then says, "We are filled with remorse, overwhelming remorse. Had we revealed the information we suppressed in order to protect Jack, that plane may never have taken off."

I am completely, utterly mystified. I can't even begin to know what to make of Harry's statement, which I think sounds like it could only be the crazy ravings of an anti–Red China lunatic, which I know Harry is not. It flashes through my mind that the hijackers of his ship years ago were Muslim fundamentalists, not even Chinese. Harry's eyes are red, and his face is strained with emotion.

"Harry, what are you talking about? What you just said is crazy," I say, sounding a little more sympathetic than I actually feel.

"It's not crazy, Aruba; it's true," he says in a firm voice, turning to look directly at me. "Aimee Cedar is in my house right now, crying as if her heart is broken, which she's been doing on and off since Saturday morning when we heard the news about the plane."

It's my turn to stare out at the ocean, trying to make some sense out of what Harry is saying. I tell him, "I never met or heard of Jack Cedar before, so whatever he may have to do with China, what could it possibly have to do with me? You're not making any sense, Harry."

"Our game, Aruba, our game," he says, and when I look at him with a blank expression, he continues. "Divorce Stories, the game we play." I realize what he is referring to, but I still am at a loss to connect it to the current situation.

"One of the first anecdotes you told me was about a client whose wife intended to sneak the children out of the country," he says. "You went to court and in twenty-four hours got the woman's bank vault sealed so the kids' passports were locked up and she couldn't go. It was a great story. I was very impressed with your legal expertise and ability to obtain such a quick and effective result."

I think back and recall telling him about my Hanson case. I had, indeed, succeeded in getting a wife's safe deposit box sealed when her husband, my client, found plane tickets indicating his wife's intention to leave him and surreptitiously take their kids to her family in Croatia.

I become instantly furious and feel adrenaline pumping through my veins. "So you just used me in some international plot? Got me to repeat my little trick?" I raise my voice, and Harry looks around to see if anyone is close enough to hear us, which they are not. As the implications of what Harry has said sink in, I am overcome with anger.

I shout at him, "You just used me in some crazy story about China? Got me to put a fraud before the court, jeopardize my career, my *life*, for Christ's sake? Who the fuck is Aimee Cedar? Who is your little partner in this game that has just about ruined me?" I am really yelling now and can barely contain myself from slugging him. He looks around in a panic, obviously worried that I am attracting attention to us.

"Aruba, please, please let me continue and tell you the whole story. Please." He reaches toward me, but I hit his arm and push it away. He ignores it. "If it hadn't been for the plane, so tragic and unpredicted, I thought you would have made a quick twenty-five thousand dollars, Jack Cedar would have been safe, and when he told you and the court that it was a case of mistaken identity, that would have been the end of it. I am so sorry to have drawn you into this. But, Aruba, if you will just let me tell you the whole story, I think, I am sure, that you will understand my motives." He stares at me, calm and seemingly full of resolve.

I say angrily, "Just tell me who Aimee Cedar is since she apparently has absolutely nothing whatsoever to do with Jack Cedar."

"She is my former wife," he says flatly, and I am so completely shocked that I am instantly drained of anger and ready to listen to his story.

"Her name is Hana Chang. She is a medical doctor, a brilliant one, and she works for the World Health Organization, the WHO," he begins. "As you know, we are divorced. There is a big age difference between us, and after the terrorist murders on my ship in 2014, I became unable to continue my life in Geneva and needed to begin a new chapter in a new place. But Hana would not move to New York because of her career and her family and friends in Switzerland. I concluded I could not leave her in that position—a beautiful young woman, alone but unable to pursue a new relationship because of her marriage ties. We divorced, but we remain the best of friends and have enduring love for each other. That will never change." He pauses and waits for me to gesture that he should continue, which I do.

"Three weeks ago, she called me and said that in the course of her work for the WHO she had been involved in evaluating claims of environmental and human devastation somehow related to the mining of rare earth minerals in Inner Mongolia, China. You may not know that these minerals are essential to the manufacture of many modern products."

But of course I do know exactly what rare earth minerals are because Jack Cedar has already told me all about this field, which I had never even heard of until last week. In a flash I realize that this is no coincidence and this subject must somehow be the basis for the connection between Harry and Jack. But is Jack a good guy or a bad guy? For that matter, which is Harry?

"While investigating the mines with a WHO delegation, Hana met an esteemed Chinese physician and researcher who had come upon evidence of certain deadly consequences possibly tied to the mining procedures. He was desperate to get his research to the West and contacted her, appealing to her for help in accomplishing that. He told her that because Jack Cedar is an expert in rare earth mining, he wished to make him the recipient of the Chinese research. He also said that as the result of reporting from a Chinese spy in the US, he knew that Cedar would be delivering an important lecture on the subject in Dublin and that the Communist party would never allow that to take place. He told Hana that if Cedar left the United

States, the CCP would see to it that he did not survive. Hana called me for help."

I stare at Harry, trying to process these revelations, some of which click into place like a jigsaw puzzle. "So you came up with a plan to keep him in the US, using me as a convenient tool for doing it." Harry doesn't know how to respond since, although I phrased it harshly, what I have said is true. "So really I have nothing at all to do with any of this except that I made a good patsy."

"Believe me, Ruby," he says in a choked voice, "I never imagined that your involvement would be anything more than getting paid a lot of money for doing your job. It was just that the job was to protect Jack Cedar, not get him a divorce. I was wrong to do it, I see that; I never considered what could go wrong. But my motives were honorable, and I truly believed the only repercussion to you would be to have made a large fee for your professional expertise. Can you understand? Can you forgive me?"

I ignore this question and ask, "So what exactly is this information that some Chinese doctor thinks is important enough to set up this whole ruse?"

"I actually don't know any more than what I just told you, and neither does Hana, by the way. The doctor told her that she would be safer if she was unable to provide details in the event that her involvement with him was discovered. She has a letter from him to be opened only by Jack Cedar. He even sealed it with sealing wax to ensure that no one else could secretly read the contents before Cedar. She has that for him. There are also two packages for him en route from Asia that will arrive in a couple of days."

Even I realize it is ridiculous that my first thought after hearing this incredible story is joy that Jack is not a Chinese spy after all, and in fact, he apparently was being used by one named George Hong. But my good cheer fades almost instantly as I acknowledge the possibility that the Chinese doctor may also in fact be a spy, using Hana Chang to funnel information to his comrade in the

United States named Jack Cedar. How can I know if Harry's wife, who has already demonstrated that she is an excellent actress by her impersonation of a woman she invented named Aimee Cedar, is on the level? Or, even if she is, if she is savvy enough to know whether this Chinese guy is actually using her the way she and Harry have used me?

"How do you know about the FBI?" I ask him, and he tells me that after the plane vanished, he became alarmed for my safety, realizing that things had gone completely awry. He had a security team from Shaw Global keep an eye on my house, and they almost immediately reported that the FBI was parked outside and that agents had entered my house several times.

"So what do you propose we do now, Harry?" I ask testily, unsure whether to believe this fantastic story or not. And then I look up and see Jack walking down the beach path, smiling, looking straight at us.

CHAPTER 37

I smile weakly at Jack and hope he is still too far away to notice my panicky expression. "So, Harry," I ask with a sneer, "want to tell me what you have in mind to do next?"

Harry doesn't answer and stares out to sea as Jack approaches us. He comes up behind me and places his hand on my shoulder in an affectionate manner.

"Good morning, Ruby," he says warmly and then looks at Harry. "Early for the two of you to be having a chat, isn't it? A serious chat, too, from the looks of both of you." He waits, but neither Harry nor I say anything, which confirms his observation.

He lifts his hand from my shoulder and says, "I think you'd better fill me in here." His voice is cool, and I realize that his temper, which I already have seen boil over several times, is percolating.

I stand up next to him and wrap my arm around the small of his back. "Good morning, Jack," I say with all the warmth I can muster and brush his cheek with my lips. Harry's revelations have made Jack's credentials shakier in one sense but stronger if I look at what Harry has just told me in a different way. It is possible that Jack is a willing outlet for information that Chinese spies want to disseminate in the United States, but it is also possible that he is an unknowing conduit for a whistleblower Chinese scientist who wants to save the world. Which is it? Until I know for sure, I will not let go of the happiness that I feel after spending the last twenty-four hours with him. I keep my arm in place around him.

My gesture has made it clear to Jack that I am not having any kind of a romantic episode with Harry, and I feel Jack relax. He looks at me, smiling again, and says, "Ruby, would you rather go back to the house and we can talk there?" He ignores Harry, whom he apparently views as a rival for my affection. Despite everything, I am delighted that he is jealous, not only because it demonstrates that he has feelings for me but also because he has no inkling that Harry might be involved in the spy trade. I think it suggests that Jack himself is not.

"No, Jack, not yet. Actually Harry has something that he needs to explain to you directly," I say sharply. "He just told me about it, just before you arrived, and now he needs to tell it to you." I turn toward Harry and tilt my head at him, one eyebrow raised in a taunt, inviting him to begin.

As if we are playing a party game, I wonder how Harry will explain his actions to this volatile man he bamboozled into a shitload of trouble, based solely upon the possibly wacko conclusions of his ex-wife. Of course I know that Harry is no dummy. Nephew of the founder or not, he did not get to be the chairman of North American operations of one of the largest shipping companies in the world by being a poor communicator. Neither is he naive, I think, and his assessment of his former wife's story may well be right on the money.

Harry stands and assumes his chairman-of-the-continent posture and body language, very effective even here on the beach while wearing shorts and a T-shirt. In fact, I note, he has regained his usual composure and radiates dignity and power.

"Jack," he begins in his sonorous voice, "as you know, I hold a significant position in a global company with very powerful political connections. In that capacity I have come into information of extraordinary significance that is within your area of expertise." He pauses for effect and looks piercingly at Jack. "What happens to that information, whether it can be used to help people around the world, is directly related to the excellence of your professional expertise and your desire to pursue scientific research to help humanity."

Jack is listening intently but seems unimpressed. Then he starts to laugh. "Pretty good stuff, Harry! Irresistible. How could any professor not go for that opening, hook, line and sinker? We're a very vain group, you know." He spreads his legs to a more casual position and smiles at Harry. I watch both of them in silence as if I am at a tennis match.

Harry is not pleased to get this cavalier response when he had been going for gravity. He doesn't smile and continues as if he has not even registered Jack's lighthearted response. "An esteemed Chinese doctor and researcher has determined a possible link between a new viral agent, possibly even the pandemic, and the mining of REE, which he believes is an area in which you have particular expertise."

Jack's entire demeanor changes. Instantly he stands upright and is listening with rapt attention. "What does this have to do with me?" he asks, either mystified or doing the best imitation of mystified that I have ever seen.

"The doctor in question has chosen you to be the recipient of his research so it can be properly investigated and analyzed in the West. He knows your resume, and he trusts you. He believes that his own government in China will suppress the information for a variety of reasons. He also believes that the government of the United States, or any government for that matter, would be subjected to political pressure to use the information to garner power or money rather than for medical advancement, so he instead chose an esteemed professor to be the one to receive it and determine how to handle it." Harry watches Jack, knowing that he has either hit the mark or he hasn't. He will soon find out which.

I watch Jack's face as he thinks over Harry's statement. Looking at him, I am convinced that he is shocked but also flattered. Coming from someone else, Harry's revelations might be instantly dismissed as ridiculous, but Harry is an important man, sophisticated and savvy. His statement is not so easily tossed aside.

To my surprise, Jack looks directly at Harry and says in a hard tone, "What exactly does Aruba have to do with this. . . story?" Harry and I are both taken aback that this is his first question. In an instant I realize that the possibility that I have not been truthful with him is more important to Jack than the flattering story about some Chinese doctor with information that could save our civilization. I am so happy with his question that my heart sings and I almost smile. But I don't. Instead I lean into Jack and wait for Harry to respond.

"Aruba?" Harry says incredulously. "Aruba? She has nothing to do with this! I just told her about it moments before you arrived at the beach. She has nothing to do with it at all." I feel Jack relax and lean toward me.

"I think you had better explain what's going on here, Harry," he says. "I am not getting any sense of a common thread between the bizarre things that seem to be happening to me and all around me since last week." He pauses. "Is there some connection between some woman claiming to be married to me and a Chinese doctor wanting to save the world by giving me his secret research? Is that what you're saying?" he says in a tone that suggests he finds this ludicrous. "And what exactly is your role in this, Harry?"

"This is a very complex story, Jack. Will you come back to my house where we can speak openly? Both of you, of course." He turns to me and says, "Aruba, since I have involved you in this without your knowledge or permission, I think I owe you complete honesty from now on, and I vow to provide that."

Before I can ask exactly who is included in "we," Jack says, "What is this research supposedly about, Harry?"

"I don't know any details, Jack. My expertise is global transportation, not science or medicine. As far as the science involved, I only know what I just told you, some connection between rare earth mining and the pandemic. My former wife is a physician with the World Health Organization, and she is the link between this information and me. She can explain more to you, although I do not believe that even she has been entrusted with details because it is so sensitive. She personally has met with the Chinese doctor a number of times, though, and has gotten to know him."

Jack is trying to decide if this story is at all credible before he agrees even to go to Harry's house, where he may just fall deeper into the morass. "What makes you think your ex-wife is privy to such information, and why would she even have access to this doctor?" he asks dismissively. "Do you know who this doctor is?"

"I know his name," Harry says, "but that's all. It's Pao Den Chin."

Jack snaps to attention. "I know who he is. Every serious science professor knows who he is. He's the star of China's environmental and infectious disease research team, and they routinely showcase his work to impress the world with their expertise in these fields. I've read several papers that he authored, and he is very impressive."

"Then come back to my house and hear the whole story," Harry says again. "My former wife is there, and she can explain it far better than I."

"How do you know it's really him? Relying on the opinion of a former spouse seems pretty shaky to me," I interject.

"When you meet her, Hana Chang is her name, you'll understand why I believe her. She's an impressive medical researcher, and she has had a long and stellar career with the WHO. She thinks the WHO has lost objectivity in this matter, has become too beholden to the Chinese, and she is risking her career to assist in delivering this communication from Dr. Den Chin. You need to meet her to decide if the story is credible to you," Harry says.

Then he tells Jack that Hana has a letter from Den Chin addressed to him and that he sealed it with wax to ensure that Jack would be the first person to read it. "Come to my house, meet her, and read the letter. Then decide what you want to do. If you're not interested, that will be the end of it. I promise you." He waits for Jack's response, but there is none. "Jack, how could you walk away without seeing what is in this letter that Hana carried around the world for you at great peril to herself?"

Finally Jack agrees to go, emphasizing that at this point he is only intending to meet Hana and read the letter supposedly from Dr. Den Chin, about which he remains skeptical. The three of us walk over the dunes toward Harry's house. When we reach the steel-and-concrete enclosure, Harry punches a code into a heavy lock that snaps the gate open to reveal a stunningly landscaped oasis surrounding a pool replete with waterfalls. Beautiful foliage and color-coordinated flower beds rim the perimeter of the yard. It is breathtaking, and I fleetingly think that since Harry felt close enough with me to ensnare me in his plot, he might have invited me over some time to enjoy the opulence of his property.

On the patio beyond the pool, a woman is sitting curled in a plush armchair, wearing a colorful robe. As we get closer, she rises from her seat, and I can see that she is a strikingly beautiful Asian woman. With one hand, she sweeps her luxuriant, dark hair off her face, and I have no doubt at all that I have found Aimee Cedar.

CHAPTER 38

When Aimee—or Hana—realizes who we are, she springs up from her chair. She has never met Jack and may or may not realize from photos of him that he is the man she has been charged with finding and protecting, but she certainly knows who I am. She steps toward me, her arms extended, and blurts out, "Ms. Jones, I hope you can forgive me. I am so very, very sorry that I have brought you into this nightmare. I thought I would protect Professor Cedar with my actions but—" Her voice cracks and tears begin to slide down her cheeks. "The plane. The plane! How could I have imagined that to stop one man from delivering a lecture they would sacrifice a plane full of innocent people." Her eyes are red and puffy, and I think Harry was being truthful when he said his former wife is distraught over what has gone wrong with their plan. I begin to speak, still not sure what I will say, but Jack cuts me off.

"What do you mean 'stop one man from delivering a lecture'?" he asks. Hana seems to have not even registered his presence, but now she stares at him and realizes who he is.

"You are Professor Cedar?" she asks and Jack nods. "Has Harry explained to you what has happened?"

Jack thinks for a moment and then says, "Why don't you tell me yourself? Your name is Dr. Chang, is that correct?" I am impressed that he has thought to let her explain from the beginning so he can compare what she says to what Harry already has told us.

Harry motions for us to sit down on the patio and assures us that the steel-and-cement enclosure around the property includes sound dampening that can only be breached with professional eavesdropping equipment. His security team checks for this regularly so we can speak freely.

We sit there for more than an hour as Hana relates her story to us, which begins with her trip to Inner Mongolia as part of the WHO mission to evaluate the negative environmental and human impact of rare earth mining, where she first encountered the respected Pao Den Chin, and ends with her leaving Taiwan with the letter from him to deliver to Professor Cedar.

She tells us that when the Chinese doctor hosted the WHO delegation in Inner Mongolia, he noticed her dubious reaction to the tour of the rare earth mine and sought to discuss with her any reservations she had. She had spent some time with Dr. Den Chin before returning to Geneva and had become convinced of his tremendous intellect and nuanced personality, which was unlike other officials of the PRC she had encountered, who were unquestioning supporters of the proverbial party line.

She had not heard from Dr. Den Chin for more than a year, and then he had contacted her out of the blue and asked her to meet him in Taiwan. He wanted to discuss a matter he described as having worldwide importance with which she might be able to help him. He said that Hana's skepticism about Inner Mongolia had convinced him of her smart and fair-minded approach to scientific research. She was reluctant to go, but his impeccable reputation and the sincerity of his tone persuaded her to meet him.

In Taiwan Den Chin told her that he had come upon evidence that might shed light on a possible link between a new viral agent he had discovered but that his government had suppressed the matter and made it clear that no further investigation would be permitted. He was defying this direct instruction, putting his career on the line, and even risking his life to get the evidence to the West where he hoped it would be possible for the scientific study to continue.

To ensure that the handling of his material was not influenced by political pressure, he wanted it to be given directly to a scientist like himself rather than a government. He had chosen Professor Cedar because a Chinese spy in the United States by the name of George Hong had alerted them that Mr. Cedar was scheduled to deliver a keynote address to the GCAC in Dublin on the very subject of environmental damage associated with the mining of rare earth elements. Hong had even given them Mr. Cedar's travel information for the trip to Dublin.

At the mention of George Hong, Jack and I stare at each other for a moment and silently share our increasing confidence in Hana Chang's story.

Hana goes on, relating that Den Chin had carefully investigated Mr. Cedar's background and scientific credentials and believed he was the right choice to receive the research material. But, he had told Hana, Cedar's life already was in imminent danger since the party would never let him deliver a lecture focusing attention on a topic they had decided to suppress. He told her that Westerners simply do not understand how the party works when it wants something to happen or, in this case, to not happen. If Cedar left his own country, Den Chin stated as if it already were a sad fact, his life would be over.

He urged Hana to use any means she could devise to protect Cedar until he received the research material from Den Chin. The ultimate public release of the material would eliminate danger to Cedar, he said, since there would no longer be anything to suppress and China would be the obvious suspect if harm befell the professor.

"And that, Ms. Jones and Professor Cedar, is the reason I asked Harry to help me figure out a way to prevent you from leaving for Ireland: to protect you," she said, looking at Jack, "until the material from Dr. Den Chin could be delivered to you." She started to weep silently and said, "Of course we were wrong, all wrong, and never even considered that something so tragic could happen." She paused and then added, "Dr. Den Chin did warn me, but I thought such a thing could not possibly happen here."

We sit for a few moments in stunned silence. The story sounds too fantastic to believe, but the facts cannot be discounted: the plane on which Jack was scheduled to travel has vanished; it appears that George Hong is indeed a spy for China; Jack is an expert in the mining of REEs and was scheduled to give a lecture on the subject; and, most compelling, Dr. Den Chin is so well known and respected that Jack has even read scientific research papers authored by him.

"So, Dr. Chang, what exactly is this evidence, and what is the conclusion that Dr. Den Chin has drawn from it?" asks Jack.

"He would not tell me any specifics, Mr. Cedar. He felt it would endanger me even more if I had precise knowledge. Instead, he gave me a letter to deliver to you, which is sealed with wax so it could be proven that I had not read the contents in the event that I or the letter were apprehended." She looked away for a moment and said quietly, "He thought very carefully about this, that he was placing me in danger. He is a somewhat melancholy and introspective man, and he told me that his feelings for the party had shifted in recent years."

"Is the letter the only information about this? A letter is not going to convince anyone of the authenticity of whatever it is he thinks he found," says Jack.

Harry and I are sitting mute, listening to this discussion. Harry has been an active participant in what is going on, but I am truly just a bystander, and I wonder what I am even doing here, sitting in this opulent backyard with these powerful, international people, not to mention Jack Cedar whom I met only a week ago under bizarre circumstances.

"Oh no, the letter is only a summary," says Hana. "The actual scientific evidence is en route and will arrive in New York in two days. Is that right, Harry?" she asks, turning to her former husband, who nods to indicate that she is correct.

So, I realize, Harry has handled the transportation for this global production number.

"And who called in the FBI?" I ask, breaking my silence. The others turn and stare at me as if they have no idea what I am doing there, an opinion that I share.

Harry answers. "It seems that they did it all on their own, Aruba. Probably because they know George Hong is a spy for China. He didn't board the plane, and neither did Jack. I would expect them to draw the conclusion that they were both involved in whatever is going on." He pauses and then adds, "I don't think they could have learned about Den Chin, but since Hong, a known espionage agent of China, failed to board a plane that has vanished and has now disappeared himself, they would surely have questions about his traveling companion. Particularly since he also failed to board the plane, and for reasons that are not exactly credible."

"I'd like to see the letter," Jack cuts in. "I'll read it and see what I think, if it's something I'm willing to take further. If not, you can keep it, and Aruba and I will have nothing further to do with this," he says firmly. I am relieved that he has taken it upon himself to include me in his ultimatum since I am at a loss to even grasp the implications of this international calamity.

Without a word, Hana goes into the house and returns moments later with a bulging envelope that she hands to Jack. I can see that it has his name neatly handwritten on the front and a thick bead of unbroken gray wax running the length of the seal on the back. Harry shows Jack into his study, which has its own exterior entry door from the patio, and tells him to take as long as he needs.

Harry returns to Hana and me and asks if we would like coffee or tea as if we are having a friendly get-together among neighbors, and we wait.

CHAPTER 39

Dear Professor Cedar,

As we are not acquainted, permit me to introduce myself. My name is Pao Den Chin. I am sixty-four years old, and until recently I resided in Beijing. My current location must remain undisclosed for reasons you soon will understand. Since the secrecy about my location and my inability to communicate with you directly may undermine your confidence in the information I am imparting to you, I ask that you speak with Hana Chang, MD, affiliated with the World Health Organization, who will confirm my position and my direct contact with her concerning the matters addressed herein. In addition, while the internet is severely proscribed in China as you no doubt are aware, I am confident that you also will find sufficient reference to me and my professional achievements in a search, which will lend me further credibility.

As for my credentials, I am a medical doctor and have received three advanced degrees in environmental impacts on health and infectious diseases, equivalent to a United States MD plus two PhDs, from the Peking University Health Science Center.

Since I was a teenager growing up in Taiwan, I have been a loyal member of the Communist party, and over the course of my career of four decades, I have risen in the party hierarchy to the position of head of Foreign Actions in Environmental Epidemiology. In this capacity and through a series of unanticipated events, I became privy to information that is not and was not likely to become available to others, even most high-ranking party members and scientists. It is this information that has caused me to repudiate my party affiliation and indeed my life in China, knowing full well that, despite my greatest efforts, I may not survive the retaliation of the party for the disclosures I now make. This grave personal risk that I have chosen to accept should provide you with an understanding of the gravity with which I view the information I impart to you herein.

I am sorry to inform you that your well-being already is in imminent peril from the party for reasons that I expect are not yet clear to you. By choosing you to receive my disclosures, I have quite considerably increased that danger to you, a fact which I regret even while concluding that it is unavoidable. I emphasize to you that the party does have a long reach and a powerful arm even in your country, as will soon be apparent to you in the person of George Hong. In this regard I sincerely urge you to immediately seek and rely upon the protection of your government.

I also note that as soon as the information imparted herein is widely and publicly known, the likelihood of retaliation from the party should diminish. There no longer will be a motive to silence you, and any effort to harm you would probably cause international condemnation, a reaction that the party strives to avoid. I conclude that it is therefore in your personal best interest to widely disclose my information as soon as possible. But of course this is your decision.

It is the aforementioned George Hong who led the party as well as me to you. Mr. Hong has been clandestinely reporting to Beijing on scientific advancements and activities in the United States for several decades and has been a valuable resource, particularly since taking up his employment at Columbia University. He reports that his Chinese ethnicity seemingly conferred upon him a heightened level of professional respect and trustworthiness at the university rather than the reverse, which he had expected. Earlier this year Mr. Hong alerted Beijing that you would be delivering the keynote address at the international science conference in Dublin and that your talk would focus on the environmental hazards of the mining of rare earth minerals, in which area you are an expert. The party did not want you to give this address as it would focus attention on rare earth mining, likely raising questions that the party prefers remain unasked.

Since the 1980s, negative effects related to the mining of REEs have been of considerable interest to the party, which had determined to make China the primary, if not the only, supplier of this material to the world before the end of the twentieth century. My documentation enclosed herein provides detail and context to this meticulously drawn plan. The party correctly recognized that demand for items that require REEs would sweep the globe with the force of a modern industrial revolution.

From the outset, the biohazards of rare earth mining were well documented, so mining was largely confined to countries that do not have good environmental oversight such as Malaysia. To limit competition, China undertook a complex plan to force the closure of the Malay mine at Bukit Merah by inciting aggressive protests from local residents and environmentalists. That action did ultimately succeed in forcing the mine to shut down, which helped to cement China's dominance as a supplier of REE.

However, in 2012, an Australian company obtained approval to commence a refinery in Malaysia, which was claimed to be able to supply up to 30 percent of the world supply within a few years. The party immediately mounted a full-scale plan to undermine the new operation. Multiple teams were dispatched to Malaysia with the goal of reigniting protests and publicizing medical and scientific data underscoring the danger to the public. As leader of the FAE, I was placed in charge of the operation.

What evolved was totally unanticipated. We discovered that the geographic area surrounding the Bukit mine had not been effectively remediated and was an ecological disaster. Radioactivity was detectable in much of the region, and there was disturbing evidence of destruction of wildlife by unrecognized disease. Most concerning was the mass, unexplained death of small mammals, in particular the prolific population of bats known to inhabit the mines.

My team was in the process of analyzing the cause of the mass deaths among the bat population when I received reports that at least six villagers in the region were hospitalized with an undiagnosed pneumonia-type illness. The victims were in different hospitals in the region, and a link was not immediately clear. However, as our investigation continued, I was notified that a Chinese national, a tourist who was on vacation in Perak, had contracted a similar, undiagnosed pneumonia and that she herself had stated to authorities her belief that her illness was linked to bats in the area of the supposedly closed mine.

I notified the appropriate party committee members that I was suspicious of a link among the REE mines, the destruction of the bat population, and the human illness, by now confirmed in at least eight people including the Chinese tourist. We concluded that while pneumonia in Malaysian villagers in rural areas would likely not draw widespread attention, the illness of the tourist, particularly since the Malay medical professionals knew that she had linked it to bats, would be hard to conceal in a foreign country. The story would likely become world news.

I was instructed to immediately shut down the entire operation, and arrangements were made to evacuate our entire cadre of more than 150 people, plus the people who were ill, including the tourist. They all were booked on a Malaysia Air flight from Kuala Lumpur to Beijing.

In addition, I had my team collect detritus from the bats and material from the remediation site and closed mine shafts, and had it loaded aboard the same flight for transport to Beijing so that it could be examined and analyzed at my labs.

I was scheduled to travel on the same aircraft. However, the day before, I was unexpectedly provided by the party with a ticket on a different route, stopping in my former home of Taiwan overnight. It is only for this reason that I was not on board the Malay plane, which, as you almost surely know, vanished in midflight and has never been accounted for. Everyone associated with our team in Malaysia, including the ill tourist and the animal and earth samples, were all lost.

When I attempted to pursue an inquiry into this purported coincidence, which I considered most remarkable, I was pointedly instructed by the committee to abandon any investigation and given a clear threat to my position and my personal safety if I did not do so. I complied.

Two years later, I learned that six miners in southern China had become infected with an unrecognized pneumonia from which three of them perished. The workers had been cleaning bat detritus in a mine shaft when they fell ill. My preliminary inquiry confirmed that there were significant similarities to the experience in Bukit, which I reported to the committee. I was summarily advised that no investigation into the incident was necessary because the mine in which the victims had been working had been closed.

In early 2019, British journalists published negative reports about the Chinese rare earth mine in Inner Mongolia, which remains the largest producer of REEs in the world by far. The adverse publicity resulted in feature stories on the BBC and mainstream British tabloids and even a report on television news in America.

To quell the growing uproar, I was instructed by the committee to host a delegation from the World Health Organization, which was being dispatched to inspect the site in Inner Mongolia. It is my belief that the tour was a sham, prearranged between the party and WHO executives to produce a report that would pacify world opinion. However, over the course of the carefully choreographed tour, I noted that one participating physician, Dr. Hana Chang, a Swiss national, did not appear to accept the predetermined conclusions. She and I engaged in several stimulating discussions about the matter.

I did not disclose to her that during my visit to Inner Mongolia, I came upon evidence of destruction of the native bat population similar to my findings years before in Bukit Merah. I was able to collect several carcasses for analysis, and the subsequent surreptitious laboratory testing done in central China confirmed that an unknown viral agent was responsible for the deaths, as I had suspected. Upon further inquiry, I learned that at least eighteen villagers from Baotou, the city adjacent to the mines, had been hospitalized with an unknown strain of pneumonia.

I was considering opportunities to study the similarities between Inner Mongolia and the situation in Malaysia when reports began to proliferate of an unrecognized respiratory illness quickly spreading in central China. It was suspected to be associated with infected bats. However, alarmingly, it was reported that the disease was transmitting from person to person and was not limited to direct contact with infected animals or the mine shafts, as I had observed in the previous incidents.

I became convinced that the new illness, called Covid-19, might be connected in some way to the mines, but it became impossible to investigate. Opportunities to communicate with scientists around the world were abruptly foreclosed by the party, which demanded that the matter be handled internally and shielded from the world's view. Failure to comply with this directive would be considered treason, punishable by imprisonment or death. My colleague and friend who performed the initial analysis that confirmed an unknown pathogen in the bat carcasses from Inner Mongolia, Dr. Keiji Takama, vanished after sharing his findings with other physicians and scientists. His whereabouts remain unknown.

The possible link of the new pathogen to REE mining operations and possibly other mining activities must be evaluated, and I urgently ask that you use your influence to induce your country and other countries with scientific resources to fully investigate it.

I also request that you specifically note that while I believe the pathogen I discovered has a connection to the rare earth mining, I never was able to confirm this possibility. Furthermore, I have not reached a theory on whether a mutation occurred as a result of the radioactive refining of waste products and other pollutants or because the mining process itself somehow unleashed a viral agent that had been contained in the mines along with the rare earth elements.

However, I state with certainty that if the party had shared with scientists around the world the information I uncovered about prior cases, some more than six years earlier in Malaysia, immediately when the seriousness of the Covid-19 pandemic was recognized, preventive measures, treatments, and a vaccine might have been accelerated, perhaps in time to save hundreds of thousands of lives. It is my firm belief, as a physician and a scientist, that this is the only goal of my expertise and my life's work and that it was intentionally precluded by the party for purely political and economic reasons.

Consequently, I find I can no longer contribute my efforts to the unworthy endeavor of the Chinese Communist Party and hope to be able to live out my life in the company of more noble pursuits.

Professor Cedar, it is important for you to understand why I chose you to entrust with this information. Having been subjected to domination by a government consumed with objectives other than improving the human condition, I understand full well that political considerations can overwhelm a state's pursuit of the common good. I believe this to be true even in your democracy, which in this regard is perhaps not very different from my own country. However, I trust that you, a man of science, not politics, will be free of these pressures, and I am confident that you will take the information and evidence I have provided to you and use it wisely for the greater good of humanity.

With deepest respect and confidence in your decisions on this matter, I remain,

Humbly,
Pao Den Chin, MD

CHAPTER 40

We look up as Jack emerges from Harry's study and walks purposefully back to our group awaiting him on the patio. Without preamble, he glances at the calendar on his watch and says to us, "Only five days remain until the preservative containers begin to degrade. We need to get to work immediately."

Jack tells us that included with Den Chin's letter is a two-page document setting forth a timeline of his research, detailing each event that he has considered beginning in 2014. Behind that is a description of two packages Den Chin has transferred to Jack under separate cover. "Parcel one" is Den Chin's scientific record book with detailed notes and conclusions at every step in his research process.

But it is "parcel two," Jack tells us, that would catapult the research to instant worldwide acclaim and the annals of scientific advances if it contains what the Chinese scientist says it contains: Den Chin claims he has sent actual biologic material taken from bat detritus infected with the unknown viral agent that apparently killed them. He says he personally collected the samples at the rare earth mining site in Inner Mongolia and supervised the testing that has already been completed. The specimens are packaged in sealed cryogenic containers that will preserve the matter for twenty-one days before deterioration begins.

Den Chin says that Hana Chang has somehow arranged for the sealed container to be transported to the United States and that she will tell Jack how to retrieve it. In addition, she has personally toured the rare earth facilities in Inner Mongolia and can supply details about the site.

"Look," Jack says, "Den Chin's letter, which I don't choose to disclose just yet, is very compelling, and if it's really from him and what he says is true, it is of incalculable importance. And if the parcels contain what Den Chin says they contain, it could be a stunning, world-changing event. Where are these packages he sent, Hana?"

But before she can answer, I jump in. "Wait a minute. We can't be certain that everything is as it seems," I say, thinking of all the suspicions I have harbored for the last week and how easily Aimee Cedar herself had duped me. "I am not a science or medical person by any means, but it seems to me we need to use extraordinary precautions with respect to these packages. Hana, did you personally take them from Dr. Den Chin, or was there an intermediary?"

"I never actually saw the packages," she says thoughtfully, apparently weighing the importance of what I have said. "I met with Pao twice in person and can confirm that it was him. But I made transportation arrangements with Harry, and the packages were given to someone else when I was not present."

"So how do we even know it was the doctor who handed them off?" I ask, drawn into the intrigue simmering around me. "Did the person who picked them up even know Den Chin to verify it was the right guy? And even it was him, how can you be certain, Hana, that he was truthful with you? It seems he's a well-known Chinese Communist Party guy, so how can we be sure he wasn't using you to plant false information, maybe even deadly material, for the benefit of the party?" I stop there, thinking it is better not to verbalize my other concern: how do we know Hana herself is on the level and also smart enough to judge Den Chin accurately?

"I'm a lawyer," I add when they all stare at me but say nothing. "It's my professional expertise to treat information with skepticism and spot weaknesses in it."

Harry ends the discomfort. "You are absolutely correct, Aruba," he says, lending authority to what I have said. "Let's discuss how we can vet this whole thing and be sure we aren't being snookered into doing dirty work for the Chinese Communists."

"Whatever we're doing, it had better be fast," interjects Jack, "because according to Den Chin's letter we have only five days until the specimens he risked his life to send us begin to degrade."

I realize that none of us has the whole story, which makes me nervous. Jack has read Den Chin's letter but not shared its contents; Harry has handled the transportation of the material but has not revealed its whereabouts; Hana has met personally with Den Chin but does not know that his allegations can be vouched for; and I, of course, know absolutely nothing about anything except what I have ended up hearing from this high-powered group with which I am now involved by serendipity.

We exchange ideas on how to move forward, and each time we arrive at a way to handle one problem, three more emerge. Finally, after an hour of intense discussion, we agree on a plan.

Jack is adamant that the most critical issue is safety when opening the parcels that have been sent. He says they need to be transported directly to a lab that meets the stringent criteria for handling infectious agents and dangerous pathogens. He has many connections in the scientific community and will get to work immediately to find one that fits the bill, but he will need to be cagy in order to not reveal why he is asking. We devise a story that, because of the pandemic, he is doing a paper on how dangerous pathogens might best be handled in the future.

Harry will ensure the safe storage and containment of the packages, wherever they are presently located, until Jack instructs him on where they are to be delivered. Not surprisingly, Harry is not at all concerned about handling this part of the process and merely emphasizes to Jack that he needs the delivery information as soon as possible.

Hana will do nothing but wait. She has already done more than her share. By now, after listening to her speak and viewing her interactions with Harry as well as with Jack and me, I am convinced that she is ethical and smart and that she fully believes she has tried to do an immense service to humanity at great personal cost. She clearly is devastated about the fate of the plane and filled with remorse that she failed to take action that may have prevented it. She also convincingly expresses contrition that she used false pretenses to involve me in a matter of far greater danger than she had ever imagined. We all acknowledge her courageous efforts, which seems to bolster her spirits somewhat.

I will handle our security and privacy, and we agree that there are several problems on that front. Most important, Dr. Den Chin's warning that Jack is in tremendous danger seems to have been borne out. It appears that at some point the Chinese learned that Jack had not, in fact, vanished along with the plane and have already attempted to finish the job. We think that realization happened when Jack confronted burglars in his apartment, one of whom openly displayed shock at seeing him. We conclude that the thieves were looking for material connected to the aborted lecture but instead found the supposedly dead lecturer alive and well. After that, the attack on Jack by three thugs, thwarted by the FBI, suggests that the CCP may have been trying to correct its previous failure to eliminate him. This, of course, is the most worrying security matter.

Second, we needed to keep attention away from Harry and also from his house, where Hana is sequestered. Harry has risked everything to help with this operation in the belief that he is helping humanity, but what if it proves to be a ruse for international sabotage or even worse? He could be facing charges for so many illegal acts that I cannot even count them all. We need to completely erase any connection between Harry and Den Chin's communications.

This would also protect Hana, I think. I never have provided the FBI with the photo of her captured on my office building's security camera, so, absent my visual confirmation, there would not be any way to confirm that Aimee Cedar was actually Hana Chang. I can think of no other link occurring in the United States that might connect her to possibly illegal acts. But then I think of Marsha, who also met Aimee Cedar and can identify her.

As if on cue, my phone buzzes in my pocket, and it is Marsha calling to tell me that my client, Mrs. Parrish, has confirmed her two o'clock appointment. "OK," I reply, barely containing my groan, "I'll be there by one."

The four of us agree to confer later in the day to discuss our progress, and Jack and I head back across the sand toward my house. We are drained and lost in thought.

Finally, realizing that we need to take a break from discussing how to save the planet, Jack says, "You look really happy about that appointment, Rube."

"You think divorce law is fun?" I respond, only half joking. "Now the Cedar case, that one is an example of fun, and I have a feeling the fun is only just beginning. But the client who is coming in today is horrible, horrible. She's no Aimee Cedar, I can assure you," I tell him. I mean to be lighthearted, but in truth I am stretched so thin that I realize the joke may turn into hysteria or a screaming tirade at any second. I take a deep breath and think, Stay calm, stay calm and talk about normal things.

"This woman," I tell him, "wanted a divorce because she felt her husband, an orthodontist, insisted on living like a pauper, way beneath her dignity and not letting her compete with her friends. When I asked her to give me an example, she said with utter disdain,

'He drives a *Chevy*. Can you imagine? I married a man who drives a *Chevy*!'"

Jack bursts out laughing. He asks, "Did you have your Chevy then, or did you get it after, as a kind of fashion statement?" His laugh is contagious, and some of the tension flows out of me.

"I'm glad you realize that my Tahoe is a status symbol chosen to impress the neighbor," I say. "I already had the car when she retained me, and I barely managed to keep a straight face when she insulted it. Whenever she comes to the office, I worry that she'll see my car and realize that her lawyer's a pauper just like her husband! A woman like that wants a prestigious divorce attorney. You know, one who drives a Maserati or a Bentley, for example."

We continue to chat, and when we reach my house, we are both in slightly better spirits. But then I get back to the problems at hand. "Jack, the danger to you is very serious. It's not a joke. You've already been attacked and had your apartment robbed. We need to figure out some protection until this is over."

"I suppose," he says, seeming to consider the danger for the first time. I gather Jack is not a worrier, although he apparently had been when it involved corn crops.

"Why don't you stay at my house while this plays out? We have no reason to think that the Chinese know anything about me. It would seem only the FBI has made that connection, and you threw them out. I imagine that if they decide to go for a warrant, it will take at least a day or two, so even they should not be around."

Jack is not sure. "I need to make some calls and thought I would do it from my office at NYU," he says. "Ruby, we have no way to know if the evidence arriving from Den Chin is what he claims it is. The parcels must be treated as potentially lethal, and they can only be opened and evaluated under the most secure conditions. All we have is Hana Chang's personal evaluation of a man we know has been a loyal CCP member for decades. She feels certain that he's had this total change of heart, and, I must say, the letter to me is very persuasive and believable. But still, it is imperative to take every precaution before we rely on this. I know a few professionals who can be counted on for discretion and might be in a position to help."

I am convinced. "OK, so stay here and work. NYU is where they will be watching for you," I say, and Jack nods in agreement. "I'll be at the office for a few hours anyway, so you'll have privacy."

I head to my office, happy to be alone in my plain old Chevy Tahoe.

CHAPTER 41

Trying to locate contact information for certain colleagues proves more difficult for Jack than he had expected. After twenty minutes of frustration, he telephones his office and asks for his admin, hoping that the unfamiliar caller ID of Ruby's landline will provide no clues to his whereabouts.

He obtains telephone numbers for Dr. Robert Karder, senior research fellow at the Applied Physics Lab, or APL, affiliated with Johns Hopkins University School of Public Health. The lab, Jack knows, is widely regarded as one of the most impressive facilities in the world for research in several areas, including public health and pandemic control. Most Covid-19 analysis is tabulated there.

Dr. Karder is a member of GCAC, and over the years he and Jack have met at numerous meetings and forums and developed a friendly professional relationship. A few years earlier, Karder had contacted Jack for help with a chemistry issue his lab had encountered in the study of vapor release associated with synthetic fuel for military vessels. They had worked comfortably together, and Jack's input had provided significant help in solving the problem.

In addition to Johns Hopkins University, the APL also has ties to the US government, which gives Jack pause, but he nonetheless decides that Karder is the best researcher to consult. After being transferred three times to different locations within the APL complex, he finally is connected with Karder, who gives him a warm greeting.

Jack tells him that he needs to discuss a science issue of incalculable importance and urgency but that, for the moment at least, requires absolute confidentiality. Karder is immediately responsive and asks Jack to call him back on his cell in twenty minutes, at which time he can be alone at a private location where he will not be overheard.

Jack decides to scrap the innocuous story he had concocted with Ruby and, without revealing names or details, tells Karder that a complicated series of events has culminated in him being contacted by a renowned Chinese environmental and infectious disease scientist whose name would be instantly recognized by Karder. The scientist claims that he has obtained and preserved specimens of a previously unknown viral pathogen that he is unable to further evaluate because his own government has forbidden research on the subject, Jack says.

At great risk to his own safety and that of others who had helped him, the doctor has smuggled the specimens to the United States in cryogenic sealed packaging that will begin to deteriorate in only a matter of days. Jack waits a moment for this information to sink in and then asks Karder if he is able to use the secure labs at his facility to safely open the cryogenic containers and confirm that the specimens are what they have been reported to be. And, if so, can he preserve the material and continue the Chinese doctor's research?

"How do you know the guy is real?" Karder asks after a long silence. He peppers Jack with a series of questions that highlight the overwhelming likelihood that the story is false. They discuss the matter in detail, and Jack is relieved to have the opportunity to brainstorm with a fellow scientist whose intellect and discretion are exemplary.

"Truly, Jack, this just sounds too fantastic to be true," Karder finally says. "And, not to diminish your superlative reputation, but why would the guy choose to transfer evidence that the entire world is desperately seeking to you, an earth science professor at NYU? I'm sorry to say it, but maybe he thinks you're an easy mark whose vanity will lead you to buy into a farfetched story."

Jack agrees that this is a definite possibility but relates the reasons that Den Chin has offered for choosing him, which do have plausibility. Researchers are all too familiar with governments hijacking scientific studies for reasons having nothing to do with science.

"Look, Bob," Jack says, "if this is for real, in only a few days the material will be corrupted and the chance to possibly unlock the greatest medical mystery of our time will be lost, probably forever. I don't think as scientists we can let this moment pass without at least trying. My question is, do you have access to the secure lab at APL, which is safe to deal with potentially communicable pathogens or other agents that might be in the package?" He waits for a reply, but Karder is silent. "Just tell me if you are able to do it, Bob, and if you are willing to do it. If not, I understand completely, but I will ask you to never reveal this to anyone. And please tell me right now so I can get to work finding another lab."

"I understand," Karder says. After a few more moments of silence, which Jack interprets as his colleague declining to become involved, Karder continues. "Yes, I think I can do it. I have the authority to take over the lab for undisclosed specimen analysis using full biohazard safety protocols. But, Jack, there is a condition: when we have determined what the material consists of, I will need to give a full report to both the university that hosts the APL and the government, which funds us and for whom we do most of our work. Is that agreed between us?"

Jack agrees and tells Kander that he only needs confirmation of the nature of the biological material within twenty-four hours of the lab receiving it. Exhaustive analysis and testing could thereafter proceed at a normal pace to be determined by Kander and the lab. Furthermore, Jack assures his colleague, as soon as the lab identifies the specimen, he himself will disclose the full story of how it had been obtained to both the government and the media. There would be no further need for confidentiality.

"I'm not going to tell you what I am advised the specimen was taken from, Bob, so you can do a blind analysis. That way it will be completely credible if you find the same thing that the mystery Chinese doctor says you will find."

They discuss the logistics of transporting the sample to the APL on the following day and hang up. Jack then calls Harry and tells him how they needed to transport Den Chin's packages once they arrive in New York the following day.

CHAPTER 42

My meeting with Mrs. Parrish is every bit as irritating as I had anticipated it would be, and since I already am a mass of nerves, I have a hard time maintaining an appropriate lawyerly demeanor.

I manage to make a show of understanding, if not sympathizing with, the difficulties that she insists her husband's penurious ways rain upon her and their two teenage children. Her daughter is endlessly embarrassed by her non-designer handbag at weekend parties; their son is lacking a MacBook Pro and is relegated to computing on a mere PC. How sad for those kids, I think in a mean-spirited way, not because they are lacking in the material status symbols their mother finds so important but because they likely will be sitting in my office in ten or fifteen years because they will lack the personal values needed to maintain a marriage.

Notwithstanding her deprived financial circumstances, Mrs. Parrish somehow ekes out $500 an hour for me and provides advance retainers promptly when asked. I realize that hefty fees enhance my image in her eyes, and it makes her feel important to have high-priced representation. I am happy to oblige her for my own benefit, and also because those fees will enable me to represent one or two more clients like Luis who truly need legal help that they can't afford.

We finish up about four thirty, and I show her out the door with a sigh of relief. Marsha brings me up to date on my messages and things that have happened in the last few days while I have been essentially AWOL. She reports on adjournments of court dates, papers received from attorneys who are adversaries in my cases, and other details, none of which seem to be urgent. She is an excellent legal secretary and office manager, and without her I would have a hard time handling the practice.

Then she asks if there is anything new on the Cedar case. She comments that there does not seem to be new information on the plane disappearance and is surprised that she has seen no mention of Jack Cedar having missed the plane. Has the FBI been back to see me? she asks.

I think quickly and realize that this is an opportunity to try to end her speculation about Aimee Cedar, who as far as Marsha is concerned is still a mysteriously missing client.

"As a matter of fact, yes, the FBI did have more to say," I improvise. "They located her, and her little game about a divorce had to do with a gripe she had with Cedar from years ago. I wasn't provided with details, but I'm confident we won't be seeing her again."

"Pretty pricey revenge," Marsha says.

"I thought the same thing," I tell her. "I'm just glad I get to keep the money."

She stares at me, obviously concluding that what I have just said is baloney, that she knows me well enough to know that I would never accept such a lame explanation. But she says nothing, and even her facial expression remains steady, which is a skill that makes her an invaluable professional.

"Marsha, you've been carrying the ball while I was absorbed with this over the past few days. Take Monday off and have a nice long weekend," I tell her, no doubt confirming for her that my story about the Cedars is nonsense.

"That's great, Aruba," she says. "I really appreciate that."

By now it is after five, and she shuts down her computer and says good night. I can't wait to leave myself, but I delay for fifteen minutes to be sure she is gone before I head downstairs since it's a good idea for her to think I'm still working.

When I finally drive out of the parking lot, I notice a black car—a Camry, I think—swing in behind me and follow me onto the Meadowbrook. I realize it is ridiculous to think I may be being followed, but I move to the left lane, speed up, pass three cars on my right, and then pull back into the middle lane. The black car seems not to react, but as I am about to lose interest in it, I notice in my rearview mirror that it performs the same maneuver, ending up just behind me but in the right lane. It stays there until I exit onto the Loop, and I see the black car continue straight ahead toward Jones Beach. I consider that I am becoming paranoid and head home without another glance at the cars driving around me.

Jack is out on the patio reading a newspaper when I arrive. He looks great sitting there, and I consider that perhaps I'd like him to stay in that spot permanently. Jack Cedar is growing on me.

He jumps up, obviously glad to see me, and without asking goes to the kitchen to get us cocktails as if he actually does live here. The drinks must be part of his Midwestern WASP thing, I think, and realize it's a habit I could come to seriously enjoy. I have no idea what other habits are common to affluent Midwestern farmers.

Jack enthusiastically tells me that he has lined up everything for tomorrow. He has conferred with Harry, and the specimens will be picked up and brought directly to a renowned lab with secure facilities to test it for a source and for pathogens. Jack says that his contact person at the lab has assured him of complete discretion and anticipates that he will be able to provide basic information on the biological material within twenty-four hours of its receipt.

I tell Jack about my day, and we end up laughing heartily about Mrs. Parrish. "Who knew that matrimonial law could be such a hoot," I say to Jack with a wink, trying out a bit of his down-home slang. It sounds hilarious to me as I utter the words, but he seems to think nothing of it.

Maybe I will get used to it.

In spite of the romantic angle that is now part of our relationship, or perhaps because of it, Jack and I decide to occupy separate bedrooms. It seems more appropriate while we wait for the arrival of the material from Dr. Den Chin and, hopefully, validation of the specimen as a bona fide source of scientific information. We say good night at about eleven o'clock, and Jack retires to the guest room where his personal items have remained since he first slept at my house.

I feel surprisingly cheerful and easily slip into a peaceful sleep. At about 4:00 a.m., a noise I can't identify wakes me, and I am instantly on alert. And unaccountably nervous. In fact, very nervous. I put on a robe over my nightgown and put my ear to the closed door of my room but hear nothing.

After a few minutes of listening, I crack open the door and peer into the house. The guest room door is closed, and no light shows at the bottom, so I assume Jack is asleep. I cautiously step into the hall and tiptoe to the living room. I see nothing unusual.

Perhaps I imagined the sound, I think, and push aside the sidelight curtain on the front door to glance out at the street. My heart begins to pound as I focus on a black car—a Camry, I am pretty sure—parked across the street. The neighbors' windows are all dark. I am confident that no one has guests to explain the unfamiliar car, and I am paralyzed with fear.

"Jack," I call out but get no response. "Jack," I say loudly, and this time his door begins to open. To my horror, I see it is not Jack emerging from the room, but a slim, black-clad man who lunges toward me as I see a second man behind him, this one big and brutish-looking. I try to scream but my throat fails to operate, so I turn and run toward the back of the house as Jack comes rushing out of the den where he apparently has been working. Light from that room floods into the living room, and in an instant he sizes up the scene unfolding. He charges at me, grabs my arm, forcefully pulls me back, and pushes me behind him. My throat suddenly opens, and I begin to scream in a hysterical cacophony of sound.

We hear thunderous smashing at the front door, terrifying us, and the door crashes open in a cascade of splintered wood. A cadre of uniformed men with weapons drawn in front of them burst into the house followed by Hamilton, holding his plastic-encased ID in front of him, and shouting, "FBI," in a commanding voice that cannot be ignored.

The two intruders stare dumbly at the new arrivals and in a moment raise their arms above their heads and stand fixed in their tracks. Stupidly, as if I am watching a TV show, the thought occurs to me that even these guys, who probably work for the Chinese Communist government, must have heard about shootings by American law enforcement agents in the course of raids that somehow went out of control. I consider that tonight I might be the one they shoot in error.

I realize I have stopped screaming, but I feel unable to breathe. Jack looks at me, grabs my shoulders, and roughly pulls me toward him.

"Breathe," he says directly at my face, but I stare at him, unfocused. He tightens his grip and blows air forcefully at my face. "Breathe, Aruba," he says, loudly this time, and I do. I collapse against him just as the towering shadow of Drost appears at the front door and then the man himself, who calmly announces to his partner standing in the living room, "Intruders neutralized."

Jack, imperturbable, says to Drost calmly, "I thought you needed a few days to get a warrant," but it is Hamilton who answers.

"We had one all along, but we couldn't decide if you were on the level, so we kept it quiet."

Drost follows up. "We've saved you twice now, Jack," as if they are golfing buddies discussing their shots. "I guess that pretty much indicates you aren't one of the bad guys."

"We've been watching the block all along," Hamilton says. "We observed the intruders parking their vehicle and approaching your house. It took us a few minutes to get the armed team onsite so we could enter. Sorry for the delay."

A few of the agents restrain the two intruders and escort them out the front door to be taken to FBI offices for questioning. Other officers search the house for evidence.

Finally it is just Jack and me and Hamilton and Drost. It is now after 6:00 a.m., and I am utterly spent. They ask if we have any idea why we are being pursued by high-powered, dangerous people. Jack tells them truthfully that he thinks the Chinese suspect that his research about REE mining scheduled to be presented in a lecture could be damaging to their control of that industry, so they want to suppress it. This is accurate of course, but both of us withhold any mention of the more important story about Dr. Den Chin. That information will be public in a matter of days anyway, and our main concern is how we will stay safe until then.

Jack expresses contrition about having previously ejected the agents and tells them how fortunate both of us are that they do their jobs brilliantly. Then, with great humility, he asks if they could kindly post someone outside the house for a couple of days. "As you can see, Ms. Jones has been traumatized by these events, and I hope you will make her feel protected until we get more answers about exactly what is going on."

They agree, and Hamilton instructs one of the agents still at the house to remain out front, conspicuously, to deter any further incidents. They leave.

I can barely stand up. The sun already is pouring through the windows, but Jack takes my arm and silently steers me to my bedroom, where we both collapse onto the bed and are asleep in moments.

CHAPTER 43

The Shaw Global Zermatt Star chugs slowly into Port Newark, guided to the berth reserved for it by two tugboats and a pilot boat. The harbormasters routinely try to assign the same pilot boat captain and tug operators to escort particular vessels since familiarity with a ship and its crew make the painstaking operation of slipping a twenty-story goliath into a docking space like a finger into a glove more efficient and safe. The tug captains and the pilot boat captain all know the *Zermatt Star* well, and when docking is secure, the captains of the tugs give friendly waves to the crew gathered on deck.

The captain of the pilot boat holds his craft beside the huge ship for a few minutes, chatting with Captain Peter Reyes who has stepped out on the lower deck platform of the *Zermatt* to supervise the docking operation.

"Glad we were able to make a spot for you on short notice, Pete," the pilot boat operator says. "I see your container hold is only about a third full. Any idea why the schedule was changed at the last minute?"

"Not a clue," answers Captain Reyes. "We were in Busan, South Korea, and I was just told that there was a change in our route, no reason provided. We went directly to Taiwan, picked up a small shipment, and headed straight here. All stops cancelled. Some of the guys had made plans at our scheduled stops and were pretty pissed about it."

"The ship owners do whatever they want," the pilot boat captain replies, smiling. "That is as long as they have the pull to get whatever they want at the port, which yours does." He nods at the huge, red arrow decorating the dock side of the *Zermatt*.

The two captains chat for a few more minutes, and then the pilot boat pulls away, heading out of the harbor to meet the next ship to which it has been assigned.

Longshoremen flood onto the decks and begin to offload the cargo, working in perfect concert to manage the eighteen-story high cranes anchored beside the ship, which lift the containers and deposit them into moving carriers rolling along the piers.

Captain Reyes returns to his cabin and collects his personal gear. The last-minute change of the ship's schedule has provided him with four unexpected days in New York, and he is planning a full complement of sightseeing. Unlike some of his crew, he prefers the extra days here in New York to port days in Asian cities like Bangkok and Hanoi, which he already has visited many times.

He slings his small shore bag over his shoulder and then picks up the sealed case marked "Personal Property of the Chairman, North America" that he has kept in his cabin's locked closet since receiving it in Taiwan. He goes topside to disembark and displays his high-level clearance credentials at the security gate where an officer he knows well calls to him, "Hey, Pete, enjoy the Big Apple. See you in a few days," and waves him through.

Outside, Captain Reyes pulls a sheet of instructions from his pocket and, as it directs, walks to "Passenger Area Six" where a small, white van marked "APL" is sitting, engine idling. When he approaches it, a driver clad in a white uniform bearing an APL logo emerges from the driver's seat and greets him. "Captain Reyes?"

"That would be correct," Peter says cordially and accepts the ID offered to him by the driver. He confirms that the name on it matches the one on his instruction sheet and then puts the container he is carrying down on the pavement. Using a key he withdraws from his shore bag, he unlocks a metal clamp that seals the container's lid. It clicks open, and, referring again to his instructions, he enters a numerical code on a second lock. It unlatches, allowing him to lift the top of the container and withdraw from it a smaller, metal box marked in large, black letters "Parcel Two," which he holds out to the driver.

"Well, here it is. Special delivery straight from Taiwan," he says with a smile and twists his arm around to elbow-bump the driver, who responds his own elbow. He places the container in his van and drives off.

Instantly a dark blue Range Rover that has been idling in plain sight across the street pulls into the spot vacated by the van and a fit, good-looking older man emerges. He extends his hand, obviously undeterred by the continuing Covid recommendations to forego traditional handshakes, and smiles broadly. "Captain Reyes," he says, not as a question but as a greeting, and Peter notes that the man radiates power and charisma.

Peter nods and takes the man's hand, which is firm and dry. He does not seem a typical delivery person, and Peter hesitantly says, "I need to see some identification if you don't mind." As an afterthought he adds, "Sir," and then feels foolish for extending this show of respect to a courier.

"Certainly, captain," the man replies affably, full of good cheer, and pulls out a letter authorizing him to receive a package that Peter has brought from Taiwan. The letter is on fancy, embossed stationery with the heading of "Shaw Global, Office of the Chairman, North America" and is signed by Harry Shaw. Peter reads it carefully and then pulls a second parcel from the case he had opened and hands it to the man. It is clearly marked "Parcel One."

"Good work, Captain Reyes. Excellent work!" the courier says in a deep, resonant voice. He takes the package from Peter and returns with it to the Range Rover. "Enjoy your extra leave in New York," he says as he pulls out of Passenger Area Six. He looks at Peter and, holding two fingers to his forehead in a cheerful salute, says in a booming voice, "I'm sure there's a bonus coming your way, captain!"

Peter stares after the car for a few moments, unsure what to make of the exchange, and then looks around for the cab stand. He is ready to head to the city.

CHAPTER 44

Jack and I sleep away half the day and then have a multicourse breakfast at the kitchen table. We take turns rummaging around in the refrigerator for more food, feeling as though we haven't eaten for days. I am relieved that it is finally Saturday and at least I don't have to worry about business. Jack had been scheduled to be in Ireland for the entire week anyway, so he has not had to juggle his professional obligations with crisis management.

I realize that Jack Cedar walked into my office last Friday and I have known him for all of eight days. I met Aimee Cedar, or Hana Chang, two weeks before that, and in this short period of time, my world has changed irrevocably.

We know that as soon as the story about Den Chin and his specimens is revealed, Jack and I will be the subject of tremendous interest, so we decide to try to have a normal day, crisis free, before the storm breaks.

To maintain secrecy about their involvement, we have agreed with Harry and Hana to have no contact with them until the lab results are received from APL, unless there is a glitch that demands immediate attention.

By the end of the day, we have had no contact from them, so we assume, with growing excitement, that the parcels were actually received in New York, that the specimens in parcel two have been delivered to APL and that the research notes in parcel one are safe with Harry as planned.

We wait. Every couple of hours, we look out at the front of the house to confirm that the FBI is still there. Twice the agents change, but someone is there each time we check.

We go for a walk on the beach but head in the direction away from Harry's house to avoid the chance of meeting him.

"You know, professor, you can tell the direction of the wind by watching how the seagulls sit on the sand," I say, trying to stump him, which I do. "They always sit facing into the wind so they can get lift beneath their wings if they need to do a fast takeoff." Jack looks around and confirms that all of the seagulls are, indeed, facing west, which is the direction from which we feel the wind.

"Very impressive," he says, "for a lawyer."

"We lawyers have knowledge and talents that you can't even imagine," I retort.

Jack answers, instantly serious, "Yes, Ruby, I have definitely noticed that."

We return to the house, grill steaks for dinner, and watch a British detective story on Netflix. We check the front of the house and see the FBI agent sitting in his car at the curb. Tonight we do not even consider sleeping in separate bedrooms.

We have a great night.

When we get up in the morning, our day of leisure has passed. It's now Sunday, but we are both in full professional mode, consumed with waiting for the report from the APL. Jack has provided my cell number to his colleague there for contact, and he keeps my phone next to him at all times.

I go online and research some of the numerous crimes of which Harry, Hana, Jack and I might be accused. It seems to me that from a legal perspective Jack and I have been victims in this scenario. True, we did not immediately share with law enforcement a renowned Chinese researcher's possible attempt to funnel secret information to the world scientific community as soon as we learned of it, but we were never actually asked. I realize it would be possible to build a case that we obstructed justice by withholding relevant information from the FBI, but I think it is unlikely since the Chinese have been trying to bump Jack off and clearly consider him to be their enemy.

I am not so sure about Harry and Hana. Harry has not shared with us how he managed to get Den Chin's parcels to the United States, but I can pretty much guess that it involved Shaw Global ships and the transport of undeclared, if not illegal, material. Harry conducts Shaw Global business from New York, and so both he and his ships that enter this country are subject to US law. He can claim that he had no idea what he was transporting, that he was duped by China and acted in good faith in the belief that he was helping humanity.

If Den Chin's material is legitimate, Harry may get a Congressional Medal of Honor. If the parcels are not what they were billed to be, Harry is in deep shit. But he is a smart and powerful man with huge resources and international connections. My money is on him to figure out a way to handle it.

As for Hana, she has no legal ties to the US. She is a Swiss national and would be much harder to prosecute. A charge could be made that she defrauded a US court by inducing me to bring a proceeding based on lies, but her government would offer her protection. She certainly misused her status as an employee of the WHO, but I guess the remedy for that would be to fire her. I doubt if any laws were broken. In any event, Harry will protect her. It is obvious to me that they are devoted to each other. Who knows, I think, maybe they will decide to hide out together on a Tahitian island for a while with a Shaw Global ship delivering fine wine and caviar to them once a week.

Jack and I begin to grow testy with waiting, and finally, in midafternoon, my cell phone comes to life, the ring startling us both.

"Jack Cedar," he says as he answers, and I can see from his expression that it is the call we have been waiting for.

He motions for me to sit next to him on the sofa, puts his index finger to his lips for me to be quiet, and switches the phone to speaker so I can hear what is said. And with this small gesture, I know that Jack Cedar is not leaving my life and that we will be together.

Without preamble Robert Karder says, "This was an easy one, Jack. It's necrotic tissue from a vesper bat, most likely the species Savi's pipistrelle, which is primarily found in Mongolia. Looks like it may have died from a coronavirus variant, but there is also some other pathogen present that we could not immediately identify. That will take more time. We tested for the known viruses that vesper bats can carry such as hantavirus, parvovirus, Ebola virus, we did the whole list, but nothing came up as a match. We used the instant testing protocol, though, because of the time constraint. Full spectrum testing might still yield a positive result. So is that what you were expecting to find?"

Jack exhales and sits back. "Yes, Bob, as a matter of fact. I was told that the sample came from a mining area in Inner Mongolia."

"Mining area makes sense," says Karder. "They like to roost in caves."

"Bob, is this species also found in Malaysia?" asks Jack.

"I don't know," comes the reply. "Hold on a moment, and I'll check my data sheets to see if Malaysia is mentioned." After a minute or two, Karder says, "Yes, they're found in Malaysia. In the areas rich in limestone in the west, such as Perak.

"Oh, by the way, we also found traces of three rare earth minerals in the tissue, but that also will take time to decipher. Is this helpful?"

"You can't imagine how helpful, Bob." Jack pauses for a moment and then continues. "Bob, I would suggest that this afternoon you advise your university and whoever else you need to inform about doing this for me. You can use my name, but please don't tell them how to find me just yet and don't give anyone this cell number. It's not mine anyway. Without the background information I gave you, your university and certainly the government agencies probably won't realize the extraordinary importance of this immediately and will just put it on the list of matters to check out when there's time."

"So, Jack, how are you planning to handle this? I do know the background information you gave me, and I think it needs immediate attention, as we agreed," said Karder.

"Completely agree, Bob. I've arranged to do a live broadcast in the early evening to fully disclose the circumstances. That's why it's important for you to reveal it to the hierarchy of the APL this afternoon, to be sure there is no appearance that you concealed the preliminary testing."

They discuss the timing and release of the information for a few minutes, and Karder expresses confidence that the prestige of APL being the lab chosen to analyze this tremendous find will outweigh questions about how he obtained it.

"By the way, one more thing," Karder says. "We also found detritus of fleas. Looks like the bat was infested, and as you may already know, fleas are a superb way to spread disease from a host to other organisms."

Immediately after he ends the call with Karder, Jack telephones Harry and Hana to tell them that we are on schedule and he will do the broadcast as planned. Then he calls his admin and instructs her to immediately contact the GCAC and let them know that he is doing a live broadcast that evening, which he urges all members to watch. He tells her to do the same with three other science committees on which he serves, as well as the science departments of NYU and Columbia. He tells her to send a follow-up email to any members for whom she has contact information.

Then he settles at my desk and works on the lecture he intends to deliver. He asks my opinion on several issues, particularly those that might have legal implications, and after about two hours we are both satisfied. We still have an hour before it will be time to head to Harry's house, but we just fidget around, unable to concentrate on anything else.

CHAPTER 45

At five thirty, Jack packs up his briefcase, we check to confirm that the FBI guy is where he is supposed to be, and we head out the back door and down the hidden path to the beach.

We walk toward Harry's house and in a few minutes see him standing beside the dunes watching for us. We join him and walk together to his enclosed yard, but before we enter it, we see news vans parked on the street for Fox, CNN, and BBC America. Harry has summoned them for what he described only as an "important news briefing." He provided no idea of the subject matter, but inasmuch as he is the chairman of Shaw Global North America, the three news services are anxious to hear what is going on and agree to send their crews. When they arrive, they are advised that Jack will be the speaker and are handed a sheet with his impressive credentials.

We greet Hana when we enter, and she is in all respects restored to the placid and beautiful woman I first knew as Aimee Cedar. She is no longer ashen with remorse and worry. Now her eyes are clear, and she is impeccably attired.

Harry has set up his library to be the broadcasting location and cleared his huge, mahogany desk of his own paperwork so Jack can spread his notes in front of him. Already in a neat stack on one side is a photocopy of the research notes sent by Den Chin that Harry retrieved from the *Zermatt Star*. The original notes have been locked in the underground safe in Harry's bedroom, hidden beneath the Aubusson carpet.

Jack uses the bathroom to freshen up and change to the tie and sport coat we brought from my house. He makes himself comfortable at Harry's desk. Behind it are twelve-foot-high wooden bookcases filled with leatherbound books, and the setting looks solid and reliable.

Shortly before six o'clock, Harry invites the news crews to set up their gear, and on the hour, a reporter from each station announces that they are interrupting normal programming to present information concerning new virus research from Professor Jack Cedar, associate chairman of the earth and environmental science department of NYU. They read into the camera a list of Jack's most illustrious credentials, and then the cameras turn to him.

He is a practiced speaker and comes across with dignity and authority as he looks straight into the camera and tells his story. He begins by relating that he has been contacted by an eminent Chinese Communist physician and scientist whose name must remain secret for now, but who is well known in the West for his professional importance. He has provided information to Jack, including physical specimens, that relate to the origins of a previously unknown viral pathogen possibly related to the origins of Covid-19. The People's Republic of China has attempted to suppress this evidence, even using lethal force, causing the doctor to disavow his affiliation with the Communist party. At great peril he has managed to smuggle the information to the West, and Jack will summarize it tonight. The material already has been examined and authenticated on a preliminary basis by a well-respected American laboratory affiliated with a major research university and the US government.

Jack then introduces his own specialty in the mining of rare earth and explains that the Chinese doctor believes there may be a connection between that type of mining, already well known to cause some of the worst environmental damage on the planet, and the origin of the pandemic. Jack is careful to omit any personal information that is not germane to the scientific story he is relating. He never mentions Aimee Cedar or the phony matrimonial proceeding that was used to keep him off the plane or any connection to the plane at all. He leaves Harry and Hana, and me as well, out of it entirely.

He then explains the introductory letter from the unnamed scientist that was hand-delivered to him. He reads it verbatim into the cameras.

As he is doing so, we all begin to receive on our phones a flurry of "breaking news" announcements about what is being shown on Fox, CNN, and BBC America. Then, one after another, bulletins announce that CBS, NBC, ABC, and their affiliates are interrupting their programming and cutting over to a lecture that is presently underway concerning evidence of the possible origins of Covid that has been smuggled out of China. They cut in to show the live feed of Jack speaking that is being broadcast on the cable stations. The cameramen, reporters, and supporting crews assembled in Harry's study fall silent and listen to Jack with rapt attention.

I hope that Dr. Pao Den Chin, wherever he is, is watching.

EPILOGUE

Ten days later, I am sitting at my kitchen table poring over the *Wall Street Journal*. It is one of my favorite times of the day, and I take my time sipping coffee, enjoying the sun streaming into the room while I read. Jack has had nonstop meetings since his broadcast, and it seems everyone wants an appointment to speak to him. He has been able to return to his Manhattan apartment, but the FBI insists on keeping a man posted outside in view of all the notoriety. We talk a few times a day and have seen each other every two or three nights.

A small article on page twelve catches my eye, and I sit bolt upright. It reports that a well-known Chinese medical doctor and scientist, Dr. Pao Den Chin, has been missing for about a month. He was last seen in Taiwan where he traveled frequently. He failed to check out of his hotel as scheduled, prompting the hotel's security team to enter his room where they found no sign of Dr. Den Chin. His belongings remained neatly placed in the room, including clothing and personal items. His laptop and briefcase, filled with files concerning the clean water project on which his office said he had been working, were on the desk, and his cell phone, by now fully discharged, was also in the room. He has not been seen or heard from since disappearing from the hotel and has failed to appear at numerous professional meetings and other commitments. He is the third Chinese medical researcher to mysteriously vanish in the last several months, the article concludes.

Tears instantly stinging my eyes, I take the newspaper and head over the sand to Harry's house. When he answers the door, I wave the paper at him and say in a tight voice, "Have you seen this, Harry? Den Chin has vanished!"

Harry takes the newspaper and glances at the article. He hands it back to me and says, "Listen to me, Ruby." He looks directly into my eyes, holding my gaze for a moment, and then says in his mellifluous, commanding voice, "Ruby, I'm telling you, don't you worry about Dr. Pao Den Chin. Do you hear me?"

I stare back at him but remain silent, thinking over his message. I lower the paper and give a slight nod.

"The Shaw Global *Alpine Star* is leaving New York on Thursday," he says affably, full of his usual good cheer. "Why don't you and the professor hitch a ride in the guest quarters? Traveling with all those containers around you can be surprisingly romantic!"

"Maybe," I say, smiling broadly now as I turn and head back toward the beach. "Maybe we'll do just that!"

CPSIA information can be obtained
at www.ICGtesting.com
Printed in the USA
LVHW021431190821
695570LV00005B/338/J